# *Grand Cru*

## *Barney Leason*

A TOM DOHERTY ASSOCIATES BOOK
NEW YORK

GRAND CRU

A Tor Book
Published by Tom Doherty Associates, LLC
175 Fifth Avenue
New York, NY 10010

www.tor.com

Tor® is a registered trademark of Tom Doherty Associates, LLC.

ISBN: 0-812-57634-9

First edition: February 2001

Printed in the United States of America

0  9  8  7  6  5  4  3  2  1

# Dedication

### For

*Christine, Karen,*
*Alexandra, and Lawrence*

# Grand Cru

*one*

HAVING BARELY WET his lips with the dark red wine, Henri Lamarque balanced the fragile wine glass lightly but firmly in his fingers, truly as if it were a chalice, swirling the precious stuff, airing it, studying its color and viscosity, or "legs" if the term is permitted. Once again, completing the tasting cycle, he put his nose to the glass and solemnly inhaled.

"I am greatly mystified," he said, suddenly leaning forward, shaking his head worriedly, sniffing again.

Clara smiled to herself, enjoying his performance, virtuoso as usual, that of the polished wine critic. She'd watched a thousand such tastings since her childhood at Morelli Vineyards. Glancing across the table, she saw that her father, in his very private, very reserved way, was equally amused, not by any humor in Lamarque's movements but by their predictability. A very faint merriment turned the corner of Alberto's generous mouth, and for a moment misted the steady eyes, set deeply in his tanned, scarcely wrinkled and unflappable face. Maybe Clara alone noticed his amusement. But that was as it should be. No one read Alberto Morelli better than his only daughter, even though she'd been slightly thrown by the unfamiliar sight of him tonight in a gray flannel suit and heavy silk tie. People often said Clara resembled Alberto, that she had his strong face and presence, a happy-making thought for he was a handsome man.

Different places—tonight, the elegant, high-ceilinged, flower-filled dining room of the Clift Hotel in San Francisco where no one seemed to speak above a murmur, especially the waiters who came and went as silently as ghosts. The Clift was the other face of San Francisco, a world away from the city's better known glitter and dash, a deliberately, determinedly patrician place—the perfect venue for doing wine business the old-fashioned way, over a good meal.

Different faces, Clara thought, different noses. But the same ritual.

They were all watching Henri. And he played priest so well. He was trim, sleek as a Jesuit, fine-featured, his black hair graying elegantly at the temples. The long, spare body was perched forward on the seat of the high-backed chair, suppressed energy coming off him like distant thunder before the lightning strike. Yes, it was true, Clara thought, even sitting down, as slim, even slight, as he was, Henri filled the room. This was a man, his every movement and expression said, who was almost violently happy to be alive. His alert posture, the face, the nose which gave his face a slightly hawkish thrust—one could argue about the nose, prominent without being alarming, she'd long since decided—and the steady, animated glow of his gray eyes jogged a youthful memory of a lordly monsignor, close friend of the Morelli family. Henri's tailored blazer, crisp white collar, striped tie, were as neat as any monsignor's vestments.

Who could not love such a man?

Over a beginning course of seafood crêpes, the six of them had already consumed nearly all of two bottles of a very smooth California chardonnay. Next, the wine dealer, their host, acquaintance ... customer, Werner Flemming, had ordered opened a magnum of vintage Château Montebanque and now, before the second course, the waiter had poured a tasting portion for Lamarque.

The beefy Flemming shifted in his seat. Apprehension, a beginning of hurt, showed on his forehead. "Mystified?" he growled. "What's to be mystified about?"

Henri put down his glass, clasping his hands under his chin. He gazed at Flemming apologetically, then glanced swiftly to his right, as if to warn Clara that the verdict would not be good. Swiftly, he lifted his glass once more, making much of smelling, swirling ... tasting. Any doubt vanished.

Planting the glass on the thick, linen tablecloth, he announced, "This is not a nineteen-seventy Montebanque." That familiar French-German accent burred his voice, tonight more French than German.

"What!"

Werner Flemming had obviously not expected to be galled in such a way, so gratuitously, even by the perverse, the famously perverse, Henri Lamarque. Flemming's broad shoulders stiffened, his robust body seemed to swell to bursting within its tightly tailored blue pinstripe. Both hands, as big as baseball mitts, thumped the table, not by any means in the subdued tradition of the Clift dining room.

Heads turned. Waiters shuddered. But Flemming was not deterred. Jowly, heavily lined face hard, he turned even more florid than usual. His voice came, like flying gravel.

"Of course it is! What the hell are you talking about?"

Shaking his head sadly, Lamarque murmured, "My dear man, not only is it not a seventy. My belief is it is also not a Château Montebanque."

Flemming turned even redder. "Now, just one moment!" His wife, the tiny—not much over five feet—shiny, bejeweled Victoria, timidly laid her hand on his arm. Flemming glared at her. But he lowered his voice. "Listen here, Henri, I bought several lots of this, I say, reputably, in New York. I've already sold a few magnums. . . . And," Flemming muttered, "I didn't bring it here in order for you to . . . to . . ."

*"Why then?"*

"To enjoy . . . to appreciate . . ."

Which was bunk, Clara told herself. The wine was here, Henri was here, they were all here at Flemming's invitation because Flemming, the wine seller, wanted Henri's okay on the Montebanque. He wanted words he could quote to his customers. No secret, Flemming and Henri Lamarque were not friends. They had been sparring from the beginning of the evening—about the near-holy responsibilities of a wine merchant and (Flemming's view) the irresponsibility of nonaccountable critics. Henri's verdict on the Montebanque was surely not going to change Flemming's opinion of the latter.

"I enjoy," Henri sighed, "but it is no Montebanque. . . . Let the others say their say."

Furiously, Flemming nodded at the waiter.

"Pour!"

Obediently, the waiter picked up the magnum.
Holding the heavy bottle in both hands, he bent
stiffly, filling each glass to the precisely correct halfway mark.

Not waiting for the others, Flemming snatched his
off the table. He tasted. "Goddamn it, it's wonderful!
You're crazy, Henri."

Flemming appealed to his wife, on Henri's left.
The day was far away when petite Victoria Flemming,
still something of a bombshell and dressed for the
role in well-cleavaged pink plumage, would dare disagree with the overbearing Werner Flemming about
anything, wine or otherwise. One of the otherwises
had been the decor of their Tiburon home. Clara's
interior design firm had been engaged a year or so
before for a minor redecorating job . . . then swiftly
unengaged when Werner threw out Victoria's plan.

"I call it outstanding," Victoria declared. "Enchanting!"

Henri winced. "Enchanting? The word is not
widely used in the wine trade, darling."

Clara felt sorry for her. Victoria was no match for
Henri. She blushed furiously and Werner fumed.
She was no match for him either, in age or the fine
art of counterpoint. It was a continuing puzzle where
and how Werner Flemming had found Victoria. She
was much younger, in her late twenties or early thir-
ties at most, while husband Werner was a sour and
ferocious middle-aged man.

At once, Henri realized he'd drawn blood. He
spoke quickly to salve the wound. And Clara silently
thanked him for it, for his deftness, his sensitivity.
Other men, Flemming for instance, would've let her
suffer.

"But I agree with you, Victoria." Earnestly, Henri

touched his quick left hand to Victoria's forearm. "I absolutely do agree. It *is* outstanding." Then he spoke to Werner, more severely. "An outstanding petit château from the Bordeaux region, I have no doubt. But, most definitely, not a Montebanque...." Ignoring Flemming's outrage, Henri looked at Clara's father. "Alberto?"

Alberto would want no part of such foolishness. Certainly, he would not follow Henri Lamarque's lead. He grew grapes and made wine but would never bother to dispute a label, not out loud anyway. As always, Alberto would be diplomatic—for business as well as personal reasons. He was a kind and polite man and Morelli Vineyards also happened to sell a goodly bit of cabernet to Flemming's California Cellar.

Taking his own, good time, Alberto tasted, not bothering with all the swirling and sniffing, holding the stem of the wine glass lightly between his callused thumb and forefinger. Then, undramatically, he said, "I like it. Whether it's a Montebanque, I cannot say. My nose is a little used up, my palate rusty from tasting Morelli . . ."

Breezily, Lamarque said, "Perhaps it *is* a Morelli and Alberto cannot tell the difference."

If looks could kill . . . Flemming growled, "C'mon, Alberto, the *truth.*"

Irritated now and not concealing it, Alberto said, "The truth is I can't say anything more. I like it. It's a good vintage, wherever it comes from."

*"And what the hell does it matter anyway?"* This from Alberto's companion, the redoubtable Florence Rampling, retired grand opera soprano, ex-wife of conductor Rogers Tidmarsh, and a few months away from being Clara's stepmother. Florence tossed her

mass of red hair and rethrew the long indigo blue silk scarf she wore over her bosom and shoulders. "Down the hatch!" Green eyes sparkled. She emptied her glass. "Great stuff!"

Flemming was partially vindicated but . . . *down the hatch?* That was the way people talked about beer or a shot of cheap whiskey. Not a fine wine. *His* fine wine to boot.

Henri lifted his glass to Florence. "So true, dear lady! So bloody true. Wine is for imbibation. *Not* debating the provenance thereof."

"Oh, yes?" Flemming sneered. "But no jollies about it when it comes to that wine column of yours, eh? Or your lectures. Provenance means a lot when you're consulting at the auction houses. *Doesn't it?*"

"Now, now," Henri shot back jovially, "have no fear, dear Werner. You will not read about this in my column. A private tasting. Lamarque is not obligated to blow his whistle. You can go right on making your customers very happy."

Flemming gazed at him, as if the words, and Henri too, needed taming.

"You know," he said heavily, "you *could* be wrong."

Henri drummed his fingertips on the tablecloth. His eyelids drooped, the proud hawk in his face taking over. Indifferently, he picked up his glass, drank, set the glass back down, saying nothing more, shrugging one shoulder—not two—a more than cavalier gesture.

Flemming pressed, "You have been wrong once or twice, admit it."

"I admit it."

"And you could be wrong about this too."

Henri flopped his hands over on the tablecloth, a gesture of weariness, of surrender—conditional surrender, however. Whatever he was going to say, he didn't necessarily mean.

"Of course." Another shrug. "Lamarque is not incorrigible."

Florence laughed. "You mean infallible."

"Yes, yes, I mean that! *Of course.* Lamarque could be wrong about this too."

Flemming was not amused by Henri's linguistic twists. "And you *are* wrong. I'm telling you, the lots were authenticated in France. Some of the magnums had to be recorked—at the estate, at Château Montebanque. And nothing can be surer than that. They're Montebanque all right!"

"Good. I am utterly so pleased to hear it. I stand corrected."

Still, Flemming wasn't satisfied. If anything, he became more irritated. This was definitely not the Henri Lamarque endorsement he'd wanted for his very fine, old magnums of Montebanque, from the lofty Château Montebanque whose cellars went back to the time of Montecristo.

Henri had put him down—worse, put his wine down. Then recanted, but only sort of, so as not to offend. Everybody understood this and Flemming chafed all the more.

"You critics. Just like I said, you're irresponsible. It's not *your* investment. What the hell do you care? *You* don't lay out the money. Just have a sip and make a judgment. If *I* get caught in the crossfire . . . so what?"

Henri smiled, but not nicely. He *was* a professional. And an honest man. He was deeply offended by Flemming's words but he would never admit it, never show it. "Of course, Werner," he said with an aplomb too obviously meant to hide his true feelings. "My sole purpose in life is to ruin you. I come, I taste, I tattle."

THE EVENING ENDED hardly better. Henri thanked Werner Flemming, too effusively, for an excellent party. Flemming's response was a bilious look, a disgusted snort.

He wouldn't shake hands. They touched fingertips.

Werner Flemming was not a big forgiver and, in this case, Clara supposed you couldn't really blame him. The suspect Bordeaux had been finished in jittery truce. There would be no Lamarque endorsement. Flemming might as well have poured his magnum of Montebanque down the gutter.

Werner had expected too much. He should've known better. But whatever his blunder, however justified Henri might have been, nobody felt good about the way it had gone. Outside the hotel, as Henri and Clara waited with Alberto and Florence for Alberto's car to be brought around—he and Florence were driving back to Sonoma that night—Alberto stood stonily silent until Henri finally demanded, "But what else could I do? I ask of you, must I not say it as it is?"

"You went too far," Alberto barked at him.

"Flemming . . . he was testing me."

"There was no need. The wine was perfectly acceptable."

"No! Not!" Henri cried. "It is not acceptable for a wine to be called what it is not."

Alberto's voice rose a bit. "*Are* you so damn sure, Henri?"

"Yes. Sure." For a moment, Henri didn't say more. Then, half-contrite, he murmured, "Whatever I may have said, I am doubtful I put some bumps in Flemming's armor."

"You mean *dents* . . ." Alberto laughed gruffly. "Forget it." Looking up, he held out his hand, palm up. "Do I feel a drop of rain?" Slinging his raincoat over his shoulders, he helped Florence with the hood of her poncho. Some poncho, mink-lined, Clara noted, feeling threadbare in her own beat-up trenchcoat—she had a better coat but couldn't be bothered to find it—and the beloved beret mashed down over her bouncy curls. "What's done is done," Alberto closed. "Better not say any more. Werner will be coming out soon. . . . I hope to hell it's not raining in Sonoma . . ."

The harvest! Werner Flemming was forgotten.

But Henri persisted. "The man is a philistine. This was not a social evening. Flemming wanted me to try his wine. I did. I gave an opinion. *C'est tout!*"

Impatiently, Alberto retorted, "You as much as said he was made a fool of."

"And perhaps he was! If so, shouldn't he be told? It *is* a bit important, Alberto. We know some funny tricks are being played with vintage wine."

"Maybe. But tonight was not the time to say so. . . . And that was *not* Morelli wine!"

"And I did not say it was. I hinted . . ."

"Hinted?"

"Yes, sir. No more than hinted. Not even that. I poked fun."

"Ha! By now, my friend, you should know Werner Flemming can't take a joke."

"Then *dommage* for Werner Flemming!"

None too soon, Alberto's car swung around the corner and Henri gladly gave himself over to helping Florence into the passenger seat, gallantly, lengthily, saying good night.

Clara walked around the car with her father. "Why don't you drive back tomorrow morning?"

Florence still had her penthouse flat in the city. They often stayed there when they were out late in San Francisco.

Alberto put his arms around her, smiling down from a paternal height. "I'm sixty-five, little daughter . . ." Her mouth came to his chin. "Not eighty-five. No, no, I've got to be there bright and early. We're a few weeks late . . . the weather. We've begun on the pinot noir. Joe Alejandro will be waiting . . ."

Joe, the estate manager at Morelli Vineyards, jolly, big-bellied Joe Alejandro, for certain would not be biting *his* fingernails. Another year . . . another harvest. Ho-hum. Joe took the weather as it came. He didn't fight it. He also found other things to do when Alberto went into the vines every morning to spend at least the early shift with the harvesters—"to get them on the ball," he always said. "And to feel the grape. I can tell you about the vintage with my fingertips. . . ." So, no use trying to persuade him.

Shaking his head, crowned with a Roman cut of graying hair, Alberto gave her a big kiss. "That Henri of yours," he grunted, for her ears alone.

*"Of mine?"*

"He takes no prisoners, that Henri."

"Yes . . . but you have to admit, papa, Flemming *is* loud and overbearing."

"True. A bore," Alberto whispered. "Don't tell Henri I said so." He ducked down into the car. "Well, Clara . . . we'll say good night."

"Papa . . . please take it easy." Alberto liked to drive fast. In this, he was very Italian. Clara was forever cautioning him about it.

"A little drive in the moonlight . . ." He looked up at her, grinning like a boy. "Florence gives me a ticket if I go over sixty." Ah, yes, Clara told herself, he does love her. "Over the bridge and we're home in forty-five minutes. . . . *You* go carefully too."

"We just catch a cab up the hill."

"That is *not* what I mean." To make his point, Alberto turned and shook his finger at Henri. "Take Clara home, you rascal. And no more insults."


Home. Clara thought about the word. Yes, of course, the peachy-rose stuccoed Tuscan-style farmhouse in Sonoma was her real home, not the San Francisco apartment which she'd never thought of as more than temporary shelter. The home of her youth, roofed with weathered red tile, galleried on three sides by a shady terrace, the home, the *house*, built by Clara's grandparents in the nineteen twenties. Low, solid, one with the earth, it was the finishing touch, like nature's own top hat atop one of the rolling hills of Sonoma Valley. Slanting away from the house, two hundred fifty acres of grapevines, mostly trellised, some still pruned in the old-fashioned "head" manner, row upon row of vines, lush, so green in spring and summer that you could

feel the color in your gut, then in autumn and winter hardy and brown. The vines were almost like bat-
tlements or at least formations of feudal troops
gathered in perfect columns as far as the eye could
see, that is, to the next ridge to the west, toward a
hollow of land and country road on the south, to
the rising sun over a matching hill in the east and,
Clara liked to think, the North Star.

Morelli Vineyards. The perfect climate, the perfect *terroir*, as the French called it, and a house of
weight and substance—that was where she came
from. That was where her mother had died ten years
before. Now, it would be Florence's home as well as
hers.

"Let's go," Henri said. "I'm taking you home, as
Alberto orders."

Home? He was talking about her apartment. "Alberto's right," she said, as if just remembering, "you
were *very* bad."

"Yes . . . but I am very good at being very bad, Clarissima."

"No you're not." Ordinarily, Henri was just very
pleasant, a pleasure to be with, an ever fascinating
companion, his sense of humor startling, his wit col-
orful, sometimes lurid. "I was surprised," she went
on, teasingly, "to hear one of the great noses of modern oenology speaking in such a way, *la belle nose sans
mercy.*"

Henri chortled. "That is very good, Clarissima. A
bon mot, if ever I have heard one." He paused. "I
am sorry. Truly. I was drawn . . . I felt myself as if
dragged to spit out the truth like a bitter grape
seed." As she didn't reply, he waited a bit. "I don't
think I was unreasonable. But even if I was . . . I cannot stand his arrogance, his Napoleonic lower lip,

the way he treats that wife. *Victoria...*" He made a face, remembering his own unkind cut. "She cannot help it. ... He and his *merde* of a Montebanque. As if I care about his great purchase in New York City. There is plenty of good Montebanque about. A *plethora* of it, in fact, showing up at all the auctions. And I am not a trained seal!"

"You made that pretty clear."

He tossed his head. "What was your father saying to you? More about that silly thing?"

Clara smiled at him. "No. He told me I should be very careful of you."

"I do not believe it." In the back of the taxi, though, as it puffed up the steep rise toward Nob Hill, he squirmed close and took her hands, saying, "Well, you are very careful of me, aren't you?"

"Am I?"

"Yes. I think you are. Sometimes, you are extremely distant."

"No." She shook her head decidedly. "We're *close*, Henri, not distant."

"Sometimes, too close for your comfort, I think." She knew what he meant. And he wasn't really wrong. Awkwardly, Henri waited for her to say something more, to issue her usual denial. "Clarissima, say you are not unhappy with me."

"I'm not unhappy with you. But tonight, that wasn't really like you." Indeed, his great charm was that he was always lighthearted, self-deprecating, unimpressed with himself or his stature in the wine business.

"Sometimes," he answered moodily, "I am not really like me. Most times, I am like me."

Henri paid off the driver and they walked past his Jaguar. He'd parked in front of her building and they'd taken a taxi, rather than brave the downtown traffic in the early evening. Henri tossed his car keys from one hand to the other. "Well, will you give me coffee, Clara? And *some* sympathy at least?"

"Sympathy?"

"I'm sad," he said. "Sad that you're upset with me. And when I think how long we've known each other . . ."

"A long time, yes," Clara agreed, "since you first came here—from France . . ."

He winked at her and chuckled huskily. This was a secret between them. Henri was not French. Indeed, Henri Lamarque was really Heinrich Marker from Grinzing, near Vienna. He had changed his name, yes, he admitted this was one of the few dishonesties of his life, styling himself Henri Lamarque from Alsace. Because, as he had confided in Clara after he came to trust her, fine noses do not come from Austria. Geography, he had declared, was such an important element in the birth and life of a nose. So it was—he had come to her, by way of France.

". . . and I am not upset with you."

His eyes filled with tears. "*My dear Clara*, if I do ever upset you very badly, you may unveil me."

"You mean, reveal you."

"Yes, I give you permission." He put his hands on her shoulders. He kissed her emphatically. "I would require it."

"Now, now, Monsieur Lemarque, I could never tell on you. . . . Coffee. Remember? Sympathy, I don't think you need. Come along now."

Within the foyer, waiting for the elevator, still curious, Clara asked him, "Anyway, you're sure it wasn't a Montebanque, not even a bad year?"

Henri didn't answer immediately. He was busy studying himself in the mirror next to the elevator door, pulling at his tie, flipping the lapels of his blazer. Clara saw herself behind him. She was nearly as tall, though not as spare. Her trenchcoat, tightly belted, described her best. She had a good waist, she was narrow at the hips, thank God, and there was enough on the balcony. Not too much. Plenty. Henri said she was voluptuous. Whatever . . . the rain was good for her skin. Rosy cheeked, red lipped, bright eyed with anticipation. The thick hair, the more curly for the damp, honey blond, her mother had dubbed it, and the beret made her just then like a next-to-the-law Parisian *apache*. Clara caught Henri's eyes in the mirror. He whirled around and grabbed her in his arms.

"My darling, let us speak no more of that stupid wine!"

Impulsively, she kissed him. Then pushed him away. "*Au contraire*, let us speak of wine. I *am* interested, you know. . . . What you said to my father about funny tricks. What did you mean by that?"

"Nothing! Tricks of the trade, no more. We are all aware there is sometimes cheating on vintages. *Nothing*," he repeated. "Clara, really? You want to discuss boring wine?" He stuffed his hands in his pockets, then seeing there was no way out of it, gave in. "All right." He shrugged mightily. "That wine, it might be Montebanque. I am not *infallible*, as wonderful Florence said. Such a woman, your father is so lucky . . . I would have to see the unopened bottle, the capsule over the cork, the cork itself, examine the label, taste in a clinical atmosphere and so on . . . and on. Ad nauseam."

"But you gave Werner such grief."

"Well . . ." Henri pulled his ear. "I must say I did have a very bad feeling about it."

"Bad feeling? I've never heard that category used at a wine tasting."

The elevator door opened. They stepped inside. They were alone. Again, he folded her in. Clara didn't resist, even kissed him back, enjoying the complicity of his lips, a stolen kiss on a moving elevator. A pleasured look on his face, Henri was about to kiss her again when the door opened to her floor. They stepped out. Clara opened her bag for her key.

"You know," Henri said chattily, "I was once talked into doing a blind tasting on a TV program down in Los Angeles. It was Merv Griffin's old show, I recall. Four of us—a vintner from Napa, myself, a wine-store proprietor, and a restauranteur. We were what you call sandbagged. We got them all wrong. We looked entirely *stupide*."

This was the apartment Clara had shared with that world-class rotten rotter Tom Addey. It was all hers now, part of their divorce settlement a year ago.

"Always so calm here, *chérie*."

Now it was, yes. Once, it had not been, had been, rather, a scene of loud voices, nasty words, and deep hurt. No question, the break had been painful. But by now, finally, her invasive feeling of inadequacy was slipping away. But its lingering effect still stood between her and Henri.

The living room was not enormous but it was of good proportions. Clara's decorator eye had chosen it for that reason. She had redone the walls in garden-green fabric, covered the floors with celadon shades of carpeting and rugs, upholstered the furniture in darker greens, chosen new pictures with green in mind. Often, she entertained would-be clients here so they could see what she was all about.

They went straight to the kitchen and Henri took his usual place on a high stool at the granite-topped counter. Clara attended to the espresso machine, very aware all the while of his strong physical presence, remembering in her loins the kiss just completed. Henri folded his hands on the counter . . . unfolded them. He jerked around on the high chair, crossed his legs . . . uncrossed them. He could not sit still for long. His moods shifted just as rapidly, part and parcel of Henri's charisma. Charisma, yes, one could call it that. Why else were people always so glad to be around him, to laugh at his remarks, to agree—or disagree—with his sharp, sometimes overcritical judgments?

From his present crestfallen look, Clara guessed Henri was intensely sorry by now that in effect he'd manhandled Flemming's wine. He had made amends to Victoria but with Werner he had been too adamant. Henri put his hand to his brow, rubbed his nose. What a face, Clara thought. More than merely lived in, his face was a map—an atlas— of his past life, its lines and creases accentuated under the overhead lighting, like footpaths across his craggy features. For one scary moment, Henri looked a lot older than the late forties he claimed to be.

"Quit worrying about it," she advised him. "Werner will recover."

"Worry? Me?" He paused. "Yes, well . . . but, listen, Clara, my little story does have a point, which is that it's risky to make judgments about wine. The whole *business* is such theatre. And, when you consider, what is theatre but deception?"

"Deception?"

"I mean in the presentation, the theatre of the tasting ceremony, the theatre props of fine, old châteaux, noble names, the fine costumes of labeling . . ."

"Were you doing *theatre* tonight?"

Henri laughed gleefully, emitting personality like fine sparks flying off a grinding wheel. "Ah! I do theatre at all times, beloved. Starting with my name, as you alone know. The theatre of Lamarque . . . versus Marker. One a *grand cru,* the other a bourgeois table wine."

"Deception . . ."

"Yes. But there is also *truth* in the theatre, look at Shakespeare." He paused, then continued earnestly, "Listen, Clarissima, *yes,* I think there may have been an imposter in that bottle."

"Is that what you meant by people playing funny tricks?"

"Yes. And Alberto knows, like everybody else, there is vintage counterfeiting. All fine products, if the price is right, are counterfeited. I think Montebanque is not exempt." He paused again. "Clarissima, I have some experience with the Château Montebanque. . . . What more can I say? A brandy, please. I beg you."

"What experience?"

"Nothing pleasant, I can tell you. Don't ask. In due course, I will tell you . . . brandy, please!"

Clara let it go, for the moment anyway. "Henri, I don't know how your liver keeps up."

"It *is* a merry chase, my beloved."

Clara poured him a small snifter of Hennessy VSOP, the best she had in the house. The espresso machine rumbled. Taking great care, luxuriously inhaling brandy fumes as he warmed it, Henri rolled the glass in the palms of his hands, as if this were where the universe began and ended, as if brandy had fueled the Big Bang. And Clara shivered, feeling left out, wanting more, wanting him.

Finally, Henri took a tiny sip of the brandy, groaning with such pleasure he might've been in pain. "How I love it here, Clara," he said, "being with you, alone, like this. Late in the night. A brandy . . . a big window overlooking city lights, the silent city, the bay, the bridge. I am so lucky, a forever-tourist in paradise."

Clara placed his espresso in front of him, sitting down with her own on the opposite side of the counter. "But nothing like Paris, or Vienna."

"Such a thought, perish!" He waved his hand dismissively. "As good as Paris. Better than Vienna. Do you know, when I think of Europe, what I think most of now as I decline in years?"

"Don't tell me—your village in France."

"Yes. Absolutely. My small peasant house in my village under Mont Blanc." His eyes went far away. "To there I will go when I am worn down, Clara. And soon. I cannot drink much more wine. Even now, you know, at parties, I water it."

"You didn't dilute the Montebanque."

"I would not. Could not. That would be immoral."

"Not if it was a fake."

"Well," he argued, "I couldn't know for sure if I poured in a lot of water. And Werner would've been truly insulted." At her doubtful look, he frowned. "But we say no more. *Finito!* I say nothing more about this."

"I know it's hard for you."

Hard? This was a most difficult predicament for a

man who had taken his vows to wine. The high priest in Henri would be vastly offended by the mortal sin of tampering, faking, counterfeiting. He would be embarrassed, even though the sin was not his own. But what was he to do about it? Where did one send the sinner? Was there a special hell for those who misused the grape? Alberto would have said so.

Not responding, Henri cuddled the brandy snifter. "Such an aroma! God! A miracle how they do this!" He sipped stingily, eyelids drooping sleepily. He smiled at her beatifically, then was in her eyes, invading, absorbing her with his own lively, interested . . . *interesting* eyes. Despite his talk of a liver in jeopardy, of declining years and imminent retirement, Henri was not used up or smug or blasé. He enjoyed the world and all its civilized trappings. Enjoyed? Adored.

"*Seriously,* Clara. This brandy . . . it may kill me instantly. I may fall on your floor, a dead man." His eyes sparkled. "And what then? How would you explain a dead nose on your kitchen floor? What would you say?"

Clara laughed. "I think I'm old enough not to have to explain a dead nose on my kitchen floor."

"Oh, Clara! Come with me to France. Tomorrow! *Tonight!*"

"And my business?"

"Forget that. We would be a *smash hit* in Petit-Pont." His village, near Grenoble.

"I'd probably never come back."

That was a fact. Clara believed it to be a fact anyway. Not that she was tired of San Francisco. And, no, she wasn't weary of life itself. Her business? She was successful enough at the decorating game—but lately had begun to think of herself as coasting along, of merely going through the motions. She'd talked about her malaise with her father. Alberto blamed Tom Addey. He blamed the divorce. They didn't talk about Martha, Clara's daughter, eighteen and away at school in the east, Martha Gates, her daughter by youthful mistake and a rushed first marriage: Tom Addey's stepdaughter. Martha had developed a deep affection for Tom. She had taken the divorce harder than Clara.

All told, it had become the goddamnedest mess. No wonder she was tired of that long chapter of her life and all the participants, including herself.

"Neither would I come back," Henri said warmly. "Together, we would be in Petit-Pont. Taking long walks. Reading our books. Making excursions. Visiting museums and churches. Fishing in mountain streams. Do you like to fish, Clara?"

"I've never fished."

"Oh hell, then skiing."

"I could ski."

"Not even so much the skiing. It is the ambiance, Clara, the feeling, a sensualness."

"Careful, you'll sweep me away."

"I wish. I wish."

"Life certainly wouldn't be dull."

But wasn't she leading Henri on, promising or hinting at more than she could deliver? If he cared. . . . It was true, she had known him a long time. They'd been chums in the beginning, not lovers, shared so many meals, evenings out, jokes, friends. Now, they were lovers but it was difficult to take him entirely seriously when he started in about "love." When she'd been married and, as far as she'd known then, happily married to Tom Addey, Henri had hovered, praising her, flattering her, often embarrassing her.

Tom had laughed at Henri, assuming he was gay, taking Henri's good manners, his flamboyance, his joyfulness, for gay credentials. Within days after the separation, Henri had begun to pursue Clara with fervor. Though often out of town on wine business, when available he was her escort and, after Alberto, a primary confidant. He'd given Clara what she'd most needed—exposure, people, conversation, diversion. Henri had helped her bridge the bad times. Now he wanted more. It wasn't about money. He was smart enough to know she had not much of that. And he seemed to have plenty of his own. Nor was it about social position—Henri was well-known and a well-known figure around San Francisco, even sought after by society high and low. Henri knew all the people he needed to know.

"One dullness from Lamarque," he proclaimed, "and you have permission to kill me."

"Kill you? Everybody is permitted to be dull once in a while."

"No! You can kill me. You must."

"Stop saying that."

He took her hands. "Clara, will you come? You know that I love you." Henri stared at her so frankly and guilelessly that Clara blushed. His eyes, dark and snapping under heavy brows, demanded attention, agreement, alliance. Quickly, he added, "I do not ask if you love me."

She shook her head. "I can't say those kinds of words anymore."

"But the time will come. I know that it will come." In the meantime . . .

Clara was moved. She was drawn to Henri. There was nothing tentative or wishy-washy about his physical attraction. His hands tightened over hers. She drew a long breath.

Henri heard her. He was delighted. "Tuscan maiden. Etruscan princess. The Titian tresses, thick, golden tresses . . ."

"Her breast heaves . . ."

"I know it! I observed! I saw your breast heave! I love it when your breast heaves!"

She came around the counter. "Drink your espresso, Henri."

"I will! I will!"

He gulped it down, rattling the cup back on the saucer, then bolted the brandy.

Clara moved closer. He turned toward her, his eyes warm, steady, expectant. She didn't disappoint. Clara kissed him carefully, agreeably. . . . There was a message there: *yes*. His answering look was a sad-eager smile. He was surprised . . . not surprised. At that moment, again, for an instant, he seemed much, much older. Not so much older in years as definitely an older soul. If, in a previous life, Clara had been an Etruscan princess, then Henri had tended grapes in the Vineyard of Eden.

"It's late," she murmured. *"Shall we?"*

So voluble, so declarative before, Henri suddenly became silent and shy. Taking his hand, she led him back through the apartment. He dragged along, as if he didn't know where she was taking him, to her bedroom, or the elevator.

But he knew very well. He knew where her bedroom was just as well as she did.

# *three*

"CLARA!" EVEN OVER the telephone, Florence's rich voice throbbed. "There's a letter from Italy. One of your cousins has invited us to stay with her in Lucaterra, as long as we like!"

"Which cousin?" There were so many.

"Maria. Maria Morelli."

Clara laughed. "There must be a dozen Maria Morellis. Papa always says our family tree is really a bowl of spaghetti. . . ."

"This Maria's house has a perfect view of the towers of San Gimignano . . ."

So did they all.

Alberto had proposed that he and Florence Rampling be married back there in the old country, in Lucaterra, the tiny hilltop town closest to the Morelli family's farms, vineyard, and winery, and Florence, being a true romantic, thought this was a fabulous idea.

"And there's a little church," she went on.

"It'll be beautiful," Clara said simply. "And you'll sing for us . . ."

"Of course. Afterward."

Florence wouldn't have to be talked into that. She'd retired from the operatic stage five years before, explaining that she'd stretched it just by going until she was fifty. But she rarely missed an opportunity postretirement to break into song. Just so, she'd been singing impromptu at somebody's birthday party when she and Clara's father had met. The voice, Alberto said, he'd heard the voice before he'd ever seen her. So, yes, she'd sing for the wedding party in Lucaterra, a short hop from La Scala in Milano, but a world and a whole career away.

"They'll love you in Lucaterra."

"I know they will!" Florence cried, her soprano voice already engaged. "And I'm glad Alberto came up with the idea for us to be married there."

But Clara knew Florence understood as well as she did what Alberto's true intentions were. Marriage in San Francisco would have been too painful a reminder for him of that other, fantastic festivity when he'd married Evelyn Cabott . . . and sad for Clara who'd be remembering her dead mother. And not easy, either, for Grandmother Mina Cabott, a widow herself, now in her eighties.

"But what about the Scolettis of Sicily?" Florence demanded. "Alberto doesn't expect they'll even show."

"Ah!" said Clara. "That's the other bowl of spaghetti. My grandmother, Sofia, she was a Scoletti, and Sicilian. Alfredo, my grandfather Morelli, a Tuscan. The Morellis like to claim a family connection back to the Medicis. Sofia and Alfredo met in Rome—actually inside St. Peter's—during a school outing and fell in love. Didn't Papa tell you about that?"

"Not as well as you will."

"The families were horrified when they found out. You know how the Sicilians supposedly despise anything that isn't Sicilian and the Tuscan people consider anything south of Siena the equivalent of darkest Africa. So . . . Sofia and Alfredo caught a boat. They got married in New York, then came to California. . . ."

"Romeo and Juliet with a happy ending."

"Except that the Scolettis have never forgiven the Morellis—dutiful Sicilian daughter abducted by a northern barbarian seventy-five years ago. We've never had any kind of a relationship with the Scolettis," Clara said, "sadly enough. . . ."

"Well!" Florence huffed. "Those stupid Capulet-Scolettis better get their act up-to-date because we're going down to Sicily especially to introduce *me*—that's on our way to Capri. Beloved Capri—I sang there once. The moon was out. My voice carried all the way to the mainland."

"I believe you," Clara said.

The plan was for Florence and Alberto to fly to Rome in mid-November, just five weeks away, then head immediately to Lucaterra to attend to prenuptial formalities. After that, they'd tour around. Venice was a destination too. No doubt Florence had "O Solo Mio" 'ed up and down the Grand Canal.

"Now, Clara," Florence continued, "the date is set for December the twentieth . . . a perfect time, Alberto says, because the grapes are dormant and we're anything but . . ." Her voice leapt, then pitched down when she realized what she'd said. "You'll be there, you've promised."

"Of course."

"And Martha." Naturally. "My son Charles . . ." From her marriage to the flamboyant conductor, Rogers Tidmarsh. "It'll be good for him to have some fun."

"He can bring his violin."

"He probably will," Florence said dryly, "and forget his socks. You've met him. Remember, he was late getting to the restaurant in New York and they had to lend him a tie? He's hopeless, I fear." Florence took a deep breath, then continued briskly. "Clara, there's something I've been wanting to say to you. I want to tell you—*I enjoy this house.* You may have funny feelings about my being here, I understand that. But I love the house. And, you know, I can feel your mother . . ."

Clara sat down. Florence's intensity had that effect.

"I'm not trying to say the place is haunted or anything. What I am trying to tell you is, I think your mother likes me. I think she's satisfied I'm here."

Clara did believe in generous and happy ghosts. "Yes . . . I'm sure she is satisfied."

"Good." The diva was pleased. "So good! That makes me happy. *Happy!* Now, here comes your father . . . *Alberto! Telefono!*"

Clara heard her father's light footfalls as he came down the hallway toward the sunroom in the back of the house. Then his voice. "That rascal," he boomed, "he got you safely home the other night?"

"Sure. How was your drive?"

"One hour, door to door. Florence told you, there's a letter from Lucaterra. . . ." He sounded just as pleased. This would mean a lot—the old family accepted him, welcomed him "home" with his bride-to-be. "Clara, everything is happening all at once. Today, another offer."

"To sell?"

"Yes." He paused reflectively. "From a big com-

pany based in New York. Bertram Hill. They own
various vineyards, labels . . ."

"A good offer, Papa?"

"Substantial . . . I won't say how much."

"Well . . ." A lump in her throat. "It's supposed to
be a seller's market . . ."

For his sake, Clara hoped Alberto would accept.
Off and on, over the past couple of years, he had
been talking, first vaguely, then more seriously, of
getting out. Now, with Florence in his life . . . but,
damn it, Clara hated the idea of parting with the
land, the house . . . it was her past too.

"For the moment, yes," Alberto agreed, "it's very
much a seller's market. But for how long? California
is turning into one big vineyard. Eventually, who's
going to drink all this wine?"

"That won't be your worry if you sell now, Papa."

"No. But Bertram Hill does worry me."

"I've never heard of them."

"Few people have, outside the industry." He ru-
minated. "Clara, you know I'm just a country boy . . .
a hick."

"Yes. Sure."

"But I read a lot. Bertram Hill are owners, im-
porters, distributors . . . big guys. I've seen some negative reports in the wine journals. I'm thinking about
getting a friend in New York to check them out. But
first, I'd like to know what Henri thinks. When will
you be seeing him?"

"Maybe tonight."

Another pause. "You see Henri Lamarque *every*
night?"

"I said *maybe.*"

"Clara, I'm not even asking." Clara smiled to herself. Oh no, he wasn't probing but she must not

think, either, that he was so dense he didn't have a fair idea of what was going on, or so bad a father that he didn't care. "You know, Clara, I like Henri very much."

"I know that. And I know exactly what you're thinking."

That at heart, in her heart, she was still a little girl. That she must tread carefully. That Henri Lamarque was a man of the world. That she must not allow herself to be hurt or taken advantage of again, ever.

"No, you *don't* know what I'm thinking. Which is, would you like to invite Lamarque to be with you in Lucaterra? Shall we invite him?"

"Invite him to Lucaterra?" Clara was surprised. Another lump in her throat, for Alberto's suggestion was no sudden inspiration. She knew it had been on his mind, that he'd discussed it with Florence. Not *go* with you to Lucaterra. To *be* with you in Lucaterra, he'd said.

"It never occurred to me. Henri is so busy . . . I don't know if he'd take the time."

Alberto chuckled. "If you asked him, he'd take the time, I guarantee it. But it's up to you . . . you'd make a couple. That's always easier for seating arrangements. In fact, you make a good-looking couple. *Striking,* that's the word."

He'd stolen her breath. "I'm not quite ready to be a couple again."

"As *I* am not quite ready to sell our vineyard . . . *yet.*" Now, he was chewing over another thought. "You know, I believe Henri was right. That wasn't a seventy Montebanque. It might as well have been a Morelli, just as Henri said . . ."

"Papa, do you seriously think Flemming would try

to pass off a Morelli cabernet as an expensive Bordeaux?"

"Why not?" he said slyly. "No big deal. Sixty-five percent cabernet, thirty cabernet franc, with a little merlot perfume thrown in . . . what's the big difference between them?"

*"Not seriously!"*

"No," he replied, "not seriously, because Werner Flemming wouldn't have the nerve. But somebody else up the wine chain might, who knows? Henri's got the right idea. People *are* beginning to talk about counterfeiting again. A depressing thought. As soon as big money gets involved, the con artists crawl out of the woodwork."

"But Papa, there's so much wine around—who needs a fake? It doesn't make sense."

"*Money* often doesn't make sense, Clara," Alberto came back sternly. "Top-flight wines, especially the Bordeaux, are bought and sold like commodities these days—sometimes the cases aren't even opened and tasted. Very convenient for counterfeiters . . . and *ideal* for money launderers. There're lots of cash transactions in the wine trade. You pay a fortune for a good case of Lafite, a year later you sell it, the money is washed clean. They come, they go, these outbreaks of faking . . . somebody gets caught, the contagion recedes. Then you hear about it again. We're there now. People pay too much for wine anyway. The *nouveaux riches*, you know about them," he went on before she could interrupt. "The brand of idiot who's got to have the most expensive, whatever it is, never mind whether it's the best—cars, boats, airplanes, one-thousand- or two-thousand-dollar bottles of Pétrus. And you're right, there's so much wine on the market, who's going to notice a few fakes? A real operator who's willing to take a small risk can easily double his money. Or triple. Quadruple. Or more . . ."

"So," Clara posed the question, "you think Werner Flemming poured a fake for Henri Lamarque to taste? He'd have to be stupid."

"Right," Alberto said, "and Werner Flemming isn't stupid."

"Unless he didn't know it was a fake."

"Ah!" Alberto laughed softly. "Leave us not speculate any further. Clara . . . there's something I want you to do for me."

"Fine . . . as long as it's got nothing to do with wine."

"Entirely different subject—your grandma Mina is hinting she wants to come to Lucaterra."

"My God! I hope you don't want me to talk her out of it."

"No, no!" If Mina decided to go to Lucaterra, she would, and nobody was going to convince her otherwise. "If she wants to come, well, fine—if it's not going to make her feel terrible."

"Why should it?"

"Well, you know why. It'll remind her of your mother. I wouldn't want that to detract . . . oh, damn it, I don't want Florence to be worried. She's already worried about you."

*"Me?"*

"Sometimes," he said uncomfortably, "she gets the idea you resent her. . . ." He waited a bit. "I've told her she's wrong."

"Papa," Clara said sharply, "I do not resent Florence. In fact, I just told her so a minute ago. I *promise* you I do not." Not quite true. But principally true, with lapses. "I'm happy for you. For both of you. I do *not* resent Florence. Believe me!" But not to protest too much.

"All right," he said. "Good. I appreciate that. She likes you a lot, you know."

*"And I like her."*

"Okay, okay. Good . . . good." He wanted away from the subject. "Anyway, please, I'd like you to go see Mina, see what she's thinking."

"I understand. You don't want any scenes in Lucaterra. I'll check her . . . what? State of mind?"

"Yes. That's it." There was relief in his voice. "And please don't forget to ask Monsieur Lamarque about Bertram Hill."

"I've written down the name, Papa."

"I need input. It's not a small thing to sell a vineyard that's been in the family for going on a century."

"I know that."

"They're very insistent. They say they won't take no for an answer."

"Pushy."

"In a sort of friendly way . . ."

Oh, yes, this Bertram Hill had better be friendly and very, very courteous. Otherwise, in his own courtly way, Alberto would slam the door in their faces.

"You will be seeing him tonight?" he asked again. "Tell him I really need to talk to him. It's urgent."

Clara laughed affectionately. "Papa, you know, he's going to be on the lookout for your shotgun."

"What? Why, Clara!" Alberto laughed with surprise. "You're something else! I wouldn't do such a thing! I would never interfere."

# *four*

HENRI STRODE TOWARD her. His walk was springy, like that of an acrobat, Clara told herself, as if he were about to perform a cartwheel. But couldn't, of course, because of the briefcase and the package in his arm.

"Clarissima! Waiting long? I am sorry."

"Only a minute or two."

He kissed one cheek. Then the other. "Here. Surprise."

"*Surprise?*" Hardly. The package was a bottle of wine wrapped in tissue.

"And glasses in the briefcase. For our drink on the ferryboat to Sausalito! We will sit in the stern and toast the city."

"And freeze. It's cold on the bay at night, Henri."

"We will huddle. We have our raincoats. We will be *warm.*"

The plan was to stop at his condo, a five-minute walk from the pier in Sausalito, pick up his car and drive a few miles north to Mill Valley for dinner. He'd made a reservation for eight P.M. In the morning, she would take him to the airport in his Jaguar, then park it at her place to await his return.

Henri reached into his pocket. "*Regards!* A note. The wine is a peace offering from Herr Flemming."

Dear Henri,
Try it again and change your mind.
                                            Kind regards,
                                            Werner Flemming

"Another Montebanque? You accepted it?"

"I could not send it back, that would be churlish of me, adding injury to injury after that most horrible evening. Besides, Clarissima," he said, "an eighty-eight. And no magnum, as you perceive. Delivered this afternoon. We will not drink it with solemnity or regard to nose. A few tastes, a *soupçon* for the cold, dark night. Maybe two. Or three. To celebrate *us*. And my good-bye drink . . ." Henri was off to Portland the next morning to be the honored guest at a gathering of Oregonian pinot noir pioneers. "Now come, Clarissima, let us go or we will miss the boat."

Purse slung over her shoulder, Clara matched his quick march through the Ferry Building. In step, they bumped hips and laughed. She caught his mood. This *was* exciting. An adventure, catching the next boat to Sausalito with her lover, Henri Lamarque.

"What's with Werner Flemming? How come his hot pursuit?"

Henri smiled at her darkly. "You are aware, my sweetness, that in the German language the word *Gift* means poison?"

"But he wouldn't . . ."

"No," he chuckled, "I do not think so."

In the best of worlds, offerings of wine weren't supposed to mean a thing. But in Werner's case,

Clara suspected, the motive would be a bit more tangled. "He wants you to back off. He's afraid you'll write something bad in your *Imbiber* magazine."

"But I said I would not do so. I promised. No, I wager Werner merely wants to be loved."

The Sausalito boat was just ploughing into view, pushing silvery waves before it. Reversed engines roaring, the craft gently bumped into its mooring. With a rattle and crash, the gangway hit the dock. A few passengers disembarked and Henri and Clara went on board, at first into the warmth of the brightly lit cabin where he corkscrewed the bottle, then, when the ferry was under way again for Sausalito, they went outside and took two seats in the stern. Alone there in the brisk wind, they watched the lighted towers of the city retreat. Ahead, the hills of Marin were a faded blue, the Golden Gate Bridge a girdle of light joining the myth of the city with the reality of the mainland.

"Our *bateau*," Henri said. "So powerful, no? Beating the waves, making for the sea."

It could have been so. They could have been aboard the SS *Kukumaru*, bound for Yokohama, for it was that kind of a misty night and their vessel slipped through swells that were long and fat and greasy. Now and then, a salty spray stung Clara's cheeks. Wind whipped the rigging just as it was supposed to, making ropes and tackle moan. The ship's horn blew. How else? Mournfully.

"It is time for our wine," Henri said.

He removing the glasses from his briefcase, giving them to Clara to hold. Despite what he'd said about not taking Flemming's bottle seriously, he took a whiff of bouquet before he poured. Even in heavy weather, Clara marveled, like a doctor or priest on a battlefield, Henri had to go through the motions.

"You could be alone on a desolate island with a bottle of cheap plonk and you'd do your tasting routine, wouldn't you?"

"I cannot help myself."

For her part, Clara bypassed the ritual, simply putting her glass to her lips . . . taking a mouthful . . . swallowing. Just in time for his inevitable question.

"What say you, beloved?"

"This time I can hear the blackberries singing." That was nice, though, in truth, it was not easy to hear the blackberries singing in this wind. But it was the phrasing that counted.

His eyes gleamed. "Spoken like the winemaker's daughter!"

"And we haven't given it even a minute to catch its breath."

Henri chortled. "Oxygen is no problem out here in the bay, Clarissima. Besides, we give it mouth-to-mouth resuscitation."

"The kiss of life."

"Your kiss would bring it to life," he came back passionately.

How could she match him? Henri's fluent, often poetic use of her language, his third, sometimes startled her. Somebody, a rival critic, Clara recalled, not meaning it kindly, had once called him Cyrano, the reference being to his prominent nose, not his poetic license. But this Cyrano de Bergerac was speaking for himself, using words that seemed to Clara to be beautiful . . . provocative. Evocative.

"Anyway," he sang, "it is *not* a nineteen-seventy of *questionable parentage.*"

"My father agrees with you about that, by the way."

"Of course he does." But Henri was not much comforted. "A perfectly good wine . . . but minor. Not even close to Montebanque's second wine, the one they call Gitane Flambé. . . . An insult to Lamarque. To Alberto. To you!"

"No. Not me, Henri. I don't take it seriously."

"Clarissima . . ." He eyed her earnestly. "You must! The point! We speak of only one bottle. *Bien.* But consider—if this bottle had been merely bad, corked or otherwise ruined, then, yes, a good laugh, an embarrassed Werner, no doubt, too bad. But the wine was not corked . . . not bad. Merely minor."

"Or simply mislabeled . . ."

"Maybe. Yes," he agreed. "Of course . . . maybe."

Disconsolately, Henri turned for relief to the running sea. All was *not* right with the world. Clara touched his cheek with her lips, even in the wind detecting his scent, a masculinity untainted by noxious cologne. She felt his well-contained body, the magnetic field of muscle and bone. But, for a second, he seemed hardly aware of her.

"Henri, you're not responsible."

He shook his head bitterly. "This bottle of eighty-eight says to forget all about it, Clarissima. In honesty, I should throw it overboard."

"No, Henri, you've got it wrong. We drink it. We throw the empty overboard."

Henri stared at her, as if detecting brilliance. "Of course! So practical a Clarissima . . ." As he lifted his glass to toast her, a hump of land loomed to their right, dark, desolate. "*Alcatraz,*" he said, "a prison of an island. Your famous Al Capone lived there for some time. Crook. Tax dodger. Murderer. A man of low ethics and no moral standards. . . ."

Clara held the collar of her raincoat to her neck.

It was damned cold out here and the wine didn't help. She shivered. But it was more than the cold. Henri was making too much of the blasted thing— or was he? An indefinable anxiety also chilled her.

"Would you be so unhappy with me if I did forget about it, Clarissima?"

"Of course I wouldn't." She'd be relieved.

At once, he looked away, at the sky, the water, receding Alcatraz, turning his Cyrano-nose to the wind, brooding. "Clara, you know that I do not hate Flemming. I endeavor *not* to hate. No, Werner Flemming I can take or leave. He is a philistine. A barbarian." He thought for a moment. "Werner Flemming should be in the beer business."

"Well! *That* does it for Werner Flemming."

"Yes. And all similar philistines and barbarians!"

Which, for some reason, made Clara remember what she was supposed to ask Henri. "Do you know anything about a company called Bertram Hill?"

Henri's eyes jumped. "Yes. I do. Why do you ask?"

"They've made an offer for Morelli Vineyards."

"To buy? What sort of offer? A good one? *Merde!* Do not tell me so!"

"Alberto wants to talk to you about it."

Henri gripped the tip of his nose between thumb and forefinger, rocking his head woefully. "Oh, God! You must tell Alberto to keep one hand on his wallet, the other on his . . ." Then he rallied. "But your father doesn't need my advice. There is a good deal of word of mouth . . ."

With that, Henri poured the last of the Monte-banque. Without fanfare, he dropped the bottle over the side. *"Voilà!"* He stood up, holding out his glass. "My darling, to your most wonderful health . . . also wealth and happiness." He drank, then heaved his empty glass into the bay. "There! As if smashing a brandy glass in the fireplace. To test the Fates." Less flamboyantly, Clara finished most of hers, then dropped the dregs and the glass overboard. Laughing excitedly, Henri pulled her up, clutching her tightly to him. "Clarissima! Sausalito *encroaches*!" The bright lights of the little waterfront city shone over his shoulder. "You must tell Alberto that he may count on Lamarque to help protect the pristine vineyards of the West. Yes, I can tell you about Bertram Hill. *Oh, yes.* Over the last decade, BHill, as they are called, has quietly, sometimes not so quietly, grown—like that creature at the bottom of the sea with the . . ."

Freeing his arms, he made tentacles of his fingers.

"Octopus."

"Yes, octopus. The Bertram Hill octopus *swallows*, grows ever larger . . . and larger, devouring all in its path." Henri meant Clara to be put off. He kept hugging her. "But they are manageable, yes. All depends on what Alberto wants from the deal."

Clara knew exactly what Alberto wanted. He wanted out from under the daily pressure. He wanted not to worry about the bank. About hiring and firing. About the petty details. "His aim," she told Henri, "is to go on as a consultant. He doesn't want to quit entirely."

"Okay, okay! But consultant to *what*? Bertram Hill knows exactly what they want, where they're going. They need no consultant to tell them that."

"Then he won't accept."

"Good! I hope not! We purists will be relieved. We don't like such international octopi sucking in all the small fries. . . . But it is happening anyway. *Inevitably.* Small is doomed. . . . *Big* is the way of the

new world. One-world-market supreme . . ." He was
standing with both arms around her, careless of people emerging from the cabin, in preparation for
docking. His voice rushed. "We must flee, Clara, you
and me, before it's too late. Like a big glowing me-
teorite aimed at planet Earth, *big* will devastate us
all. . . ." He squeezed her. "Clara, come with me to
Mont Blanc!"

Bumping pilings, the ferryboat shuddered.

"Not this year," Clara said.

But maybe next. Henri knew her song. Sadly, he
picked up his briefcase, his left arm still around her
waist. They moved toward the gangway. "Then, shall
I tell you all about Bertram Hill?"

"I wish you would."

HENRI RECITED THE *histoire* of BHill over
glasses of champagne and a plate of smoked salmon
and brown bread.

"You see, Bertram Hill is, or was, a very old and
respected name in the spirits business. The original
Bertram Hill was an Englishman who moved his
shop from London to Boston and then New York
City in the middle eighteen hundreds. The family is
long dead but the name goes on. For a time, BHill
was run by an Irish scoundrel named Jimmy Moriar-
ity, nicknamed the Professor. In the twenties, during
Prohibition, ownership went to another Irishman, I
forget his name, then his son. Next the war years.
Postwar, BHill passed into the control of a man
named Mercer Puce, a New York dilettante and afi-
cionado, and finally into bankruptcy ten years ago
due to his mismanagement. At this point, the present owners stepped in . . ." He paused a beat. "The

Pinjatta brothers. Franco and Maximilian, who is known as Maxey."

"Bertram Hill begets *Pinjattas*? And *they* want to buy Morelli? Who are they?"

"The Pinjattas, they are Venezuelan. Originally from Colombia, via Mexico. Their beginnings were in South American wine—the Chilean, Argentine. They went on to Spain. They own sherry in Spain and port in Portugal. From the Rioja area of northern Spain, they invaded Bordeaux. . . ."

Clara blinked. "You're going to tell me *they* own Château Montebanque, aren't you?"

"Exactly." His voice dropped meaningfully. "Bertram Hill has owned Château Montebanque for fifteen years . . . and already they have a big ambition to be nominated by their Bordeaux neighbors to the select group of first growths. . . ." He shook his head. "They will not make it. If they were French . . . maybe, after another generation."

"And now they're invading California. But why Morelli? We're so small, Henri, not much more than one of the boutique vineyards."

"Ah, but one of the finest of the small California estates. Morelli would be a prize!" Henri cocked one knee up on the sailcloth-covered couch, the better to face her. "And, of course, Clarissima, there might be other uses for an excellent Morelli."

"At this point, I don't dare ask what you mean."

Henri laid both hands on her forearm, as if to prepare her. "Shall I make you a terrible hypothesis—a *suppose*? Suppose an unscrupulous winemaker or dealer, a wine *entrepreneur* we can call him, suppose he wanted to expand his profits in an inventive way. Suppose he had unlimited access to the right bottles, labels, appropriate corks. Suppose each week he faked up several hundred cases of imposter wine, as I like to call it. Suppose he wholesaled such wine for one, two hundred dollars a bottle, that is twelve or twenty-four hundred a case, against an outlay of two hundred dollars' worth of superior but nonvintage cabernet enlarged with good merlot and cabernet franc . . ."

"That's a *horrible* hypothesis. But," she objected, "you're basing all this on *one single* bottle of funny Montebanque."

Leaning closer, he whispered, "And suppose Mr. Entrepreneur distributed this wine through compliant wine dealers, ten cases here, twenty there . . . one hundred elsewhere, here in America . . . in the Far East . . . *worldwide*. Suppose. *Just suppose*."

"I'm doing the arithmetic . . ."

"No need. I can tell you. If he is very impudent and makes two thousand dollars per case, one hundred cases equals two hundred thousand dollars. A neat sum. Even only once a month, faking a thousand or so cases a year, a mere drop in the world wine bucket . . . *suppose*. Over a year he clears more than two million. The wine retailer makes another million, or more."

"Henri, are you saying this is Bertram Hill's sideline?"

Henri pulled back. "Not for a fact, Clarissima. So far, what have we? Rumors. One magnum of wine with false credentials. Much insider talk. Alberto must draw his own conclusion."

"Well, I know damn well what that's going to be— after you tell him all this."

He smiled. "But more, Clarissima. A *trumped* card! Werner Flemming acquired that magnum, his shipment of same, from . . ."

Clara saw it coming. "None other than . . ."

"Yes. Bertram Hill."

"How do you know that?"

"*I know.*"

"So, then, maybe your hypothesis is more than a hypothesis."

Henri shrugged in that perfect Gallic way. "*C'est ça. Rien ne va plus, chérie.* We know of some previous trickery. A few years ago, an amount of Gitane Flambé, their second wine, was, we might say, mislabeled as Château Montebanque. The balloon burst. Pinjattas severely chastised." He grimaced. "Is the same happening again, in different form? We ask. We speculate. But we must not, *cannot,* make such an accusation until the time is right, until we are sure. Or does Lamarque forget about it, as Werner Flemming recommends?" Pensively. "It might not be good for Henri Lamarque's health to close the hypothesis. Do you understand?"

"Understand? *Jesus!*"

Henri laughed acidly. "Château Jesus, if you please. May we refer to the miracle of the wine served to the wedding at Cana in Galilee? Château Jesus, of the bottomless barrels . . . if you believe in miracles."

"I do," Clara said, "but not as performed by Werner Flemming. Henri, you've got to see Alberto. He needs to know."

"I will see him. I will tell all. Clarissima, I like it no better than you. But it is not for you to worry, I assure you. All will be well. Bertram Hill is a mere entity. The Pinjattas are but men. Alberto will know what to do. He is brilliant." Henri took her hands, holding them tightly in his own. "How I admire your dear father. No! I *love* Alberto! He is like a father to me . . . a father-in-law someday, I can hope." He stared at her soulfully.

"Henri! You've just scared the hell out of me. This is no time to propose."

"I propose *all* the time! It is my habit."

"Really?"

"Yes. I propose to the same woman many times. Not to many women."

"Hasn't anybody ever said yes?"

The question stopped him. "Clarissima . . ." For a moment, he stared out the picture window at the end of the room. Beyond the darkened bay, busy with lights. "That is another long story which I must tell you. But not tonight, please. I almost married. But did not. Of the chaos of that moment, I prefer not to think. I know I must explain but it is something I don't fully comprehend for myself. But I will say that that is the number one reason I came to this country from Paris. . . ." He looked so troubled that Clara didn't press him. But he went on anyway. "You already know why Heinrich Marker made his way to France from Austria, to pursue the professional demands of his *nose*. But why he came here . . ." As if to escape a bad memory, he jumped to his feet. "It is such a long and depressing story it leaves me bereaved. It was not a case of *cherchez la femme*," he tried to joke, "but more *laissez la femme*. Leave . . . no, *flee* the woman."

"Poor boy . . ."

"No! Rich boy! Now I have you!" He dropped back on the couch, taking her hand again. "Clarissima, I worship you."

"You shouldn't. I order you not to worship me!" Then, seeing his eyes, how he was looking at her, she remembered the other thing. "Henri, will you come with me to my father's wedding in Lucaterra?"

His eyes popped open. Instant, joyous tears welled up. He burst out, "I accept! I accept wholeheartedly to be with you in this wonderful place. Lucaterra! The *terroir!* It produces a distinctive wine of the countryside! The Vernaccia, a white of magical resonance and which also reduces to a wonderful grappa . . . Clarissima!" His voice caught. "I accept with pleasure. With joy. With enormous excitement. I am honored!" He was glowing like a lightbulb. "I will be part of the family. Henri Lamarque, Heinrich Marker, a man without family, not even a third or fourth cousin removed. A man alone, emerging out of the fogs of Europe . . ."

Clara stopped him. "Nothing that complicated, Henri. It's just that I think I'd miss you if you weren't with me."

"The local chianti, hard to the palate, a modest hill wine but behind it, a hardness and strength. And the sangiovese, with a softness, an afterkiss like that of an Etruscan maiden . . ."

# *five*

A S CLARA ENTERED her office the next morning, a skinny young man leapt to his feet. "Steve Pinjatta!" he exclaimed.

He looked at his watch. She did the same. It was eleven-fifteen.

How weird. But the name stopped Clara only a tick. It would mean absolutely nothing to her. "I'm sorry... I wasn't expecting... we didn't have a date, did we?"

*"No."* The answer came from Daisy Chaney, Clara's assistant. Short, bright, energetic, her dark hair gamin-cut, Daisy was Clara's gatekeeper, buffer, and valued second opinion. "No, Mr. Pinjatta did *not* have an appointment and when he called I said you might not get here until noon."

"So I just walked over!"

Daisy's eyebrows jumped, as they did when she was not amused. But she didn't say anything more, merely glancing at Clara as if to ask what a girl was supposed to do with a clown like this.

"I was at the airport and I stopped to see a client."

*"No problema."* Young Pinjatta grinned cockily.

"Daisy has been giving me some pointers about the city. I'm new out here."

He was disarmingly young, youthfully slight, narrow shouldered and insubstantial within a navy blue double-breasted suit. A stylish, two-toned shirt and bright red tie didn't provide any extra weight, nor did the gold collar pin which looked as though it had been driven through his prominent Adam's apple. Beaky nose and large, weepy eyes finished the job. As they shook hands, his fingers seemed so fragile that Clara imagined crunching them into knuckle dust. One thing though, she wouldn't forget Steve Pinjatta right away. He was a foppish figure and, on this first sighting, there was absolutely nothing predatory about him, not what Clara had been expecting in a Pinjatta.

"And what brings you to us, Mr. Pinjatta?"

"Please call me Steve. . . . We're gonna be doing some business together."

"Oh, you've just moved out here? And you've bought a house. Where? Anything you buy in San Francisco just now is a wonderful investment . . . but I'm sure you know that already . . . is it one of the old Victorians? They do up very nicely."

"No! Nothing like that, Mrs. Addey. I explained to Daisy . . ." She was looking sour. "I'm living . . . I'm staying with an old school friend. Temporarily."

"Oh, I see. Then . . ." She arched an eyebrow.

"You don't understand," he blustered. "I represent Bertram Hill. Don't you know about Bertram Hill? My God! Oh, Christ!" He glared at Daisy. "But I thought . . . I understood . . . isn't Alberto Morelli your father?"

"Yes, he is."

"Hasn't he mentioned us? We want to buy the Morelli vineyards! That is, Bertram Hill does. We've made Alberto Morelli a terrific offer!"

Clara did her best imitation of genuine surprise. "An offer for the vineyard?" He nodded eagerly. She hesitated. "Then I guess you'd better come in my office and tell me all about it."

"Hey! That's better." He winked at Daisy. "We're back on track here."

To seem polite, a bit forthcoming after all, Clara poured Steve half a glass of Morelli merlot and one for herself too, a little booster if she was going to be dealing with a disreputable takeover artist. She had placed the young man on the battered black leather and chrome-framed couch, a relic from an earlier modernist age, and seated herself in an antique rocker on the other side of the chrome-and-glass coffee table. Facing him to the windows gave her an advantage.

He fidgeted with his legs, then self-consciously tasted the wine. "Umm . . ." Sneaking a quick look at the bottle. "A Morelli merlot. I thought so. I love merlot." Bull, Clara told herself, he wouldn't know merlot from cough syrup. Front, all front, no substance. The Pinjattas had sent a boy to her—what nerve! "There's not a lot of merlot in California, is there?"

"I wouldn't say that," Clara replied frostily. "Morelli has quite a bit . . . enough to make a few bottles."

Holding his glass close, Steve crossed his legs, exhibiting long, calf-covering blue socks, the same shade as his shirt. His shoes were black patent-leather loafers with floppy tassels, an affectation Henri would sneer at. Steve studied the room, as if it were no more, no less than he'd expected. "You're in the decorating business."

"That's kind of obvious, isn't it?" Clara gestured at the clutter—catalogues strewn across the coffee table. Big picture books, fabric swatches, wallpaper samples, pieces of wood molding, scissors everywhere. Framed interior design posters covered the walls. There was a dismantled chair in the middle of the floor and a big drafting table that took up one whole window corner. Office, yes. Workshop too. "And you're in the wine business . . ."

Cutting into his answer, from outside came the sudden clatter and clanging of a cable car heading uphill in front of the St. Francis Hotel.

Steve giggled jubilantly. "Listen! A cable car! That's San Francisco, right in a nutshell, isn't it? I love it!" Yes, he *was* a boy. "What a *great* location for an office. What you'd call a prestige location," he added admiringly.

An *expensive* location. In a restored older building around the corner from Union Square, smack in the middle of San Francisco's perplexing downtown, such a jarring mixture of poverty and plenty, they were within walking range of all the galleries, department stores, theatres . . . and, yes, within hearing range of the cable cars.

"Yeah, Clara, I'm in the wine business. The booze business." His supercilious smile warned her he was likely to be stubborn—but perhaps not particularly clever. It seemed like all he'd learned so far was how to keep his foot in the door. "Listen, Clara, level with me. Really, hasn't your old man mentioned our offer?"

"You mean *Mister* Morelli?"

"Well, yes, of course. Alberto Morelli."

"No. He hasn't mentioned it." A business lie didn't count.

"But we understood you're a partner in the business."

"Silent partner."

Close enough to the truth. Legally, Clara was part owner of Morelli Vineyards. But she'd never played an active role. Alberto kept her informed. But, without their ever having discussed it, it had been understood how much her two marriages had demanded of her time and energy. How she'd been channeled by her second husband, Tom Addey. Weekend after weekend, she and Tom had come up to their tiled and beamed country cottage—Alberto had had it built on the property as a wedding present—but Tom had wanted neither of them to have anything to do with the business of the vineyard. So, decorating had become her thing. But Tom was gone now. Clara was back to her old self. And, whatever people might think, or how it might look, she *did* care about the place where she'd grown up. She was vitally, even desperately, interested in what happened with the family vineyard.

"By the way," she asked, "how did you locate me? I never use the name Morelli in the business."

"Werner Flemming tipped me off. He's a friend, you know. And Flemming's Cellar is a big, big customer out here." Young Pinjatta gulped more merlot, leaning forward ingratiatingly. "I'd like to get you on our side, Clara. I hope you'll encourage Alberto to accept our offer."

"That decision is entirely his."

"But he'd listen to you. You're his daughter. Werner told me Alberto adores you."

How would *Werner* know? Clara didn't react, instead poured more wine and sat back, waiting. Embarrassed, Steve played with his cufflinks for a bit. Finally, Clara said, "I suppose you'll be talking to my father. In what *capacity,* if I may ask?"

."Capacity? Why, I'll be running West Coast operations for Bertram Hill."

"You have West Coast operations? I've never heard—"

"Why *would* you hear if you've never even heard of Bertram Hill?" He stared at her impatiently. "*Of course* we have West Coast operations! We do a load of business in the Far East . . . Japan. Those guys are crazy for Scotch whisky and expensive Bordeaux. 'Course lately"—frowned professionally—"we've got an economic downturn in the Far East. Export markets are a little shaky right now. You know: economic restructuring, reform of the banking systems . . . you've heard all that, I'm sure." Naturally, he assumed she *hadn't* and didn't care anyway. "It's in the papers every day. In fact . . ." He was primed to expand on the theme but seemed to run out of expertise, so turned to Los Angeles and what a powerhouse Bertram Hill was in southern California. "Hell, we do Scotch whisky, Russian vodka, French brandy, Spanish sherry, Portuguese port, German beer . . . we import caviar from Azerbaijan and truffles from Italy and pâté fom France, chocolate from Belgium and Switzerland, cigars from—"

"Florida."

"Right! Florida. Bertram Hill would *never* break the embargo on Cuban cigars, don't worry. We follow the rules . . . despite what you might hear from unfriendly sources."

"What unfriendly sources?" she demanded.

"Not saying! There's been some negative stuff in

the papers. I'm not trying to keep it a secret. Your old . . . Alberto Morelli's probably seen it. Total crap! Company like ours . . . *hell*! We've got customers up and down the West Coast . . . ask any of them. Bertram Hill is clean as a whistle. We deal in all the *good things,* Clara. And yes, we have vineyards too. In Chile, Argentina, Spain, Portugal, France . . . and *no*—that's the answer to the question you haven't asked—we don't own any California vineyards. Not yet. Morelli will be the first."

"*If* Morelli sells. Who's second?"

"Come in—you'll find out."

"That's something my father will want to know before he makes a decision."

"In due course . . ." He seemed to shrink away from answering and Clara was suddenly conscious of his peculiar eyes, languid but evasive.

Severely, she said, "You can save yourself a lot of time and trouble if you're *very* up-front with Alberto Morelli—and me."

He grinned. "The silent partner turns noisy, eh? So you do have a say."

"My father will ask my opinion before he makes a final decision."

"*Morelli will sell,*" he insisted. "You *have* to sell. The offer is super! It covers estate taxes, takes into account inheritances, all that stuff."

"Are you making us an offer we can't refuse?"

"Of course!" He missed the allusion. "And you know why? Because we're gonna build a California powerhouse wine business. Morelli is going to be the cornerstone. We want Alberto Morelli on our team."

"You'd buy him out. He'd be gone."

"No, Clara, believe me, he won't be gone. He'll

be on the team as a consultant. Isn't that what he wants? That's Werner's feeling . . ."

Werner again. "Listen!" Clara leaned forward. "Werner Flemming can't possibly know what Alberto Morelli feels."

Steve's sallow face lengthened. "He buys Morelli wine, doesn't he? Anyway, Werner says if we want to build anything out here, we gotta have Morelli." He dumped merlot in his mouth. "Why? Because your old . . . your father is respected. He's an authority. When Alberto Morelli speaks, people listen."

Clara wondered what idiot had prepped him. Flemming? Was his aim to sabotage the thing?

"Mr. Pinjatta—"

"Steve!"

"Listen . . . Steve, we're small . . . tiny . . . insignificant compared to the biggies. You know about the Gallos and the Mondavis, the Sebastianis, don't you?"

"That's just it, Clara, nevermind about the Gallos and the rest. We're gonna create a big, new consortium of California wine producers. Our market is Planet Earth!" Steve was agitated, working himself into a sweat, straining to make his case. "We're prepared to make a *huge* commitment."

"And *you're* going to be in charge? Aren't you awfully young to be running such an operation?"

"Sure. Yeah. I'm pretty young. You hold that against me?" he demanded. "So, maybe I didn't go to Harvard Business School—but I've got an MBA in my pocket from Florida State. . . ." Clara just stared at him, not believing her ears. "And don't worry, I've already fired my share of deadwood. Everybody knows I'm a ruthless bottom-lining *prick*! I don't apologize for it. I'm ambitious!"

"That's very reassuring," she murmured.

"In a few years, you know, I'll be running Bertram Hill. Don't tell the old man I said so." He laughed breathlessly. "I came up through the ranks. My father, he's Franco Pinjatta, he had me sweeping the floors. I worked in our shop in New York. I was a delivery boy. I went down to the docks to meet our containers. I've humped cases and cases of booze. . . ."

By the delicate look of him, not all that many.

"I attended to customers. I did window displays. I've been on buying trips with the old man. . . . I've already tasted a few hundred barrels of wine—"

Clara held up her hand. "I get the picture." God knows how Alberto would react to this young squirt with the big, boastful mouth. "You must be older than you look."

"Christ, *everybody* says that. I'm twenty-eight years of age. I wouldn't be here if they thought I'd fuck it up . . . sorry." He glanced at her. Got no reaction. "My uncle's just waiting to jump all over me. Uncle Maxey. He and my father are twins. Funny thing is the old man's completely bald and Maxey's got an incredible head of hair. I don't look like either one of them." He paused to make his point. "That's why I think I'm adopted . . . anyway, what I'm saying is if I screw it up, I'm history."

Suddenly, he did look his age. Young. Vulnerable. Nervously, he helped himself to more wine, then reached into an inside pocket of his tight suit and pulled out a pack of cigarettes.

No, no, Clara waved her finger. He sagged back miserably, tucking the cigarettes away. Then sat, as if struck dumb, clenching and unclenching his fists.

His face pulled and twitched. His lippy mouth quivered.

"Look," Clara said more kindly, "I'll tell my father you were here. That we talked."

"Oh, Christ! Come on now, Clara, you can do better than that. You know it'd be for the best. Alberto's over sixty and he's got nobody to take over."

"Speak to my father," she said stiffly.

He sighed. "He'll listen to reason, won't he?"

"Sure . . . but what makes you think this has got anything to do with reason?" Steve wouldn't understand. He'd attended a playboy business school and fired a couple of poor warehousemen. "You see, this has very little to do with reason or logic. It's about grapes and wine and the land."

"I know about that!"

"No you don't."

The only good argument for selling—Steve did have that right—was that, frankly, there was no one to carry on, Alberto's greatest disappointment. He never alluded to it but if there had been a man-child in the family, things would have been different. Therefore, in her heart of hearts, Clara knew that when, and if, Alberto did decide to sell, it wouldn't be to Bertram Hill. No, Alberto would listen. Then he would send Steve away.

Without realizing it, she'd been staring at him, pitying him for the rebuff that lay ahead. "Unfortunately," Clara said, "this is not a very good time to see him. He's in the middle of the harvest."

"I know that . . . whenever he's got a spare hour or two."

"Hour or two? This is the time of the year we count in minutes."

"He can't just ignore us!"

"He won't. He'll consider the offer. Trust me."

"Well," he grumbled, "you sure don't make it sound very hopeful."

"Isn't that what springs eternal?" Clara got up. "You'll talk to Morelli. Don't worry."

"Talk to him? I'll grovel."

"He doesn't take to groveling."

"Only kidding! Only kidding!" He jumped to his feet. "Hey, Clara, it's noontime. How about I invite you out to lunch? You name the place."

"No, thanks. I'm already four hours behind."

"Raincheck?"

"Does Bertram Hill give rainchecks?"

Henri would've liked that.

HER COTTAGE. A long, raftered room. Fireplace smoke-stained underneath the mantel. Easy chairs. A low sofa. White stuccoed walls, here and there pictures from the Tom era she hadn't bothered to remove. Her favorite spot, a cushioned window seat. Directly outside, close enough to touch, a rough wooden arbor supported a web of grape vines which in full summer shaded a battered table and benches. Now, losing leaves, the intricate skeleton, the bone structure of the vines, was exposed like an X-ray shot of Mother Nature.

Bordering the arbor, an expansive rose garden twice as big as the house itself, laid out in intricate color patterns and still producing this late in the year, told a tale of its own. The garden, a mix of modern hybrids and old varieties, had been planted by her mother as soon as the wedding-present cottage had been finished. Clara remembered the wonderful names: a pink Brigadoon, white Rose of York, red Chrysler Imperial, yellow Midas Touch. Meticulously, lovingly, Evelyn Morelli had added to the roses until the very end, the latter marked by a six-foot wall of old brick, which could've served as her tombstone, covered by a prolific Lady Banks climber whose pure white blooms were a favorite of grave-haunting butterflies. Butterflies, souls in flight.

Sun poured down on the south-sloping incline, penetrating the thinning grape arbor, invading the house, warming the room. Heat soaked into the saltillo floor tiles to keep the room warm into evening. The little house was a marvel. Everything worked like it was supposed to. It had been meant to be their house—hers and Tom's—and they were to come up to Sonoma whenever they liked. They could be alone. Or not. The elder Morellis lived just up the hill in the main house, the Casa Morelli, with its panoramic overview of the property. At first, Tom and Clara's castle had performed its magic. Tom had spent weekend after weekend painting, not noticing or caring when Clara went off to help her father. Martha played with Clara's mother, even then ailing. It had been ideal, except for her mother's illness.

Then things had changed. Tom announced he was bored, began painting with a kind of frustrated fury. Clara had pulled back, offering him all of her time. To no avail. He'd begun blaming her, the marriage, her daughter Martha, for blunting his talent. Talent? That was his problem, though she'd never said so until the bitter end. So it had ended. Her mother had died. Tom was gone. He was painting elsewhere now. His gallery was closed and he lived at Stinson Beach. He had found a rich woman. Good. Everything had turned out for the best—except for Martha who was still adjusting to adulthood. But Clara wouldn't think about Martha just now. Instead, thank God for sunshine. For warmth. Like a primitive, she would bask in the sunshine and think no disturbing thoughts. She put her coffee cup to her lips. The coffee was good, comforting, like a bookend. It opened memories, closed them.

Orderly as a blueprint, the land on the other side of the wall dropped into a hollow which the years had carved into the hillside. During the rainy season, it banked torrents of run-off. Ducks flew in for a few weeks and now and then a loose goose. Three or four hundred yards farther on, the green metal roof of the winery lay flat and solid against the land. Big as a football field, at harvesttime the winery was the center of the Morelli universe. It housed the crushing apparatus, the press, stainless-steel fermenting tanks, cooling units. Lab and offices were located on a mezzanine. There was a separate barrel room, another for the bottling line—for Morelli bottled its own product, leading with the prime estate cabernet, of grapes grown, harvested, crushed, fermented, pressed, aged in oak—and bottled right on the property.

Listening carefully, Clara picked out familiar sounds—the whine of the forklift as it shifted pallets, the rumble of the conveyer belt and thumping of the stemmer-crusher. And the bad-tempered, Falstaffian growl of the tractors. At intervals, a tractor rounded the eastern hill below the big house, huffing and puffing, dragging a trailerload of grapes behind it.

Even on a Sunday, it didn't stop, especially if the harvest was running late; this year it was ten days or two weeks behind normal schedule. But what was normal? In grape territory, the calendar was a slave to the weather, not shopping cycles or national holidays. The first day of summer didn't mean a thing if spring had been cold—hopefully not exceptionally wet as well—and thus summer late, causing autumn and the harvest to lag and winter, when it came, to be dry . . . though another, renewing spring couldn't be far behind.


C LARA? C LARA . . ." Alberto was banging at the heavy door at the end of the big room.

"I'm here! Come on in."

"Ah, good," he said, when he saw her, "you're up."

"It's ten-thirty, Papa."

"Just sitting here?" He put his hand on her shoulder. "Doing nothing? Hey, we're picking grapes!"

"And you've been out with them this morning, haven't you?" She could tell from his hands, stained purple to the cuffs of his flannel shirt. "Sit down for a minute. Have some coffee."

"No, thanks." But he did sit down on the edge of the window seat. "Nice here."

"Always. I hate to leave." To his unspoken query, she said, "Right after lunch. I've got to get back."

"Henri, I suppose."

"No. Didn't he say?" Henri had called Alberto from the airport Friday morning to talk briefly about Bertram Hill.

"The only thing he said," Alberto grumbled, "was that I had better bring a long spoon if I dine with the Brothers Pinjatta. He promises more. Later. In person."

"He'll be back in a couple of days."

"Then why don't you stick around?"

Clara shook her head. "There's a cocktail party tonight. Cousin Cabott has gotten one of the new software billionaires interested in his research. I'm supposed to meet him. A man named Michael Tyler.

Supposedly, he's building a huge new house and wants help decorating."

Alberto looked skeptical—Cabott Root was different, to say the least. "Speaking of which—Grandma *Mina*?" Mina was Cabott Root's great-aunt. "I guess you haven't talked to her—" Interrupting himself, Alberto jumped up. "What's going on? It's gone so quiet." He glanced at the clock on the kitchen wall. "Not lunch break yet." Then a tractor spoke up. Alberto eased, smiling guiltily. "Not that I'm preoccupied." He didn't sit down again. "C'mon, Clara, get your coat. Let's have a walk around before lunch."

There was no fighting it. Clara put down her coffee and reached for her windbreaker. She was already in turtleneck, jeans, and jogging shoes. "I thought you'd never ask."

Alberto was already at the front door. "So Cabby is hard up again, is he?"

"The research center is."

"There'll never be enough for Cabby. But . . . ." He shook his head wryly. "I shouldn't talk. I never worried about it either, didn't even think about it if I could help it. Now that I'm older, I realize what a monkey I was. Your mother and I worked so hard over the years we never had time . . . never took time to spend it. Evelyn worked too hard . . ." His voice dropped to a whisper. "Goddamn it, I regret it now, I can tell you."

"Papa," Clara protested, "you know there's no such thing as a vacation on a winemaker's calendar. And Mama *never* complained."

This was feeble reassurance and he didn't accept it. "The trouble is—and you should learn this now—there's *not* as much time as you think there is."

With that, he slammed the door and stuffed his hands in his workpants.

Moving away from the house, Clara felt the morning sunshine on her back. Around them, the acres and acres of grapes spread as far as she could see. The vines were beginning to change color. The topmost leaves still held their green, signifying that the grapes were still soaking up sunlight—and making sugar—but underneath the foliage was turning yellow, a yellow which eventually would go to orange, amber, and brown. Soon enough, as October expired and November built and December arrived, all the leaves would fall, baring the precious vines to dormancy.

Softly, not argumentatively, Clara said, "Bertram Hill's money is there, if you want it."

"Yes. Theoretically." They started up the rutted and dusty track which led past Casa Morelli to the crest of the property. "The Pinjatta boy wants to come up and see me. And now you tell me he's a little twerp."

"Twerp, or not . . ."

"Yes, the offer." Alberto halted, facing her soberly. *"Fifteen million."*

Clara heard. Curiously, what struck her first was the astonishing thought that goofy young Steve Pinjatta could be anywhere in the vicinity of fifteen million dollars.

"That's a lot," she said simply. "Why does it make you so gloomy?"

"Not gloomy. Disturbed. It's more than I like to think about. Maybe too much. And that makes me suspicious. Still, in all . . ." He rubbed his chin. "I'll talk to Jim Fontana. If Jim thinks it's a solid proposition, I'm going to be very tempted. Think about it—fifteen million . . ."

"I am thinking about it."

And worrying. He kicked at the ground. "Would it hurt you so awfully much?"

Clara felt a tear or two at work behind her eyes. "It'd hurt . . . but I'd get over it." She reached for his hand and they walked on like that, hand-in-hand. "Papa . . . please . . . don't do anything till the grapes are in and you can think straight."

He laughed heavily. "Ah, there you have it. Funny thing . . ." Suddenly, he stopped, then pulled her off the road and into the midst of the vines where the canes and shoots reached well above their heads. Smiling broadly as the light and shadows played on his face, Alberto reached among the leaves to grab and heft a bunch of nearly black grapes. "*The zin.* Smell it? Heavy with juice. But we'll give it another ten days, or two weeks, maybe longer if we're lucky and the rain holds off. Young Joe is out here bright and early every morning checking the Brix sugar— I don't like the alcohol going much over twelve or twelve and a half percent. Gets too powerful for the normal wine drinker. Here . . ." He freed a handful of grapes. "Have a taste."

Clara popped a couple into her mouth. Juice exploded. It was sweet enough, but tart. The acid fought back, puckering her lips.

"They're getting there," she said. "Beautiful . . ."

Alberto grinned at her. "See. You *know*! The taste. It's something you don't ever lose. Like I was saying . . . *funny thing.* When I'm feeling low, after a bad year or between seasons, I always think to myself that the wine business is a drag, like selling beans or shoes. Then, after bud break and a good summer, when the grapes begin to peak and everything's set for the harvest, I'm happy again. Fulfilled, you might say. And I'm thinking that there's a good deal after all to be said for making good wine. That maybe it is a noble profession, like people say . . ."

"And you can think straight again."

"That's right." He picked a few more grapes, giving her some, tossing the rest in his mouth as they headed back to the road. "So, don't worry, I'm not about to leap before I have a good look. You heard Florence last night. And Henri thinks these Pinjatta characters are a bunch of crooks."

"He just wants you to be careful." Clara decided not to reveal Henri's horrible hypothesis. She'd leave that to him.

Thoughtfully, Alberto said, "One reason I'd like to accept—we could pay off Mina."

Yes. Sometimes, it had been very tough. Twenty years before, Alberto had been bailed out of a real deep hole by Grandma Mina. The deadly phylloxera plague had been another challenge. Morelli had been lucky compared to some—nonetheless, at great expense, acres of vines had to be ripped out and replanted. Again, Mina had played banker. By now, the old lady owned twenty-some percent of the estate and Clara assumed Alberto would want Mina to bless a sale of the property, if it came to that.

"She's never asked—has she?"

"No, never. That's why I'd like to make it good, if I can, while she's still alive to know it."

"*If* you can."

"That's it," Alberto grunted. "Florence says no, don't sell, hang on. But I'm not sure she really means it. She might be thinking I'd sell just to please her and she wouldn't want that burden and so tells me not to do it. Like last night . . ."

The previous evening, yes, after a long, leisurely, really *family* dinner—rack of light pink Sonoma lamb, roast potatoes, peppery gravy, a spinach-and-cheese soufflé, garden salad . . . a jug of crisp pinot noir, big pieces of New York cheesecake (Florence's specialty)—the three of them in the old paneled dining room hung with family pictures, Alberto had put on music, some Beethoven, Florence insisted. She did *not* wish to listen to Florence Rampling singing Aïda, not after a good meal. When they were settled with coffee and small brandies in front of the glowing fireplace, houselights dimmed, the music as her background, Florence had announced, very dramatically, that she could not imagine an Alberto Morelli without a vineyard.

"What would you *do* with yourself? A caged lion, a lion without a cause, a lion without a role. And, if you did sell, what would happen to Joe Alejandro and his family? His daughters about to go to college? His son, young Joe, a budding oenologist, as you people call them? What about this house, Alberto? Seventy or eighty years old, built by your own parents? *Clara's house*? Oh no. Oh no. I don't think you can sell Morelli Vineyards to those upstarts! The Pinjattas? What are they, some kind of stuffed donkeys?"

Remembering, Clara put her hand in the crook of Alberto's arm. "You know, I think Florence means *exactly* what she says."

"I guess so . . . Clara, do you think I'm making a big mistake? No, not about selling . . . *about Florence.*"

Masking her surprise, Clara said, "No, of course not. Why are you asking? I thought your mind was all made up."

"It is. I'm hooked—line and sinker. But you know, Florence is very strong. You think—too strong?"

"Too strong?" Clara laughed. "You're not exactly a wimp, Papa. You need a strong woman to stand up to you. Florence says what she thinks. I like that. Don't you? Of course you do."

"People say a widower, so lonely, can become irrational and remarry out of a kind of desperation, only to find himself more miserable than before . . ."

"But it's not like you're rushing headlong into it . . . You've been all alone for ten years." She squeezed his arm. "I've always been a little scared you'd fall for one of those neat little social ladies in San Francisco."

He snorted. "You think I'm out of my mind?"

"I did worry a bit about Francey Shingles down the road."

"Not seriously!"

"No. Not seriously. Then you found Florence. And I happen to agree with her about the vineyard. This time of the year—you'd be going crazy."

"So—*you* don't think I should sell either."

They had reached the top of the hill a couple of hundred yards to the west of the Casa Morelli. There, barely two years before they'd been killed in an *autostrada* disaster near Siena, Clara's grandparents had planted a sturdy wooden bench. There, they'd often spent the end of a long summer's day watching the sun go down.

Far below, at a certain spot in the spread of pinot noir, the tops of the vines shook as the pickers—you couldn't see them—worked with their sharp knives, cutting bunch after bunch of ripe grapes off the trellised canes. This was the last of the pinot noir acreage, thus located to take advantage of the cooler northern slope, available ocean breezes, and the warm but not blistering summer afternoon sun. The pinot ripened first and was harvested first, then the merlot, finally the south-facing cabernet, cabernet franc and zinfandel which were made to soak up the sun until the very moment of picking.

Alberto paced in front of her, one eye on the harvesting, the other observing her. "There's a lot of blood invested here, Clara. My parents . . . my brother's . . . and you remember all the stories about the Old Count."

"Remember?" Clara responded warmly. "Those stories were my first fairy tales. I can remember Grandmama Sofia talking about the Old Count with his pegleg, then Mama . . . I used to search the *cave* for his treasure, scared to death I might find his ghost."

The *cave*, a tunnel, a labyrinthian wine cellar dug into the chalky hillside behind the present winery one hundred and fifty years before, was the oldest, the most revered feature of the vineyard, and still very much in use. And the Old Count, Count Cazimir de Quasimoto, who'd left a leg on the battlefield at Waterloo. Count Cazimir had come to California for the gold in 1849. He'd survived the unruly times, a fever of anti-French hatred, staying on with his new wealth, building a mill and then, when the water ran out, turning to the vine—but with no great success. After his death, the place had lain derelict for years, was haphazardly revived around 1900 and finally sold to Sofia and Alfredo Morelli in the late twenties.

"It was my mother who got them into the land," Alberto reminisced. "She was the cunning one. My father had the charm. That's how he stole her away from the Sicilians." He grinned. "Just like I stole Eve-

lyn from the Dexter Cabotts—though by now the
Cabotts have forgiven me, unlike the Scolettis. They
never forgave my father."

"Surely, by now . . . Florence said you're going to
visit them."

"If they receive us. Not that it matters anymore . . ." He plopped down beside her on the
bench. "You realize, of course, Florence doesn't understand a goddamn thing about running a place
like this. It's easy for her to say don't sell . . . Easy for
you too."

"No, it's *not* easy, Papa. Believe me."

"Sometimes," he said gruffly, "the cash flow is a
trickle. You know how hard it is to keep afloat.
That's why—"

"I know all the reasons *why*," Clara said sternly.
"Everybody says . . . Henri says the first thing this
Bertram Hill would do is raise prices."

Alberto wagged his head stubbornly. "We have,
you know. Hell, every year. But I like to keep it in
bounds—good wine for good prices. That's always
been the Morelli motto. And hell, we are okay. Don't
get me wrong. We're not about to go bust."

"I know that." Clara turned. From this spot, there
was also a good view of the winery and, on its far
end, the rustic tasting room—not open, as it happened, during this busy time of the year. There,
Clara liked to think, the Old Count also haunted.
Anyway, nobody dared seriously disagree that the
present tasting room, humble and unpretentious,
had once been his living quarters, not if you accepted that his pegleg had made all those marks in
the old pine floor. "I wonder what the Old Count's
motto was . . ."

Alberto laughed happily. "Well, Count Cazimir always told *me* that two glasses of good red wine per day act as Nature's own antioxidant. That moderate consumption of good red wine is beneficial to heart, lungs, and digestion . . ."

As Clara watched, a tractor chugged up to the winery door. More grapes. From experience, Clara knew they'd be aswarm with bees, insects of every variety attracted by the pungent smells. She'd been stung a half-dozen times every harvest. Young Joe, on holiday from the university, was unloading the pallets onto the conveyer belt. His mother and a couple of his sisters were at work doing Clara's tedious old job, standing beside *her* mother at the belt, picking spoiled fruit and leaves out of the unending flow of grapes to crusher.

"It'll be a good year," Alberto quietly said.

"Count Cazimir will be happy."

Joe Alejandro—Big Joe—had emerged from the winery. He was wearing rubber boots and a grin Clara could see from way up here. He waved.

"Let's go," Alberto said. "Joe needs me."

"He *doesn't* need you. He's just waving."

"Come on, Clara!" Alberto was on his feet. "Let's go down and taste some new wine."

MY BEAUTIFUL COUSIN!"
Immediately, at the very ornate archway into the miniballroom of his neo-Venetian palazzo, all filagree, Byzantine windows, stained glass, and heavy furniture, laughing wildly, Cabott Root grabbed her to him in a bear hug. After all, he always said, they were *second* cousins, maybe even more removed than that—so what was the problem?

"But where's Henri, darling? There's somebody he's *got* to meet."

"Henri is out of town."

She didn't elaborate. No point, for Cabby was already miles ahead. He kissed her again, hugging, muttering, "Oh, bother! But what can we do . . . best-laid plans. Etcetera. Etcetera . . ."

"And your dear wife?"

That was Nan. Clara didn't like skinny Nan and, more and more, she got the feeling that her cousin Cabby didn't much either. There was one child, a precocious girl of ten. The little family kept out of each other's way inside their architectural curiosity located in the no-man's-land between Russian Hill and North Beach.

Cabby rattled loose change in his pocket, then gestured dismissively, making his white silk shirt billow like a sail. He wore it open-collared. All the men in the room were buttoned up tight in their business suits, but neckties weren't for him. Cabby looked as much like a mad artist, a Van Gogh, as he did a physicist and mathematician. Family lore had it, in fact, that one strain of the Cabotts, back in New England, had included more than one certifiably insane Mayflower descendant.

"Over there," he said of his wife, "gossiping away like the Bavarian peasant she is. *Her set.* Look at them, San Francisco's best, in their tweed suits and sensible shoes. And you! In your medieval cape and velvet skirt! So admirable. So sexy!" Cabby neighed. "But never mind about *them.* I want you to meet my guest of honor, Mick Tyler. Here . . . have a drink . . ."

A white-coated waiter was at her elbow. Clara took a glass of champagne off his tray.

Cabby steered her around. "Mick!"

A chunky man, not as tall and broader than Cabott Root, wheeled away from a little group of people—one, a man Clara knew from the Bank of America, the second Nan's doctor, an internist and very important figure in her life, and the last an associate of Cabby's at his Pacific Rim Research Center.

"Clara . . . want you to meet Mick Tyler. Mick, this is my talented cousin, Clara Addey."

Mick thrust his hand out, palm up, a little trick the upwardly mobile had stolen from the Indians. The open palm meant he wasn't armed, in other words wasn't planning to stick a knife in your gizzard, moreover that he was honest, aboveboard, a true-blue American entrepreneur with whom you could trust your very life. *How!* That would have been the appropriate Indian greeting. Instead, Tyler said, "Hi."

His brush cut couldn't have been any shorter. The face was square and open, not fully open though— like a broken window, perhaps, with dangerous daggers of glass sticking up. Tyler looked like an astronaut *should* look. Blue-eyed. A ready if somewhat programmed smile. Dressed in a blue button-down shirt, blue-and-gold striped tie, workaday blue suit, and brown wing-tip shoes, he was the personification of Mister Let's-Get-to-Work America.

She touched her hand briefly to his hot palm. "Hello."

"Mick," Cabby was saying, "is one of the newest, brightest stars in Silicon Valley. He's founder and CEO of a tiny softwear outfit that's capitalized at a little, bitty five billion." He laughed loudly. "At least when the market closed Friday. Tomorrow, who knows, it'll probably be worth ten."

"Or zilch," Tyler said.

". . . and he's interested in the work we're doing at Pacific Rim!"

"Gravity," Tyler said blandly. "I'm fascinated by gravity. It's what keeps us glued to the planet."

"Control gravity," Cabby cried, "and you'll outrun the speed of sound!"

"Which will be going some," Tyler murmured.

"But listen, Clara," Cabby bubbled, "Mick's company, Soft Landings, has set them all on their ear. Bill Gates is shaking in his shoes . . ."

Tyler chuckled modestly. "Actually not, Cab. In fact, we moved to the Bay area to get out of range of Microsoft's firepower, if that's possible."

"You see, Clara, what Soft Landings does—"

"She's not interested, Cab."

"But I am."

"You really want to know?" Tyler looked doubtful. "Well, in simple terms, we simplify. Consider all the innovation, ever-faster chips, new software, this system on top of the last . . . we do shortcuts. We try to make the cyberworld easier on the user. Simpler . . . softer."

"Get that?" Cabby practically bellowed. "Sheer inspiration! Simplify the digital clutter that's messing up our lives . . ."

Embarrassing. Cabby would go to any lengths. He was desperate for money. Cold War over, Pacific Rim Research was no longer indispensable. These days, its work was simply arcane and Cabott Root merely an eccentric genius who ran a nutty think tank on the West Coast. Clara hoped he could get Tyler to cough up.

She tasted the champagne again. French, maybe Dom Pérignon. Cabby was extravagant. Nan didn't rein him in. Why should she? She was perfectly willing to spend Cabott and Root money. Fortunately, royalties from Cabby's "little" inventions seemed to flow in at fortuitous times.

"Anyway, now listen, Clara. Mick's building a huge house over in Tiburon. How many square feet was that?"

"I dunno. Ten or twelve thousand."

"That's why Henri should be here, damn it!"

"Yes," Clara said. "But he's at a pinot noir fest in Portland."

Tyler gulped. "My God, I wish I was with him."

"The point is," Cabby raved, "Mick's putting in a *huge* wine cellar and he's got to stock it but he doesn't know his ass from deep center field about wine."

"I know what I like."

"Sure you do," Cabby jeered. "It's all status, this wine business, *all* status. You guys, half of you don't know what you're drinking. It could be a great French number or a bottle of cheap bellywash from Mexico . . . which, by the way, is what I prefer."

Take care, Cabby. Her cousin was *not* a great salesman in his own behalf. He went too far, too fast. He was too extreme. "Like this champagne?" she teased. "A Dom? How much a bottle, cousin mine?"

"Haven't the slightest!"

"Seventy or eighty, at least," Tyler said.

"Money . . . money." Cabby waved his hands, as if he couldn't be bothered to think about the stuff. He turned, rocking on his heels. "Oh, hey! There's Doc Langer *und Frau.* Got to leave you now. Tell him, Clara! Henri Lamarque's his man!"

When he'd gone, Clara said, "My cousin is a little nutty."

But she couldn't have wished for a better kind of cousin. Careless about money, yes, eccentric, yes, but not totally bonkers, Cabby was kind and he was loyal. Tall, well over six feet, disorderly and funny, Cabby was also a genius and took full advantage of it. His friends at school had nicknamed him Square Root, or the Root of all Evil, backhanded acknowledgment of his intelligence and testimony to his hell-raising. Cabby didn't care. He had other things on his mind.

Tyler shifted his glass from one hand to the other. He looked to be drinking whisky on the rocks. "But he's right about the wine. I will need help. Right now, I buy a couple of bottles at a time. That's different from building a cellar. I've been talking to the people at Flemming's Cellar. They're helpful. And Werner Flemming seems like a knowledgeable guy."

"Oh, sure."

"But when I'm ready, I'd like to meet this Henri fellow."

The newly rich, Clara couldn't help thinking—not snobbishly or enviously—did need help with the niceties. Notice, Hector hadn't mentioned the library of Tyler's new house. No need. In the decorating trade, dealing with a client like Mick Tyler, you'd probably send somebody to a warehouse and buy a few yards of books. Fill up the shelves. Didn't matter what the books were. The same went for the wine. Build a wine cellar. Fill 'er up. Or was she completely misjudging him?

He asked, "Didn't Cab tell me your father is in the wine business?"

"Yes. Up in the Sonoma Valley."

Tyler snapped his fingers. "As opposed to Sonoma *County.* Different wine district. See, I know a little bit about it, after all."

"We own some acreage in the county as well."

His eyes lost their wariness. "God, I'd love to have a vineyard."

So, maybe, after all, Tyler was an exception to the rule about poor man becoming richer but no wiser. "You want a vineyard? I'll sell you Morelli."

A joke, of course. Partial joke, anyway. But wouldn't that be a kick? The mere thought of undoing the Pinjattas was enjoyable.

Tyler's eyes sparkled. "*That's* your father's place? Morelli Vineyards? So your real name is Morelli."

"Maiden name."

"Are you really for sale? Not that I . . . *hold it!*

Don't get carried away here, Tyler! A vineyard? No, no." He grinned. "That'll come later—after I'm grown up."

"No, no, we're not seriously for sale. But . . ." Why not? "As a matter of fact, my father's just had an offer from a big firm in New York."

*"Who?"*

"A company called Bertram Hill."

"Bertram Hill is a big wine and spirits importer."

"So we hear." But enough of that. "I doubt it'll come off. . . . Tell me about your house. You know, I'm a decorator."

"Cab told me so, yes."

So Cabby hadn't neglected her interests after all. "Not that I'm looking for a job," she assured Tyler. *"Really!"* Feeling like a goofus. "Tiburon is choice . . . but you already know that."

Werner and Victoria Flemming, for example, lived in Tiburon, though they were not on anything like twelve thousand square feet. Across the bay from the City, the suburb was known as one of the most affluent in the Bay area.

"Actually, I'm in Belvedere, not Tiburon."

"Even better."

"I put together a couple of pieces of property. Tore down the houses. One was a real dog, a split-level monstrosity with an A-frame add-on, all redwood and glass, a deck in front big as an aircraft carrier." He looked at her solemnly. "You think it's immoral to tear down and rebuild?"

Clara shrugged. "Some houses deserve to be torn down. Put them out of their misery."

"Good! I'm happy to hear you say so. I'm putting up a Frank Lloyd Wright knockoff. Solar. Lots of cement and steel. Not a lot of redwood. Redwood is scarce and a *damn* expensive building material." He paused for a breath. "I prefer to see my redwoods vertical . . . not turned into decks."

"I agree with you there too."

"So, what about it?" he asked abruptly.

"About what?"

"Helping me with my house?"

She was more embarrassed than before. "I'm serious. That's *not* why I came tonight."

"I know that. I'm asking, can you help me? Have you got time? Time is the rare comodity."

"Well . . . truthfully, I don't have much time." Having denied she was looking for a job, she couldn't just leap at it. "I'll have to think about it—and don't you have to discuss it with anybody first?"

He chuckled harshly. "You mean like a wife? There isn't any wife. There was. Now there isn't. I'm divorced. I *discuss* things with my accountant." Eyes level, gauging her every blink, he continued. "I believe I'd enjoy working with you. No bull! I like being around talented people."

Clara smiled. "Talented, I don't know. Competent, yes."

He nodded, as if satisfied. "What about we go have dinner someplace?"

He'd mentioned time. Time: he didn't waste it.

BY NINE O'CLOCK, they were sitting at a table in the back room at the Balboa Cafe on Fillmore, close enough to the kitchen to see the sweat on the chefs' faces. This was not one of Clara's usual places. Henri preferred a far quieter scene. Tyler, on the other hand, said he loved the Balboa, which reminded him of Seattle and restaurants in New York.

"Young crowd here," he said. "I try to hang out with a young crowd. This business, they get younger and younger and before you know it you're out of touch. You know what I mean?"

"I do." Clara thought of Martha.

" 'Course, a lot of them are burnt out by the time they're thirty-five, either that or rich enough to retire and devote themselves to the environment." He grinned at her challengingly. "I'm thirty-five."

"But not burned out."

"No. You?"

"Not burned out, no. Thirty-eight."

So far, she admitted, no real chinks in his nice-guy armor and if Tyler had an agenda she didn't see herself as part of it. But there would be an agenda, no doubt. He was probably a control freak, a neatness nut, and as conventional as the family car. "Your business is pretty cutthroat, isn't it?" Clara asked.

"Cutthroat?" He laughed, the sound more a combative growl. "I'll say. Like playing pirates. Pamper your talent or the pirates raid and they're gone. You buy loyalty. . . . Yeah, sorry to say: *buy.* These people are prima donnas."

"It can't be much fun."

"But it is, if you thrive on competition. My partner and I started up in a garage, just like Hewlett and Packard. Now, within five years, we employ five hundred terrific people. We've got a bulging production facility out near San Jose and a new sales office in the city. It's been one long rush, Clara." Tyler picked up the wine list. "What should we drink? I like chardonnay."

Clara had already decided on grilled salmon. "Chardonnay is fine."

"Then'll we get a bottle of something with the

meal." Decision made, Tyler caught a waiter and ordered the wine. Then leaned across the table so Clara could hear him well. "Tell me about Bertram Hill."

Clara repeated what she'd told him before. "My father's probably going to turn them down—even though they seem to think the offer is so good we couldn't possibly refuse."

"Which you can."

"Of course." Unwise, perhaps, to open the Pinjatta file to Mick Tyler. Maybe unwise to have dinner with him at all, but why not? Henri was out of town. Besides, she wasn't married to Henri. Why shouldn't she have dinner with Mick Tyler, who might become a client, not only of hers but also Henri's? Anyway, he seemed a sympathetic ear. He listened intently, as if the tale were the most interesting he'd heard in weeks or months.

"I know about takeover bids," he said with finality, "and you're *not* vulnerable. The vineyard is privately held."

"That's right. My grandmother owns some. But it's entirely family."

Tyler's lip curled scornfully. "Then, screw 'em. Look, I am interested in wine. Really. So I follow the news. And I remember Bertram Hill did have a run-in with the government, or the wine authorities, or somebody. *Jackals!* The woods are full of them."

"I don't think it's that big a deal."

"Maybe not." He permitted himself a cold smile. "But don't forget one thing—when people want something bad, they do bad things to get it." He waited a bit, then demanded, "What's your friend Henry say?"

*"Henri."* she corrected him. "Henri Lamarque."

"Does he like the idea?"

"No, not at all."

"You should listen to him. I suppose you do. Is he," Tyler probed, "like your *best* friend?"

This was her chance to head him off, to stop something that Clara reckoned he was in the mood to start. "After my father, yes."

"Daddy's little girl, huh?" His voice was light. Somehow, he avoided making the question sound like an insult. "Do you and Henri live together?"

Her answer surprised her. "You might say so, yes."

"No hope for me then, I guess."

"Afraid not."

"Well . . . can't blame me for trying." He wasn't apologetic about it, continuing in a businesslike manner. "I want to meet him. Hell, I *have* to meet Henry . . . *Henri*. Not that I couldn't collect my own wine. But it takes time. And I don't have time. You don't have a problem with that, do you?"

"Of course not." She granted herself a little snappishness. "You asked. I answered. End of story."

"Good," he said. "Because you know, you just might need my help with this takeover thing."

"No. I told you. It's going no place."

"See," he pressed, not hearing her, "I do like you, Henri Lamarque or not." He gave her space to say she liked him too. "If Bertram Hill turns out to be too persistent, too aggressive, I want you to let me know. I'm a specialist in fighting off unwelcome gobbles. And I want to meet your father."

"But . . . really," Clara argued, "you should not get involved. Why would you?"

"Because, as I just said, *I like you.* I like Cab Root. Let me tell you something, Clara: I didn't make it in this cyberspace business by being a dummy about people." He cast her a warm look. "And I admire the hell out of guys who make wonderful wine. They should be honored and supported."

Alberto's response, however, would not be as friendly. Third parties, he would lecture her, casually met outside parties were not to be introduced into family affairs.

"I'm afraid I've told you too much."

Tyler put his hand on his chest. "Your secrets are safe with me. And listen—I'm sure you've got a good lawyer." Clara nodded, yes they did. "Well, I know tricks lawyers don't dare use, can't use—if it comes to the nitty-gritty."

"It's not going to any nitty-gritty," she insisted. But she had a bothersome feeling about him. "I shouldn't have mentioned it. Forget what I said. Please."

He reached across the table, touching her hand as if this were the most natural thing to do. "Clara, no! *Let* me take an interest in this. Do me the honor! I'm so impressed by Cab Root. By you. I want to meet Alberto Morelli. And Henri." Now, it was impossible for Clara to be negative, particularly when he added, "I'd love to be *with* you guys."

"Mick . . ." Clara tried to make light of it. "This is so sudden . . ."

"Best things in life are sudden!" His hard blue eyes lit up again. "Look, maybe *I'll* make an offer to buy Morelli Vineyards. Hell's bells, you *cannot* sell to Bertram Hill. . . . Besides which, you're going to help me decorate my new house."

Clara began to feel uncomfortable, as if somebody had turned up the heat. The Balboa suddenly was noisier than before. "Well, that's not certain. I've got to study my calendar."

"But I am going to need a decorator. Why shouldn't it be you? Is that *unreasonable*?"

"Not unreasonable, but maybe we're jumping the gun."

He shook his head impatiently. "No! And don't forget, a lot can be accomplished *very quickly* if you've got a little cash and a monster credit line in your pocket."

She'd been looking for a flaw? There it was. Mistaking her good-humored response to his personal questions, he'd gone too far. Yes, he *would* turn out to be a control freak, the sort who commanded and demanded and would never take no for an answer. Working with such a man would be hand-to-hand combat all the way. "Now, wait a minute," Clara said. "My practice is *not* to go overboard. My purpose would *not* be to spend all your money."

"Great! I don't like to spend more money than I have to."

"And I'm *not* making any promises."

"Fair enough," he replied. "Just as long as you're not trying to kiss me off. Are you?"

"Mr. Tyler . . . Mick . . . we've known each other all of two and a half hours and already you're leaning on me."

"Am I? I desist." He winked wickedly. "Don't worry, we'll get along. I'm easy."

"I don't really think so."

"You're wrong, Clara. I'm only hard when the jackals start yapping. People like Bertram Hill. Want to know what I'd do to them? First thing I'd do— and they wouldn't know what hit 'em—I'd run up their stock, way up, then sell off at the high. They'd crash and burn."

Clara froze. "But that's not even legal, is it?"

Face set, he muttered, "You get together a few straw men. And, let me tell you, it's over so fast . . . Anyway, I'm just giving you a for-instance. I don't even know if their stock is on the market. But such things can happen. They do happen." He winked again, touching his forefinger to his eyelid. "Good heavens, oh, no! I'm not saying I'd actually pull a stunt like that . . ." Wily grimace. "But it can't hurt for the jackals to know you've got backing, i.e., the wherewithal to go after *them.*"

Clara drank some of the excellent chardonnay. It was dry up front, she thought, preparing a report for Henri, with a touch of crisp fruit in the rear seats.

"So far, the Pinjattas haven't yapped."

"Okay," he acknowledged, "but I've got no reason to believe the wine business is any different, or more enlightened, than any other. Be surprised at *nothing* because nothing is ruled out."

"We'll be on our toes," Clara promised, turning to the menu. "What are you having, Mick?"

"A huge filet steak. I'm hungry."

"I'll bet you eat it rare . . ."

"That's right. The bloodier, the better."

# *eight*

"SURPRISE!" STEVE PINJATTA uncoiled from his chair. "I talked Victoria into letting me come along."

Victoria Flemming hadn't warned her. But Clara didn't flinch, deciding once again that she wouldn't be put off by Pinjatta tricks. "I didn't know you two were friends."

A blush gathered on Victoria's fair cheeks, coarsening the peach blossom of her complexion, showing at the dark roots of her brassy blond hair. Maybe Victoria hadn't had any choice. If Steve had insisted on crashing their lunch date, it would've been difficult for Victoria to turn him down, particularly as Werner Flemming was so close with the Pinjattas and Bertram Hill. So close, it occurred to Clara, that maybe this was Werner's idea.

Somehow, she doubted it. Victoria looked just too happy. "We met when Steve first moved here from New York. He came straight to Flemming's."

"Vicky's shown me *all* the sights . . ."

Well, so it seemed, Clara thought. Victoria was practically cooing, as if announcing an egg. "Steve and I are *great* friends," she said ardently. "But we're not broadcasting it, Clara. You understand?"

Victoria's expression was so warm, her eyes so hopeful, pleading, that Clara realized she was supposed to like Steve, to like the two of them together. Victoria was a schoolgirl bringing somebody to meet mommy. But mommy *didn't* approve. Opposites. Victoria such an innocent—being generous, so one assumed—and Steve, already marked and scarred by a world he scarcely knew. More than before, he registered in Clara's mind as a roué, even though he'd probably fail every roué qualifications test. Where Werner Flemming truly squelched Victoria's shallow personality, saturnine, pouting Steve inspired the lovesick teenager in her. She chattered. She was playful, flirting even then, when it was fairly obvious their relationship had passed mere flirtation. Steve absolutely basked in the attention.

The two had apparently been at the restaurant for a while, by the looks of something with vodka or gin and a slice of lemon in front of Victoria and Steve's scotch on the rocks, or whatever it was, now mostly melted rocks.

Victoria goggled at Clara. "I thought it wouldn't do any harm if Steve joined us. He's a nice boy . . ."

"I'll leave if you wish." He didn't mean it.

"*Silly* boy!" Victoria cried.

Clara had not been thrilled to drive across the bridge on a workday to meet Victoria in Tiburon. It was midweek. Henri was due back in the late afternoon and she was trying to get caught up before going to meet him. Then Mick Tyler had called and kept her on the telephone a half hour talking about his house and being nosy about Bertram Hill. Finally, she'd broken away and here she was. God knows why. Victoria had never been a riveting luncheon companion. Maybe out of duty, since the Flemmings had been clients. Or simple curiosity, Werner Flemming currently being much on their mind.

"*Boy?*" Steve mewed. "I'm *not* a boy!"

"But you *are* a boy!" Victoria laid one hand on his arm, stroking the sleeve of his grayish tweed jacket. "A boy doing a man's job."

Why hadn't Victoria just postponed their lunch? They'd have been more comfortable alone. Clara was odd man out, an intruder. Or—this hit her— was she an excuse for a rendezvous Werner Flemming wouldn't have been very delighted to hear about? And now what? Was Clara supposed to sit and watch while they caressed each other under the table?

"Clara," Victoria urged, "order something to drink."

"Just mineral water. I'm driving."

"Your trusty BMW?"

"My trusty *old* BMW."

Steve looked interested. "A classic?"

"No, just old. It won't be a classic for a few more years."

Brightly, Victoria piped up, "This is the restaurant Clara and I used to come to almost every day when she was helping decorate the house. Remember, Clara?"

"Oh, yes." Where Victoria would plot how they'd get Werner Flemming to agree to a decorating fix he didn't want to pay for. Generally, he had paid, anything to humor his new wife, until the day came when he'd quit paying.

The waiter stopped by. Clara asked for her mineral water.

"Steve picked me up today," Victoria said. "I don't

have to drive. Steve'll take me home in his new Porsche convertible."

"*Lucky* you."

"Steve," Victoria said, "let Clara see what you've got."

"No, no!" Pretending great embarrassment, Steve showed off his white teeth, too large for his narrow jaw. His smirk was not infectious. "It's still premature. A secret, Vick, highly confidential."

"Go on!"

He fluttered long eyelashes at Clara. "You're not going to be mad?" As if to tantalize, he slowly removed a white envelope from the inside pocket of his jacket. From inside it, he took a single square of stiff paper.

It was a wine label, designed in three colors, light gray, earthy tan, and pastel red. The red script spelled out:

BARONE ALBERTO MORELLI

Beneath the titled name, a fanciful pen-and-ink drawing of a country house or château caught the eye. Whatever it was supposed to represent, this was definitely not the Casa Morelli. Printed in smaller type: Cabernet Sauvignon. Estate Bottled. Private Reserve. Distributed by Bertram Hill, New York and Los Angeles.

"Well, what do you think?"

Speechless, Clara shook her head. Stomach muscles tightened.

"I had it done on spec," he boasted. "Aren't the colors sensational?"

"Beautiful!" Victoria whispered. "Awesome!"

Clara snapped forward. "Beautiful or not is not

the question! For God's sake, you haven't even talked to my father yet. . . . What the *hell* do you think you're doing?"

Steve reared back, coughing and clearing his throat. "I had it made so I can take it up there to show him what kinda stuff we've got in mind for Morelli Vineyards. We're *serious*! This oughta prove it. You don't get these things made for nothing, you know."

Clara pushed her chair back. "Alberto is no *barone*!"

"So what? It's just marketing. He could be a *barone* for all you know! We can market the hell out Barone Alberto Morelli!"

"You show my father that and he'll tear your head off. You're getting ahead of yourself, sonny boy. The deal's not done. *If* it's ever done. You're coming on too strong."

His lips bulged. "You don't know about coming on strong, lady!"

Victoria began to tremble. Her made-over nose twitched with alarm. Breathing hard, she put her hand on Steve's arm. He shook it off. He was angry too. He had been deflated in front of Victoria. Too bad. Clara had been brought here under false pretenses, caught in a Pinjatta-devised trap, then presented with something like a fait accompli even before she'd had a proper look at the San Francisco skyline on this newsprint-clear day.

"Where did that label come from?" Clara demanded.

"It's . . . it's easy enough to get labels made." He flicked his finger at the one on the table. "Take it. It's for you."

"Please, Clara . . ." Victoria made herself heard.

"The boy thought it would please you."

"It does not please me, Victoria. Now, I think I'd better leave."

"Wait a minute!" Before she could get up, Steve said, "You don't know, I guess, that Alberto talked to my old man yesterday afternoon. He's not half as negative and snooty about this as you are."

"*Snooty?*" Clara barked a laugh.

Tight-lipped, he backed off. "Negative then. *Goddamn negative!*"

Clara shrugged coldly. "I'm sure your father didn't say anything to Alberto about that thing." Pointing at the label, she remembered the word Mick Tyler had used. *Jackals!* There should've been a picture of a jackal on the label.

"You didn't even know they talked, did you?" he sneered. "That's how involved you are."

"I did, as a matter of fact," Clara lied calmly. Anyway Alberto had probably called and left a message.

"Then you know they hit it off like a house on fire. The old man'll be coming out here in a few weeks for a face-to-face meeting. They talked about a trial run of a couple thousand cases ... I hope," Steve said sarcastically, "*that* doesn't offend you."

"Hardly. And we'll just see how far that gets us."

Suddenly, Steve, then Clara, realized Victoria was silently crying.

"Vick! Hey, dollface! What's the matter?"

Tears, big sticky gobs, ran out of the corners of her eyes. His concern made the tears gush more freely. Victoria popped open her pocketbook and dragged out a wad of tissues. Voice all choked up, she moaned, "I so wanted you to get along. For us to have fun."

"Ah, Vick ..." His own puffy lower lip trembling,

Steve glared aggrievedly at Clara, blaming her. He pulled at his tie, ran his forefinger around the inside of his shirt collar.

"Stay for lunch, Clara," Victoria begged. "Please . . ."

Don't, Steve's eyes were saying, get the hell out of here.

"All right," Clara said. "I'll stay for lunch."

"And no more business," Victoria decreed, instantly dry-eyed. "I'm sick to death of hearing about the fucking wine business. That's all anybody ever talks about." She took the tissues away from her face. Her makeup was faultless. How had she done it? "Our night at the Clift, an absolutely wonderful dinner, and then Werner and Henri got into a big hassle about that Montebanque . . ."

Steve jerked forward. "What Montebanque? *Our* Montebanque?"

"Yes!" Victoria was eager to tell. "It's always about the wine, isn't it, Clara? Wine, wine, and more wine."

Steve's face became what Clara had expected of a Pinjatta face—feral with curiosity. "Henri? That's Henri Lamarque, isn't it?"

"Yes," Clara said.

"The so-called wine critic."

"*Not so-called,* sonny boy."

"We know about him." Young Steve rounded on Victoria. "Just what the hell happened that night?"

"Well," Victoria spouted, "we were at the Clift Hotel. Werner wanted Henri—and the rest of us—to taste one of the new magnums of Montebanque. And—"

Steve's face was all nose and teeth.

Clara cut in. "It was only a little dinnertime discussion. *No big deal.*"

"No big deal to start with," Victoria declared. "But then it got to be a very big deal. And that's what I'm saying. Everybody gets so excited about a goddamn bottle of wine. Except for Clara and me and Miss Rampling—Alberto Morelli's fiancée. The former opera star—"

"Werner didn't say anything to me about this."

"He wouldn't, would he, sweetie? He was *very* embarrassed. Henri said it wasn't a sixty or seventy or whatever it was supposed to be."

Clara said, "It was *supposed* to be a seventy."

"Oh, yeah? What the hell does Henri Lamarque know, for crissakes?"

"What does he know? Actually," Clara said bitingly, "if *you* want to know the whole story, Henri said he didn't think it was a Montebanque at all. Not a sixty. Not a seventy or eighty or even ninety . . ." Steve's mouth went slack. *"Not any kind of Montebanque."*

"You're kidding! How can that be? He's out of his goddamn gourd! What did he think it was, for crissakes?"

"A good Bordeaux. But not a Montebanque—as advertised on the *label*." Clara dared him to answer.

Steve's eyes lidded disingenuously. "Come again? Listen, *darling*, if the label says Montebanque, then it's Montebanque!" He shook his head violently. "No, no! *No!* Lamarque is wrong! *Or worse,*" he muttered blackly. "That guy has always had it in for us. We date back, you know. Ask him about it, Clara! Just ask him! Anyhow, his taste buds are shriveled. These critics!" he all but shouted. "These *guys!* We hate them! They're dangerous. They should be muzzled."

Clara had no thought now of leaving. "Don't talk

like a stupid ass. How do you know where Werner
got that Montebanque?"

He bit hard. "He bought it from us! From Bertram
Hill in New York City! So—what're you trying to say?
Accusing us—"

Victoria's tears began to trickle again. "Stevie,
don't be upset. Clara is a close friend of Henri's."

"Tell me something I don't know!"

"Stevie . . . Stevie," she pleaded. "In the end,
Henri did say he might be totally wrong. Didn't he,
Clara?"

"That's right." But she was being too patient with
thickheaded Steve Pinjatta. "This was not a formal
wine tasting. Henri was putting forward a casual
opinion—at Werner's invitation, by the way. Like
any sensible person, he admitted he might be
wrong."

This was a little easier for Steve to swallow but he
continued to grumble and complain. "I'm telling
you, there's no mistaking a Montebanque. It's a top
rank Bordeaux—soon to be made one of the first
growths when those French appellation guys expand
the circle of the Magic Five."

Peppily, Victoria said, "*That* I know about. Château Lafite-Rothschild and . . . who are the others,
Stevie?"

"Oh, I dunno . . . Lafite *and*—" He began to answer, then chopped himself in midsentence. Terrified, he stared past Clara. "Holy shit!"

Whatever Steve had seen, apparition or reality,
Victoria saw it too. Her lips moved, forming silent
words: *son of a bitch!*

Werner Flemming's solid figure loomed at Clara's
elbow. Not looking very sociable, he lowered himself
into the fourth chair at the table. "Well, I've found

the younger set." His voice was heavy, mocking. "I thought you'd be at your usual place. And Steve Pinjatta too." He paused. "How are *you*, Clara?"

"Fine, Thanks." She couldn't imagine any other reply. "And you?"

Werner didn't answer. Taking his time, he studied Victoria. Burning with insult, or pure hatred, his eyes lost focus. His face was as red as a side of beef. "How'd you get over here, Victoria? Your car's still in the garage at home."

The pink shade of Victoria's cheeks had faded to dead white. Her voice, a moment before so assertive, became tiny, close to inaudible. "Steve came and picked me up."

*"Neat."* Werner tracked around to young Pinjatta. "I tried to call you this morning."

"I was out," Steve muttered. "Obviously . . ."

"I didn't know you bought a car. When did you get a car? What kind of a car?"

"A little red Porsche."

"I was going to tell you where to go. Get you a good price."

Steve vented a high-pitched, near-hysterical giggle. "I got a good price. It's a ninety-six. I got it for a song. Cheaper than your Bentley anyway." He giggled again. "Easier to park too—"

Werner cut him off, turning back to Clara. "Is this business or social? I hope Victoria hasn't come up with more redecorating ideas."

Timidly, Victoria said, "I'm looking at the kitchen, Werner. It's really—"

"Forget it, Victoria. You don't know anything about decorating. Or dressing, for that matter. Everything you know, I taught you."

"Werner . . ." She was ready to cry again.

"Anyway, we're selling the house."

*"We are?"*

Bad news. Very bad. If Vicky's face had been por-
celain, it would've crumbled. Werner Flemming was
a very cruel man. Out of her own embarrassment,
Clara offered a kind of explanation for the meeting.

"It's mainly social. You know Bertram Hill has
made an offer to buy Morelli. So Steve and I have
been getting acquainted . . . thanks to Victoria's invitation."

Why did she bother? She didn't owe them cover.
Anyway, Werner didn't believe her. His jowly face
jelled into a scowl. "So I've heard." A wrinkle of mal-
ice deepened around his mouth. "It's all over town.
Rumor. Fact. I heard it just a day ago from a fellow
you just met, Clara. *Michael Tyler.* He appeared to
know more about the offer than I do myself, despite
my association with BHill."

"That's right," Clara fired back. "He asked me
about you."

Flemming adjusted his shiny glasses. "And you
said?"

"That I did know you, of course."

"My, my, what a lovely recommendation. . . . So
tell me, has Alberto decided to accept the offer?"

"Not yet."

"Yes, a big decision. He should think it over very
carefully. . . . You never know about a company like
Bertram Hill." Behind his metal-framed glasses, Werner's eyes glittered maliciously. "Have you taken Michael Tyler on as an advisor . . . along with *Henri
Lamarque?*"

"Of course not—and Henri is not an advisor either. Not in any official way anyhow."

Flemming laughed, sounding something like a

meat grinder. "Oh, no, there wouldn't be anything official about it, would there? Just a *dear* friend, that's all." Clara didn't try to respond. "Yes, Alberto should be very careful. As I've learned myself, selling, or taking on a partner, is the most important business decision you're ever going to take. *Right, Steven?*"

"*What?* Yes. Oh, absolutely!"

Steve was in agony. He hung on Werner Flemming's every word, responding jumpily to his slightest change of tone. He squirmed so that even the furniture must have felt his pain. But only the very guilty should suffer so much. Was he guilty, then? Had he actually cuckolded Werner Flemming?

That same question must also have been on Werner Flemming's mind. Having delivered himself of these several mouthfuls of bile, he went silent, becoming the impassive Buddha, perfectly opaque, his conclusion hidden behind his shiny glasses. But, suddenly, he roused himself. He looked at his watch. "You're still having drinks? Haven't you ordered yet? It's one o'clock. Are you planning to eat?" To Victoria: "Or just run?"

"I'm not very hungry," Victoria whispered.

"Nonsense! Have some fish, you must eat." He addressed Clara: "Doesn't she look a little thin, and scrawny?"

Clara wouldn't have said so. Victoria looked as juicy as a big-breasted hen. And must be equally intelligent, starting an affair with the likes of Steve Pinjatta.

"When I married her," Werner said, "she was a knockout. I picked her off the chorus line, did you know that? The Midget Kickers, they were called."

Clara glanced at Victoria, pitying her more than before.

"She worries too much," Werner said. "Always worrying. Worrying gives you lines, did you know? And warts."

Bravely, as if trying to divert Werner, Steve announced, "I'm having the mahi-mahi. I love it!"

*"Good for you. You do that."* Werner treated Steve to the same malevolent stare he'd painted on Victoria. "I myself will have a nice bit of swordfish. I like the texture of the meat. Firm. Nothing squishy about it. Almost like steak. And, eating it," he went on, "I picture the fearsome fish, that big blade on its snoot, spitting its prey like so much shish kebab... Where's the waiter?"

Steve jumped up. "Waiter ..." He waved his arm. "Waiter!"

Flemming grabbed his sleeve, pulling him down. "Easy. Don't shit yourself."

"Well, the goddamn waiter ... goddamn lax around here, if you ask me."

"Werner," Victoria said, "I guess I'll have the lobster salad."

Flemming studied her. His eyes drilled into her. Then, he said, "I thought you weren't hungry. Now, you're hungry. And you pick the most expensive item on the menu." Werner's face glowed red, like a traffic signal. "Jesus Christ! You'll eat me out of house and home. You said this morning you were going to have a sandwich for lunch because you were watching your weight and now you're not. You're going to get fat. You're going to eat yourself into *obesity* ..." Werner chortled ungraciously. "I'll roll you along the street like a bowling ball."

"Oh, Werner! You just said I looked scrawny!"

"And I'll be broke because I can't afford lobster salad. No white fish for you, huh? Only the best!"

Real tears were running down Victoria's face. Weepily, she gazed at Steve—expecting him to do . . . what? If he were a man? Steve looked ready to burst. He sat, trembling, staring at his hands. If he could've . . . what would he have done?

*"Sorry!"* Werner bolted up out of his chair. "I seem to have lost my appetite. And a minute ago, Victoria wasn't hungry. We'll assume, for the sake of argument, okay, that she still isn't." He stared at Steve. "I'll take her home. It's on my way—since I live there."

Saying no more, nodding at Clara, smiling gruesomely, Werner yanked Victoria up. She didn't resist, didn't dare a look at Clara, or Steve Pinjatta. She hurried along beside her husband, a shimmying little figure next to his angry bulk.

Steve collapsed. He put his head in his hands. "I'm ruined." When he looked up at Clara, his big bold eyes were humbled, his narrow features pinched. There was a whiteness around his mouth. "He's gonna fry my ass."

"Because you took Victoria out to lunch?"

"Out to lunch? We didn't have any fucking lunch, did we? My God! If Vick squeals . . . if Werner tells the old man . . . I'm totally dead meat."

Clara crossed her arms over her blazer. "No gory details, if you please."

"Nothing gory about it," he gasped, near hyperventilation. "Love. You know about *love*, Clara?"

"Love? You do not fall in love with a married woman with a husband who's your business client. Especially a woman married to somebody like Werner Flemming."

"Oh, yeah, thanks a lot." Despite his anxiety, he managed an ungrateful leer. "What the hell am I gonna do?"

"Call it off. Right now."

"It's too late. He'll know."

"What will he know?"

"Everything, she'll tell him. He'll get it out of her."

So it must be true. The boy had put the horns on the man. "Whatever happens, sonny boy, it's over."

He agreed, then shook his head in distress. "Vick . . . Vick. She's just such a hell of a woman. And it's a horrible thing for her to have to live with a fossil like Werner Flemming. Jesus! A fossil who's still alive and kicking, and looking for his kicks once in a while. Vick can't stand it. She says he's like a big, old, smelly bear."

"Victoria knew what she was doing. She married him. I suppose nobody forced her to."

"Yeah, thanks . . ." Steve swiped at his eyes with a napkin. "Don't you get it at all, Clara? Vicky's a fun girl. She *needs* fun. And what's she got? Werner-fucking-Flemming." He pulled a silk square out of his breast pocket and honked his nose into it. "I'm crazy about her. I don't know what to do. Love . . ." He crooned the word. "You know something, Clara? She's got a little horse tattooed on her butt. Did you know that?"

"No."

"A mustang, she says, a wild horse . . . I love it!"

*nine*

NATURALLY, THERE WAS wine. Henri could've returned with a suitcaseload of it but had settled for two bottles of Rugged Coast pinot noir, oddly named, given that the vineyard was located in the mild inland Willamette Valley. One of the bottles, opened, two glasses, tasted, stood before them.

"Clean and pure as flute music, don't you agree, Clarissima, a wine with a light tread and wide footprint—if I can put it so."

In very good spirits, eager to talk about Oregon and Oregonian winemakers, Henri had deliberately put aside what she'd told him in the car about the disastrous nonluncheon with Steve Pinjatta and Victoria, the appearance of the wrathful Werner Flemming who threatened to fry Steve's ass.

Henri slid closer, even though they were as close as two human beings could get without overlapping. They were snuggled—was there another, less smarmy, word for it?—deep in the couch in her living room with its own view of the Bay. Clara hadn't dressed again, merely throwing on a long white cotton robe, her sushi robe, Henri called it. He was wearing the mate, in blue.

"Make a note," he said. "I will write that—light tread, wide footprint. Inspiration! My God, do I need it. It is *so* difficult for me to find new and original ways to describe wine in not my native language."

"Your English is very, very good."

He ducked his head down, using his nose to nudge aside the robe and plant a wet kiss on her breast.

"Thank you," he whispered, "but no, I fatigue from searching for words. A whole new vocabulary is needed for description of wine. The present words have become what you call boring, old hat."

Clara felt his cheek, the bristly beard. He kissed her again in the same, pleasing place. "Henri, everybody says you write better about wine than anybody since the Romans."

"No, no, I don't, Clarissima. I am tired of scrambling for words and I am tired of wine."

Clara smiled, not believing him for a minute. "Then why don't you go over to assigning them numbers like everybody else?"

He was shocked. "What! Lamarque would use numbers to express quality? Clarissima, that would be even worse than inadequate words! A wine is no longer of wide footprint and light-footed? It is a ninety-two or -three or -four?"

"There are so many wines now . . . you can't describe them all."

Henri smiled archly. "Lamarque will only deal with the nineties. He will not bother with the eighties. And what does it signify anyway? Nothing. It would depend on what the critic had for breakfast or for sex the night before. Bah! I refuse to indulge myself—"

"Engage."

"Engage myself in this numbers game of wine." His beard tickled again. After a bit, he drew away. "Listen! I *engage* myself only in the one-to-ten game for women. You, Clarissima of the velvet skin, the Tuscan tresses, like old gold, the depth of body, the glorious breasts, like Titiano, you, Clara Morelli, are a big, big *ten*." He clutched her desperately. "You know why I love you best of all?"

"Because I'm willing to talk about wine." Correction: she was willing to listen to him talk about it.

"No. Your skin. In your skin, I feel the texture of antiquity."

"You're saying I've got a patina."

His voice drooped. "Clarissima, you know very well what I mean. I'm speaking of the scent of Italian history, of your blood-old Etruscan ancestry. . . . My nose catches the flavor of your skin, your skin, yes . . . *body* . . . of old wine, old wood, old stone . . ."

"Now I remind you of a seventeenth-century wine barrel."

"No, no!" He frowned reprovingly. She *must* take him seriously. "Your ancestor Etruscans were a very romantic, if mysterious people. You feel that when you visit their tombs, see the recumbent sculpts—all such happy-looking dead people."

Humoring him. "Not much point in looking miserable once you're dead. Nothing much else can go wrong."

"Please, Clarissima, pay attention to me. These ancestors of yours, they had a flavor. They teach us: enjoy life! Celebrate! Live each day! And so," he declared, "I am finished with the wine. I concentrate on you. . . . Gather ye rosebuds, a poet said. Life is short. Enjoy!

Because after that, another poet said . . . *Sans Wine, Sans Song, Sans Singer, and—Sans End!*"

"None of that talk."

"I am manic-depressive."

"Henri!"

Groaning, he buried his face in her stomach. His breath was warm. Then, he suddenly rolled over, throwing his feet on the couch, staring up at her. "I think it is the postcoital sadness."

"That'll go away too. Maybe it's the wine. We'll switch to champagne. Something bubbly. There's a bottle in the refrigerator."

"Clara, no, no, thank you. Frankly, tell no one, I do not much like the bubbly anymore. Or even white wine. Too acid. And I am too . . . jaded." He groaned again. "Too awful, is it not, for one of my profession to confess."

"Henri, I don't take you seriously for one minute. I've never heard you say a single bad thing about chardonnay."

"Chardonnay?" He rocked his head in her lap. "It is there, like Mount Everest."

"Oh, is that so? What about all the great Chablis?"

*"Mon Dieu!"* He clapped his hand to his forehead. "*Touché.* But truly, Clarissima, there are not so many perfect chardonnays. I think there are more good reds than good whites. Am I wrong?"

"I think white has its place . . . with fish. In the summer, it's nice in spritzers. People drink it at cocktail parties. They christen ships with cheap champagne."

"Clarissima, you are pulling at my leg, are you not? No mind. Thank God my future father-in-law is a red-wine specialist. No whites for Alberto Morelli."

"He tried a Riesling once. Didn't like it. Too feeble, he said."

"*Feeble.* Yes, a *good* word. I will use that too. But not in my column on the magic Willamette Valley. Nothing is feeble about the Willamette Valley."

The column in the weekly *Imbiber* was his outlet, in more ways than the obvious one. Not everybody knew that Henri had founded the magazine some fifteen years before, then suddenly sold it—he said the business aspects of a magazine bored him—and moved west, continuing as columnist and commentator. He still traveled widely at *The Imbiber*'s expense.

"The Oregon growers are heroes," he went on avidly, "doing battle with a fickle, tricky climate and the American wine drinker. Americans cannot believe that very fine wine can originate from such a faraway, far-north, un-European wilderness. They do not realize that southern Oregon is of the same latitude as Burgundy. Ah, well . . ." He turned his head, nudging that nose into her belly, breathing deeply. "Toothsome. Delicate but bold. Reserved but subtly adventurous. Calm, but underneath passionate. Straightforward . . . nuanced. Fragile . . . sinewy." He looked up at her.

"For this wine? All would do."

"No, not for the wine. *For you.*"

"Me? I'm *sinewy*?"

"But fragile, I tell you. Strong—but at the same time . . . breakable."

"*Breakable?*" How close to the truth he was, though she'd deny any such fragility. "I'm some kind of a china doll?" Clara knew what he was trying to say. She didn't mind hearing it again.

"I wouldn't hurt you, that's what I mean." She laid

her hand on his chest, caressing. His body tensed. "Clara . . . not so fast!" Aroused, he slipped away from her. Clara couldn't think why. She was ready for more bed. Reserved? Yes, but adventurous. Robe billowing behind him, Henri crossed the room to the windows.

This was a perfect place for a telescope.

He bent to the eyepiece of the instrument. The robe fell open. But he didn't bother about it. He was very frank with his sexuality, unlike other—the few other—men she had known. Watching him, a warm tide swept over Clara, a wash of physical reassurance. Making love in the eventide would do that for you. Lazily, she drew her legs up under her, reaching for her wine, putting it to her lips. She felt like purring. If she'd been a cat, she would've purred her fur off.

"I hope nobody's looking this way."

"I am *voyeur!*"

It was a powerful scope, indeed the voyeur's delight, except there wasn't much to see from this vantage point, only a mismatch of apartment-house roofs, roads, cars on the roads, a tangle of warehouses by the waterfront, then the Bay, Alcatraz, the Golden Gate Bridge, the peninsula of Marin, beyond that the open sea. People believed Clara when she said she'd bought the telescope to watch the sailboats, not to spy. People thought of her as good, too good, perhaps, to be true. Sometimes, it was unflattering to be thought so well of.

"I am aiming at Belvedere, at this new friend of yours. Mick . . . who?"

"Tyler. He's anxious to meet you. I gave him your office number."

He was glued to the telescope. "And you dined at the Balboa with Mick Tyler."

"Yes, I did. After Cabby's party." Was it possible he was upset? "Now, Henri . . ."

Blithely, he stopped her. "I will be pleased to hear from him." He swung the telescope this way and that. "Now I will zero in on the Flemming establishment in Tiburon above where hangs such a pall of black fury. . . . Ah, I have the Flemmings in my sights. The deck. I see the barbecue cooker. I see the front room. Ah, do I see fair Victoria? Yes! Fair Victoria. What! With two black eyes? No! Impossible! Werner Flemming is not such a brute. Do I see brutish Werner, lurking behind her? No . . . Yes! *Um Gott ist willen! Werner, he is on the floor!* A big knife is sticking out of his chest! No. Impossible! Is Victoria a killer? No! Who else do I see in this bloody room? Do I see the young Pinjatta? What does he look like, this Pinjatta? An overdressed popinjay, if I am not mistaken! Is it he?"

"Could be."

"Or is it a policeman in plain clothes, also well dressed, the fashionable constabulary . . . more likely, from what you've told me, it is young Pinjatta on the floor with Werner Flemming's corkscrew in his heart."

"I warned him."

"But will he heed, Clarissima, will he heed? This Pinjatta sounds like a veritable idiot." Frowning gloomily, Henri put the cap back on the eyepiece of the scope. Resashed his robe. For a moment, he stared into the early evening's slate gray, following the blazing torches of the commuter ferries tumbling along toward Marin. "Truly, I would like to meet this Mick fellow . . . but what are we to do about the young idiot and his *stupid* label?"

"Nothing. He'll go away. His main worry now is that Werner will tattle on him to his father."

"To the fearsome Franco Pinjatta who hates the very guts of Henri Lamarque?"

Henri picked up his wine and paced restlessly back to the window. Finally, Clara thought, he had to deal with what she'd told him about Steve Pinjatta and his overwrought reaction when he'd learned of the Montebanque episode. It was obvious the Pinjattas hated Henri. Hate had positively leapt out of Steve.

*"Franco Pinjatta,"* Henri mused. "There is a tale that Franco was once the terror of the Andes, that he murdered his way into the wine trade."

"What is it with you and the Pinjattas? Steve says you've got a vendetta—"

"Vendetta? *I against them?*" He laughed quietly. "Rather the other way around. The Pinjattas hate me . . . why? I will tell you. I almost married one of them. It would be Steve's cousin, the daughter of the twin, Maxey. Her name was, is, Carmen. That was in Paris when I was very young."

He was very matter-of-fact about it, as if talking about an old parking ticket. Clara took the . . . what should she call it? News? Revelation? No, she took the *disclosure* calmly. Given Henri, it would've been more of a surprise if he hadn't had previous involvements. Besides, it was in another country and the wench was . . . "What happened?" she asked simply.

"They will say that I jilted her. *No.* I simply decided that marriage to Carmen Pinjatta would not be heavenly. I told her so, long before there was any sort of formal *entrothment.*"

"And so they hate you . . ."

"And for other things too."

"Why didn't you tell me before?"

"No reason." Henri shrugged manfully. "It is not a life episode I am so very proud of."

"What was she like?"

"Beautiful. But very neurotic. Headstrong, like her operatic namesake." Henri dropped down beside her again. "I could say she seduced me and be telling some of the truth . . . I was stupid and naïve, an Austrian trying to be Alsatian and a *nose* to boot. No more than a pimpled boy, I was fascinated by wine already, you know, being from the suburb of Grinzing, which is the wine bar for Vienna. And then . . ." He paused to see how she was taking it. "First I must explain—I had lost so many family during the war . . . as a young man, I began to realize I did not belong in Austria and with a realistic view of past history that I was not even Austrian anymore. So I wandered to the south of France, then to Paris. I found the Pinjattas by chance. At this time, they had just begun their inroads to the Rioja in Spain. I encountered Carmen." He shrugged. "And then it ended. But they did not forget. After I had wandered to New York, my confrontation with the Pinjattas took another fatal dimension . . . I was now a *nose* and the Pinjattas had come to Bordeaux . . ."

The story was simple enough and by no means a new one in the annals of wine. A quantity of the Pinjattas' second wine, the imaginatively named Gitane Flambé or Flaming Gypsy had been mislabeled and slipped into a large export shipment to New York of Château Montebanque.

"Bad things happen," Henri shrugged, "more often than the French like to admit, less often than charged. We connoisseurs, *par example*, never forget the *scandale* of the epoch, on the order of treason or other capital crime, in which several esteemed Bordeaux producers dosed an anemic vintage with virile North African plonk. Aha! And so! Lamarque was put in a most terrible position, Clarissima. The drama occurred at a tasting event at the Hotel Pierre in New York City—just as, on lesser scale, at the Clift in San Francisco all these years later. Lamarque has spotted the *failure*—*fraud* such a dirty word. What to do? My reputation is at stake. Not that the Lamarque nose is so spectacularly gifted that it identified the substitute as Gitane Flambé—but keen enough to know a Montebanque from an imposter. *What to do?*"

"And?"

Henri shook his head sadly. "Lamarque must blow the whistle on the Brothers Pinjatta, residual guilt over his affair with Carmen Pinjatta to the contrary."

"Good!"

"Yes, good. But, beloved one, all hell burst loose. The Pinjattas go wild. I am called a charlatan and worse. Career and huge lawsuits are threatened. But Lamarque stands by his gun. Aha! Ergo! Soon enough, one questionable bottle leads to another. Finally, *à la fin,* the *scandale* is referred back to France . . . now, the Pinjattas try to make of it a mild business misadventure. But the Appellation-control bureaucrats do not believe in misadventure, even much in accident. They pounce, charging deliberate substitution. Deep *scandale* sweeps the Bordeaux region, ah yes, and has still not been forgotten, severely limiting the Pinjattas' ambition to be crowned as a reigning first-growth château . . ."

"And they blame you."

"Of course. Entirely."

"But it was a serious thing. And they *were* guilty."

Anybody even on the margin of the wine business knew about the Appellation d'Origine Contrôlée, which sets the AOC standards advertised on most French wine labels. Years earlier, to do away with misrepresentation of provenance, adulteration, all these faults and more, the elite French châteaux had been led to establish various systems of appellation control. Specific grape-growing locales were defined and, within these areas, rules to govern everything from labeling to how vines were to be tied to their trellises, how many buds left on a cane, even, to be ridiculous, the hours of harvest. But the aim was worthy—to establish trust within a nation of wine drinkers.

"Yes, guilty, it would seem," Henri agreed. "But the Pinjattas argued that the horrible event happened a mere year or so after their acquisition of Château Montebanque. Their minions were forced to plead error and confusion resulting from the transition. No excuse at all because the like had not occurred in the recorded history of the château . . . the Appellation was not impressed. There was no good explanation for how two or four or ten thousand—nobody knew the exact figure—liters of Gitane Flambé came to be in bottles labeled Montebanque."

"And they were nailed."

"Yes. A fine was levied. A minion or two were sacrificed, the Pinjattas found not to be personally culpable. They were hurt. But not destroyed." Henri paused darkly. "In the end, they took petty revenge. They forced me out of my magazine. Making much of a wine review which was not even written by me, they threatened my backers with a lawsuit which would have meant huge legal costs. And that is why

I sold my share and came West. I was allowed to keep a column . . ."

So he did have every reason to hate the Pinjattas, every justification for a vendetta. But there was this: "Henri, if Franco Pinjatta murdered his way up the wine ladder—"

"You ask *why*? Why he did not have Lamarque, as you say, bumped off?" Smiling dismally. "Well, murder is easy in South America but not so easy here."

"You're so sure of that?"

"I am sure of nothing. But I do believe the Pinjattas have been civilized. They want to be part of the Establishment. They make grand monetary offers now . . . and use their attorneys as muscle."

"We've got to tell Alberto all this."

"Better not. Not just now."

"I don't mean about Carmen. The rest of it."

But Henri was not sure. "Alberto will remember the scandal—it was on the minds of all wine people. My fear would be to get Alberto aroused. His instinct would be to boot Franco down the stairs . . . in itself," he said meaningfully, "perhaps not a wise way to end a negotiation with the Pinjattas. For the moment, Alberto should *please* play it straight. Let the matter run its course. Remember, Franco is now— supposedly—an upstanding member of the New York community."

"Faking wine? Cheating? That makes him upstanding?"

"For us, no. But in New York, where people are more and more impervious to chicanery, it is different." He looked at her inquiringly. "You forgive me?"

"For what?"

"Carmen."

"Nothing to forgive."

"Good. *Bon!*" He picked up his glass. "To you, my lovely." Then sank back, more at ease. "Now tell me, do you think the young idiot Pinjatta actually went boom-boom with luscious Victoria?"

Perhaps he thought he was changing the subject but he wasn't, not really. "Well, he told me Victoria's got a horse tattooed on her bottom."

"Ha, ha." He laughed, faintly amused. "*C'est drôle.* I never saw this boy, you know. I think he was at that school in Switzerland, Le Rosey, where go the extraneous children of wealthy marriages turned sour. So we can know that this Pinjatta has the habits of the playboy elite and little of the crudity of the older generation of Pinjattas—or their ruthless driving force either. No doubt Victoria showed him the tattoo to entice. My feeling about Victoria is that she works her wiles upon men. She does not seem so, but I believe she is a courtesan of some talent."

"Then why is she so scared of Werner?"

Henri smiled cynically, very like a Frenchman. "Because Werner is too much of a bore to be flattered by the wiles."

"She must have wiled him once. She got him to marry her."

"Indeed. I wonder how that happened."

"Maybe he fell in love with her and she didn't have to wile him. A deadly serious man falls in love with a tease, not the first time it's happened. I'm beginning to feel sorry for Werner."

"No! This is Werner's own fault. He treats Victoria with disdain, as if he truly despises her. If Victoria wanders, who can blame her? A happy marriage? I think not. Werner is at fault. I do not pity him."

"You're merciless, Henri. But I'm so glad you're

back." It was time she said so. "I've missed you."

His eyes leapt excitedly. "Truly?" He thumped his chest. "*Mon Dieu!* How could I leave you? What a swine I am! Next time I say I must go away, you can kill me."

She touched his cheek. "I wouldn't go that far."

"Clarissima, yes! I give you permission. When you see me packing a bag, unless you are also packing a bag, I give you permission to kill me."

"We'll both be packing soon for Italy."

"Yes, yes. I am looking forward . . ." He stopped pensively. "We will travel together, Clarissima, but once we are there, in Lucaterra . . ." Again, he paused. "Not to embarrass ourselves, how will we be accommodated?"

"The short answer is that I'd feel damn silly going to Tuscany with you, then sleeping like a nun in a single room someplace."

"Would Alberto be shocked though? And what about the Italian family?"

"What about them? Henri, I thought *you* were the European. Don't forget . . . Tuscany. The weather. The food. The wine. All conducive to—"

"Clarissima!" As if in a swoon, he slid off the couch. On his knees before her, taking her hands, he whispered, "We could solve all the problems. We could marry too. *I love you.*"

He nudged his body between her legs, taking her around the waist, pushing his face into her belly. His shoulders were shaking. Clara couldn't believe he was crying. She hugged him closer. He dropped his head. His lips were warm on her skin. His tongue made her shiver. He caught a nerve or two. She trembled.

In a moment, he pulled away. "I am decadent. Am I decadent? I will ask your father!"

"Ask him what? Whether you're decadent? Best not."

"For your hand, Clara, I will ask him if he will approve of me."

"No, please, not just yet."

"You are at least open to the idea, no?"

The question. "Yes," she said, "I am open to the idea."

This was further than she'd gone before. Henri was joyous. *"Then when?"*

Next question. How much longer did she need? It wasn't as if she were in mourning, God knows. But would there be some sort of signal that *now* was the time? She had to tell Henri something—and give herself a deadline. That was only fair. "After Luca-terra, we'll make up our minds. Is that all right? I don't want anything to detract from Alberto's celebration."

"Detract? I think he would be very happy for you too, Clara. *If* he approves of me."

"I know he approves of you."

"Did he say?"

"He asks about you a lot."

"Good. I ask about him too."

So saying, he dropped his head again. Clara closed her eyes, surrendering. It was all very acceptable, including the scrape of his beard on her thighs, maybe *especially* the feel of his beard. After a moment, she whispered, "Henri, aren't we something?"

He made a contented noise. "Yes, *too much.*"

"You get here . . . five minutes later, we're in bed."

"I take that for a good sign . . . no? An omen for future connubiality . . ." Henri hiked himself up on the edge of the coffee table, an arm's length away, eyeing her greedily.

Keeping her own desire in place for just a few more minutes, like holding her breath underwater while wanting so much to breathe, Clara asked, "This wine, Henri, has a slightly tropical edge, a sensualness, a lushness. Is that *possible?*"

"With wine," he replied eagerly, "everything is possible. Coffee beans. Chocolate. Tobacco. Young cedar. Old oak. Fruit of every variety. Diesel fumes. Scotch whisky . . ."

"You're pulling my leg."

"I would, yes," he agreed. "But I will quote you in my piece. An easterly, mysteriously tropical wind blows out of the Rugged Coast. In its vapors, one detects a scent of mango, of breadfruit, of rich tropical rot . . . weird indeed for a wine from near the coast of temperate Oregon."

"But possible."

"Yes, Clarissima . . . possible. *Everything* is possible."

As he watched her, his eyes gleamed boldly, but with a shyness too, something even like apprehension. Who and what was this *person* he had set loose, this person possessed, this woman now teetering on the brink, dizzy with sudden, great desire? Did he recognize her? Henri opened his mouth to speak. Clara knew he was going to tell her again that he loved her and wanted her. But she stopped him.

She slipped down in front of him, kneeling, putting her finger across his lips.

"Don't say anything."

*t e n*

S OMETHING'S RINGING IN your purse, dear," said her grandmother Mina. "Are you timing your visit to poor, old granny?"

"Grandma!" Clara reached down. "It's the damn cell phone."

"You've got one of those things?"

"Sure." She thumbed the proper button. "Hello . . ."

"It's me." The voice came in powerfully. "Mick Tyler," he added, in case she hadn't recognized him.

"Well, hello." She made a face at Mina, expressing annoyance at the caller, at the phone itself. "Where are you? Can I call you back from the office?"

"I'm in my jet. Thirty thousand feet over Indiana," he said brusquely. Well, he hadn't advertised a private jet. "Sorry. I'll just take a minute. I wanted to tell you I spoke with Henri Lamarque this morning. Hope I didn't blow it."

"No," Clara said coolly, "that's fine."

"I liked him . . . *very much.*" As if congratulating Clara for Henri, he sounded very much the CEO he was. "I wanted his opinion on an interesting proposition from Werner Flemming—which is, I've got first crack at buying a huge, old wine cellar owned by a New York banker type, dead a few months ago. I apparently can get it from the estate before it goes to auction. . . . What do you think?"

"I wouldn't know. What did Henri say?"

Tyler chuckled. "He was cautious. Didn't commit. I'd of been disappointed if he had. We're gonna get together."

Her now-familiar Tyler reaction set in. He'd called several times that week, again about Bertram Hill. He had some guys, you see, in New York and they . . . well, once he got a bee in his bonnet, no holding him back. There was no way, it seemed, Clara could dissuade him from poking his nose into the BHill thing. Not that she didn't like him, it wasn't that. Better to say simply that Tyler was not a soothing person. He'd be a stiff leather boot compared to somebody like Henri—supple as a leather glove.

"I told Flemming I wouldn't make a decision till I talked it over with Henri."

"Oh." Mina was listening in, eyes snapping with curiosity. "Flemming won't care for that."

"Can't be helped." His voice faded. "Have you thought about my house at all?"

"I'm still waiting for the drawings."

"I know. I know. I called your office. Who was that I talked to?"

"My assistant. Daisy Chaney."

"Sounds nice."

"I'll tell her you said so."

Static. "So long, kiddo." Without hearing her good-bye, he broke the connection.

Thank God—Clara's first thought—it was Friday and Tyler was out of town. Saved by the bell! She still wasn't ready to say yes or no to doing his house.

It should be remembered that in decoration, as in musical composition, two strong heads were not better than one. But you couldn't phrase a turndown so bluntly. You lied. You acted the hypocrite, like everybody else. As to Henri and the wine cellar, Henri would have to make his own decision.

"I'm sorry, Grandma."

"Who *was* that?" As in, how dare he, or she, interrupt us with that infernal instrument?

"A client. A potential client. He was calling from his airplane."

Mina sniffed. Even worse. "He shouldn't call when you're sitting here talking to somebody, should he? It's not polite."

"But he didn't know where I was, Grandma."

Which was an unsatisfactory explanation. Mina would have it her way, no matter what. Like the rich dowager she was, Mina lived her life on her own terms, kept slightly in line by a devoted butler named Hugo. A housemaid came in by day. Few people knew Hugo's family name, which happened to be Wanamaker. Some, those who dared, suggested Hugo was actually Mina's Mr. Brown. The old lady even looked a bit like an elderly Queen Victoria, though Hugo, a medium-sized gray man in a black suit, was not much like pictures of Mr. Brown in kilts. God knows what went on behind Hugo's poker face or within Mina's house when the maid had gone home for the day. No one but God *would* ever know. Mina and Hugo made a discreet, *fin de siècle* couple.

"Must you go?"

Clara was packing the cell phone back in her purse. "I've already been here way too long."

It was never easy to get away. Visitations to her grandmother's fussy old mansion in Pacific Heights required time. Mina did things in an orderly, measured fashion and others were expected to tailor their schedules to hers. Clara did so willingly, when she could. They were very fond of each other. Clara, Mina's only grandchild, the very image, she said, of her own dead daughter, was *beloved*. Mina threatened to leave Clara all her money, the house, her jewelry . . . everything. Clara wanted none of it. She wanted her grandmother to be around forever.

"Did I not hear Henri's name mentioned?" Mina inquired.

"Yes, this man wants Henri to help him build a wine cellar."

"From scratch?" Mina echoed doubtfully. "No piece of cake, Clara. But if anybody can do it . . . I like Henri. He'll he coming with you to Italy, won't he?"

Surprised, Clara asked, "How did you know?"

Mina touched her nose. "I know most everything. . . . So we'll all be together."

No surprise, Mina had decided she would definitely travel to Lucaterra for Alberto's wedding. She'd announced the decision to Clara over a pre-luncheon bourbon-and-soda cocktail. Hugo would be with her. It was essential, Mina said, that she be there to affix her stamp of approval to Alberto's marriage. After all, her daughter, Evelyn, Clara's mother, was no more and for that very reason Mina was obliged to be on hand to wish new happiness for Alberto. Besides, Mina *liked* Florence. Who wouldn't like such a stellar figure? Did Clara too? Of course, Mina concluded. It would've been unreasonable of her not to.

"Papa will be very pleased."

"I'm surprised he hasn't called."

But Alberto wasn't communicating very well just at the moment, a sure sign he was totally involved in harvest. Clara herself hadn't talked to him in a week or more until he'd telephoned the night before to say he and Florence would be in San Francisco the next day. Steve Pinjatta was pressing for a meeting and Jim Fontana, the Morelli attorney, had advised they not put him off any longer, even though it was a pain in the neck for Alberto to break away. Wisely, Fontana wanted them to meet in the city. It would've been impossible at the vineyard anyway.

"He knows you've been thinking about going," Clara defended her father. "This is his busiest time right now and . . ." Should she tell? "There's been an offer for the vineyard."

"I didn't know that." Mina's lower lip stiffened. "He hasn't said a word!"

Clara lied a little. "He doesn't intend to worry you about it until there's something definite."

"Worry me?" Mina was indignant. "As if I've got anything else to do—why shouldn't he worry me?"

"He just wouldn't, you know that. Now, look, Grandma, really, I've got to get back to the office."

"Yes." Mina nodded imperially, dismissing her. "Go then. Hugo will show you out . . ." As if Clara didn't know the way. "Tell that father of yours that I'm going to be in Lucaterra. I *will* bless this marriage—and in person!"

That was a positive. Clara wondered how Alberto would take the news. She'd soon know. He'd promised to bring her up-to-date after he'd finished with Steve . . . finished him off, she hoped.

Clara was back at the office by three. Then, suddenly, it was four-thirty and still no word from Alberto. She dropped her pencil. Wadded up a piece of drawing paper upon which she'd been sketching. No use pretending to work. The minutes ticked by. Her mind wandered back to Mick Tyler. Addey and Company was doing well, Clara reminded herself again, not a time to get overloaded with clients, to run the risk of being put down as a slapdash performer. Yes or no to Mick Tyler?

Daisy bustled in to get her to sign a letter but otherwise didn't interrupt.

"Thanks . . ." All at once recognizing salvation, at least a solution, even as it stood before her, Clara whirled around. "Daisy . . . wait! I've got a brilliant idea. The man who called from the jet . . ."

"He said his name was Tyler. I'm sorry. Should I have told him the cell phone number?"

Clara shrugged it off. "Yes, Mick Tyler. I might've mentioned him. He's a high-flyer in the computer business. He wants us to decorate his new house, over in Belvedere. . . . So, what do you think?"

"Me?"

Daisy should not be impressed by position or great wealth. Her father was a muckety-muck at the Bank of America and Daisy had been brought up with her share of the trappings. She didn't really need to work. She could've gone the usual route—dabbled a while, then married. But Daisy wanted more. She'd do her own thing, she'd told Clara, but not in anything as phony as public relations or one of the dignified professions. Daisy had her own drummer. Clara admired her, hoping daughter Martha would finally go the same way.

"Well, you heard him. What'd you make of him?"

"He sounded like he's in a hell of a hurry."

"He is in a hurry. There must be a hundred . . . a

thousand . . . just like him, suddenly so rich and he doesn't know how to spend it."

Daisy nodded, unimpressed. "You don't want to do the job, do you?"

Wise girl. Perceptive, at least. "I don't know. Another big project right now? And my trip's coming up . . . anyway, he's going to be sending us architectural drawings. I said we'd look at them. No promises . . . Mick said you sounded very nice."

"I don't know where he got that idea." Daisy was more annoyed than embarrassed. But, yes, if it came to that, she could handle a Mick Tyler.

"I want you to study the drawings, very carefully. You know, sooner or later, you're going to have to face the music. Things won't stop while I'm away. My thought is, you're going to have to start getting out, stroking the clients . . . I know you're familiar with the term. And I also know you didn't come to work here so you could sit around all day answering the phone. I'm thinking we're going to have to hire a full-time secretary . . ."

Daisy finally smiled. "I'm ready," she said.

"You can start with Mick Tyler. You *may* like him."

ALBERTO ARRIVED JUST before five. Saying hello to Daisy, he kissed Clara's cheek. With a weary grin, a small groan, he sat down on the couch, saying no to a glass of wine. "Well," he announced, "Jim Fontana and I met young Pinjatta at the Top of the Mark for a drink before lunch. I thought he'd like to see the views. Naturally, he's already been up there." He shook his head wearily. "What a waste of time! After all the pressure to meet me, he was more interested in talking about himself than their offer.

He blabbed his whole life story, then went on about how he loves San Francisco and wants a place of his own and blah, blah, blah . . ." He glanced at Clara. "It seems that years ago his mother ran away from Franco Pinjatta and he was sent off to a horrible, cruel school in Switzerland. . . . Did he tell you he was adopted?"

"Yes, but I didn't pay any attention."

"He's too loony for me. Not much like his father, Franco."

"So you really did talk to Franco Pinjatta . . ."

"Sure. Why?"

"Steve Pinjatta told me you agreed to let Bertram Hill handle two thousand cases of your cabernet. . . . He took me by complete surprise."

"*Agreed?* No way!" That familiar bite in his voice, Alberto hardened, reminding Clara that her father was not a wholly patient man. "That little bastard! Where does he get such an idea? He mentioned it today—and we shot it down. What Franco proposed was buying a couple of thousand cases for a special promotion. To show their good faith, and all that. I said I'd think it over. Now, Clara," he admonished her, "take it easy. I'm not going to be reporting in every time I—"

"All right . . . I was just . . . I don't want . . . How's the harvest going?"

"*Clara* . . . everything's going to be okay. Believe me. Including the harvest." Alberto smiled happily. "Looks like we'll have fifteen hundred or so cases of pinot noir; last year we got practically nothing. Yields are generally up—not too high, I hope. I'd rather have less than a glut, makes for better wine. Comparable to seventy-one, I hope . . ." seventy-one, the boosters liked to call it Sonoma's wine of the century. "We're finishing the merlot, beginning the zin, and the cabernet is perking. Should be ready beginning of November—I'm going to let it sit as long as I can."

"But all done by the time you leave."

"Hopefully, yes. And the Bertram Hill business too. Today, Jim and I didn't hear anything we didn't already know. We had a quick lunch with the kid, then went back to Jim's office to talk it over. Concluding what? Nothing . . . Clara, I've *got* to talk to Henri. Can we arrange it for tonight? We'll stay over."

"Oh! No." She shook her head guiltily. "That's impossible. Henri's driving up to the Anderson Valley. He's got some chardonnay to taste."

"He was just away. He's off again? So soon?"

"It's his work, Papa."

Daisy ducked her head in the doorway for a second. "Good night, both of you."

Clara called after her, "Don't forget to think about what we discussed."

After the outer door closed behind Daisy, Alberto burst out again. "That kid Steve is absolutely infuriating. All he could say, over and over, was we were going to be so happy in the Bertram Hill family. I can't figure out if he's bright or very stupid. Compared to his father, he's like a flighty girl."

"Henri does not like them."

"I know that, Clara! But what else? Besides warning me, it seems like he doesn't want to talk about it. He *must* know more."

"He does, Papa. Lots."

"Well, then?" Alberto stared at her inquisitively. "When's he getting back this time? He's only going to the Anderson Valley. Are you—" He stopped, then restarted. "No, I'm not asking."

But he *was* asking. "Yes, I'll be with him, Papa. Maybe . . . can he . . . can *we* . . . stop Sunday afternoon to see you? We'll be on our way back to the city."

*We.* Alberto ingested the word, chewed it, swallowed it. Accepted it. "Yes. Sure. That would be just fine. We'll look forward to seeing you both."

"Remember," she reminded him in case he'd forgotten, "Henri is coming to Italy with me." Meaning, why shouldn't she go to Sonoma with Henri?

He got the point. "Yes. But . . ." But nothing. "Okay, okay . . ."

Clara wanted to hug him. Then, for his sake, or her own, changed the subject. "Did Steve show you the label?"

Alberto snorted scornfully. "Yeah. That! He was honest enough to say you hated it. Another of their good-faith gestures. *Barone Morelli* . . . me, a baron? Please . . . I told him to stuff it." He waited a bit. "You know, Clara, I've always preached that the wine is not of Alberto Morelli, like blood or something. It's *wine.* There's nothing miraculous about it. It comes from Morelli Vineyards. You open a bottle and you drink it. If you like it, that's because the grapes were picked at the right time, crushed by well-washed feet, and fermented at the right temperature. Nothing to do with me personally. *Barone* Alberto Morelli. Hogwash!"

"You pick the grapes, Papa, you blend the wine— even if you're not a *barone.*"

"The grapes were planted long ago. The sun is the sun, water is water. Let's give the credit where credit is due."

"Joe Alejandro?"

"No. *God* and Joe Alejandro." Alberto frowned

fiercely. "But forget the label. You know what else? And this is worse—the pipsqueak has had the colossal nerve to approach my friend, Oscar Bridges. *Behind my back.*"

Bridges owned Twin Bridges Winery in Sonoma County wine territory, to the west of Morelli's holding in Sonoma Valley. Alberto and Oscar were cronies, if it could be said Alberto Morelli was the type of man to have a crony. Over the years, Alberto and Oscar had talked merger but nothing had ever come of it.

"The kid told Oscar I've already agreed to join their consortium, the idea being to finesse him into signing up. I told him in no uncertain terms to knock it off! Any more funny tricks, and all bets are off. . . . He just smirked and said we'd be coming in, don't worry. That Franco just won't take no for an answer. That when I meet Franco, I'll understand."

"You're *really* still considering it?"

"Considering . . . yes," he admitted uneasily. "Jim thinks it can't hurt to establish a base worth. Fifteen million? Not bad—the figure might come in handy next time I'm trying to borrow money." He winked ruefully. "What bothers me is they're so damn sure of themselves. Do they know something I don't?" Alberto leaned forward with the question, cupping his chin in his hands. "Can they make trouble? Is there some lousy scam they can pull that we're not ready for? I'll say one thing—young Pinjatta is jittery as hell. He's arrogant. At the same time he's scared of his shadow."

"He's scared to death of his father, and his uncle."

Nodding, Alberto slouched back. "Jim says forget about the horrible personalities—spoken like a lawyer, of course—and focus on the money. If they offer fifteen million, maybe we can get more. Jim says let's be greedy and if it works, well . . . it might be a big mistake to pass it up. But I don't know about that. Can we trust these weird Pinjattas? Jim Fontana can't answer that one . . . maybe Henri can."

"Papa, all I know is what Henri says. They're slippery customers. He's had bad experiences with them. They've pulled some fast ones in France and been in trouble with the Appellation authority . . . Henri will explain. One thing, the Pinjattas don't like Henri any more than he does them." She didn't say the Pinjattas *hated* Henri. Nor had she forgotten the frightening story—Henri called it rumor—that the brothers had bloodied their way into the business. As Henri had warned, such a revelation might be too strong for Alberto—and Fontana would probably demand proof.

"Okay. Noted." Alberto relaxed a little more. "I think I will have that glass of wine." As Clara took glasses and an open bottle of his reserve out of her cupboard, he went on casually. "Actually, I have another idea about all this . . . a *great* idea. I won't tell you just yet what it is—but I think you'll be surprised when you hear. . . . Now, what about Mina?"

Clara put the glasses down and poured. "You will be happy to hear that Mina—and Hugo—will be in Lucaterra for your wedding. She expects *you* and the Italian branch to arrange accommodations."

"Oh, joy!" Alberto looked bemused. "Well, I guess I'm happy . . ."

"A two-bedroom apartment will do, either in a house or hotel, or *pensione*, but preferably in town. Mina doesn't care for the country—it makes her sneeze."

"So I've been told, over and over." Alberto sighed.

"She hasn't been up to Sonoma for twenty years . . ." The year both of the elder Morellis had died, for the funeral. "She and Hugo drive to Tahoe every year, but, oh no, never to Sonoma. She says the lake air is sinus-friendly."

Mina had a house on the lakeshore. In early May, the practice was for Hugo to load all Mina's geraniums in her Mercedes—invariably driven by a chauffeur named Jack—while Hugo and Mina got in the Rolls . . . and off the caravan went to Lake Tahoe. Used to be, with Mina at the wheel of the Rolls. Hugo did the driving now.

"Here's hoping the allergy season is over in Lucaterra," Clara said.

"For its own sake, it better be."

# *eleven*

SATURDAY NIGHT, SHE and Henri stayed at the Boonville Hotel, a century-old stagecoach stop on the rugged road between Santa Rosa and the Pacific, rebuilt, refurbished, renovated. This was the first time they'd been away together. Clara didn't need reminding. She'd been thinking about it all day Saturday, then at dinner—and after dinner felt like a girl, nervous, skittish. It was not the same as being home, having him in her own bedroom. This was like . . . almost like performing in front of strangers. Actually, she hadn't meant to be with him—but Clarissima, could he leave her so soon again? For their high purposes, he explained very seriously, the hotel was perfect. Their room, at *his* request, was blessed not only with a comfortable and comfortably sized bed but also a view of the soft undulating hills which cupped the old cowtown like the palm of a hand, those hills dented and creased and folded by millenia of ice, then rain and wind and the light stride of prehistoric and more recent inhabitants. Clara couldn't help wondering if he'd ever been here before, with somebody else.

Clara knew the territory. She'd visited often

enough, for the Boonville rodeo, the sheepdog trials, or to shop in the little town, since one of the old Cabott properties, she thought the last of the Cabott ranches with a beautiful, old mission-style hacienda, was located only a few miles away, in the hills off Route 128. The ranch had devolved to her cousin Cabby Root. He called it Cabott's Warp.

Sunday, at eleven, they drove to Robert and Holly Danziger's sparkling—stylish, Clara wanted to call it—Dancing Water Vineyard, a half-dozen miles farther west, close to the Navarro River, over a few hills from Philo in the midst of hillsides turning amber, gold, and crimson.

The Danzigers had spared no expense in laying out their vineyard or equipping their winery. The approach to the house was spectacular, along a road bordered by poplars—like the Loire, Henri commented. The house itself, a French château, already looking weathered, or prematurely aged. The winery had been built of stone. The Danzigers, it seemed, had money to burn after a generation of toil in the vineyards of the New York Stock Exchange. Everything at Dancing Water was modern, shining, expensive. Touring the winery before brunch, Clara was reminded of how badly Morelli was in need of renewal, expansion, not only of the winemaking capacity but of storage. Lack of such space, space to store more oak, Henri constantly harped, was the main reason so many smaller wineries sent their varietals into the world without proper education, that is, *aging* in barrel or bottle.

Just as extravagantly, the Danzigers had adopted the west for themselves. Holly Danziger was dressed in jodhpurs, a leather jacket, and soft boots—actually, she did keep a couple of horses in a barn

on the other side of the winery—and Bob in faded
blue jeans, cowboy boots, denim shirt, big hat . . .
the works.

Under the awning on a lawn outside the kitchen,
next to a pool, and after a meal of light soup and
salad, a tender sirloin barbecued by Bob Danziger
on his super new gas grill, a bottle of Mondavi-
Rothschild Opus One, Henri leaned back and declared all was right with the world.

"The Anderson Valley, after all," he declaimed, to
Bob and Holly's delight, "it is not Napa or the Alexander Valley or the plains of Sonoma. This place
is comparatively new to the grape and something
very different. As vineyards filled the maps of Napa
and Sonoma, prices of land skyrocketed. Ergo, grape
growers must look elsewhere and so descended on
this most natural of places, an area of climatic spe-
cialness. When it is blazing hot across the hills in
Napa and Sonoma, even very hot and windless in
the geographically closer Alexander Valley, this tight
little valley is generally cooler. Ocean breezes funnel
through the configuration of hills, the Navarro River
playing as air conditioner and humidifier. So, the
weather is well suited to full-bodied whites." He
smiled. "At least, this is what you will tell me."

Finally, after more talk of wine—Bob Danziger
couldn't get enough it—he and Henri had gotten
down to business in a cozy tiled and pine-paneled
tasting room. "The word is out . . ." Danziger
couldn't resist boasting. "This is our first *great* vintage. Bankable, as we say in the trade."

Henri just smiled and rubbed his nose. Perhaps,
he'd confided to Clara in the car, the Danziger chardonnay would do something remarkable, turn his
head, something a chardonnay did not often do. *Per-*

*haps*. Now, sitting with Bob Danziger, Henri tasted. He was most respectful of the wine, one reason his opinion was valued by most everybody—*most* everybody. Not all. Thinking of the Pinjattas. Henri was deliberate. Studied. Even philosophical. His face said all these things.

At length, he turned to the lord of Dancing Water. "You are right, Bob. It is outstanding. It makes me weak in the knees."

Danziger was so happy—and proud.

Later, Henri told Clara he'd been quite sincere. The Dancing Water chardonnay, to be released in a year or so, was already outstanding. *"But I still prefer the reds."*

ALL WENT WELL, until . . .

At first, it was hard to remember.

Henri had been driving at a moderate clip, taking the road as it came, handling it so smoothly that Clara, unashamedly subdued, satiated by the food, too much wine, the pampering of the night before, had fallen half asleep beside him in the green Jaguar. It was about four in the afternoon and they were heading up into the high country—called the Yorkville Heights—between the Anderson Valley and the freeway. The rapidly ascending road was not the safest in California by any means and portions were even treacherous, etched by tight curves and narrow straightaways.

Not minding that Clara was dozing, Henri carried on volubly about the Pinjattas and Bertram Hill and what he would say to Alberto. *Objectivity*, that was the word! What to do about such a *quandary*. Good word, quandary. For Alberto, Henri would put all his cards on the table. Quite bluntly, he was going to advise Alberto against accepting the Bertram Hill offer. Ever since that night at the Clift Hotel, even leaving aside his bad memories of Carmen, his long-standing memories of the Pinjattas had been afflicting his *stability* like a corked aftertaste. Doing business with the Pinjattas was bad for business. Merely talking to the Pinjattas could reflect badly on Alberto's good name.

Finally—and, yes, this *could* happen, Henri fulminated—did the great Alberto Morelli wish to risk the indignity of seeing his gold medal estate reserve poured into bottles decorated with Château Montebanque labels and sold for ten times its proper price to unsuspecting Japanese geishas—or, even worse, his wine mixed with rough Mexican red, as the French had been known to mix the Algerian with their own, and delivered as Barone Alberto Morelli to pizza parlors in Atlantic City?

There was no end to the *shenanigans*, good word, that inventive rascals could foist on the world's wine market. Should Alberto Morelli become accessory to a fraud of the wine? Never!

Skillfully, meanwhile, as he laid out the case to the near-supine Clara and, as routinely as if he'd been a race car driver, Henri negotiated the serpentine, climbing, narrow two-lane stretch, maneuvering the Jag through tight curves, speeding, slowing, keeping his foot away from the brakes, like any skilled race car driver would, allowing gravity to do its duty. "This," he murmured, finally noticing, "is a very tricky bit of the countryside."

Rousing herself with a big yawn, Clara half turned in her seat. Putting the Pinjattas aside for the moment, she had something she wanted to say. She'd been drowsing over it. And, yes, she was about to say *yes,* she'd decided just then, no, better, she'd decided the night before, on the verge of sleep beside him in the soft bed that, yes, she was inclined to say *yes.* That she thought she loved him and wanted to be with him, though exactly how she would've said this, she didn't know. And didn't find out, either, because the words didn't get said.

A dusty black pickup with outsized wheels had been trailing behind them. Now, on a last curve before the crest of the hill, the pickup pulled out. Accelerating noisily, it came abreast of them. Clara remembered two men in the cab, the driver and his passenger, the latter leaning out, long blond hair blowing in the wind, gesturing crudely with his right hand, his mouth open, shouting something foul.

She remembered Henri. *"The son of a bitch, he is trying to pass!"*

At a place like that. On the hill. On a blind curve. Clara froze.

Pulling up, pulling up, passing, the dusty pickup veered into them. Crashed against them. And again! High fenders and running board screeched across the hood of the Jaguar, forcing them to the right, into the guardrail. Cursing, Henri fought back, braking, accelerating, ramming the Jaguar into the pickup.

Clara remembered the roaring engines, the shriek of clashing metal.

Still hanging out of the cab, the blond man was laughing wildly at her, showing teeth like fangs, a gaping red mouth. Clara realized there was something in his hand. *"Henri! He's got a gun!"*

She saw the belch of smoke and fire. Heard a

high-pitched pinging sound. Saw a hole in the windshield.

The Jag shuddered and bucked. The guardrail gave way.

For a sickening moment, the car hung, teetering, long enough for Clara to register in her mind the pickup skidding, straightening, and disappearing over the hill. Slowly, the Jag began a roll to the right.

She remembered Henri yelling. "Keep your head down! Hang on!"

The Jaguar rolled again, and maybe a third time, she wasn't sure, then somehow straightened out. Henri struggled with the wheel, trying to make some sense of the downward rush. Clara remembered them breaking through bushes, taking out small trees ... then, suddenly, with a bone-shaking, bone-rattling crunch, they stopped—

Clara remembered no more.

Yᴏᴜ ᴀʀᴇ Cʟᴀʀᴀ Addey?"

The voice was unfamiliar and official. Clara thought she must be in a government office, or in court, or speaking by telephone over a long distance.

"Yes ..." She heard *her* voice. "I'm Clara Addey. Addey and Company. How can I help you?"

The woman's voice was very quiet. "Mrs. Addey, do you hear me all right? Can you please open your eyes."

"They're open."

"No, they are not. Please open your eyes."

But they were. Open. Everything, her senses anyway, said her eyes were open.

Black became gray. Gray became blazing whiteness, hurting her head. Then, she remembered again that one awful thing which had been on her mind—the screech of metal. The sickening earth-thumps as the car turned over, then again. The flying trees. Henri Lamarque shouting . . .

Nausea swept up. Clara felt the grab of her stomach muscles. The hurt made her fade. Then she was brought back by the feel of wetness, the sick acid taste, and smell of vomit. Her vomit. Disgusting.

"That's all right," the quiet voice said. "That's okay. That's better."

When she stopped heaving, somebody wiped her face, put something cool on her forehead. She heard another voice. Hers? She swallowed. Her throat hurt. "Am I by any chance dead?"

A solemn chuckle. "No. You're alive."

"The whiteness . . . I thought Heaven was white. Or is this Hell?"

"You're in Memorial Hospital in Santa Rosa."

"A hospital." This wasn't possible. "I'm in a car, rolling . . . rolling. Henri?"

"You were in an accident. A bad accident . . . can you open your eyes and look at me?"

Clara opened her eyes. Above her, she saw a face, the composed face of a lovely young woman, a woman beautiful enough to be an angel. A woman with sad and sympathetic eyes, dark hair cut at the shoulder, the shoulder covered by a white costume of some sort. Surely, she was an angel. No wings. Clara realized she was looking at a doctor's smock, a dangling stethoscope. This *was* a hospital. A pity in a way. Death would've been so easy. She'd been almost there. "How did I get here?"

"By helicopter. They lifted you and Mr. . . . is it La—"

"Lamarque," Clara whispered. "Henri Lamarque."

"I'm your doctor. My name is Laura Spelling."

"Is Henri . . ." How did one ask the question when one wanted a certain kind of answer?

"We think he'll be fine."

"Ah . . . that's good." Clara felt she was smiling. Even that hurt her face.

"You were in a very serious accident, Mrs. Addey. You were on the road to Cloverdale. North of here. On Route 128."

"I know that. I know that road very well." Clara remembered something else. *"It wasn't an accident."*

"No?" The woman doctor looked concerned. "Why do you say that?"

"Henri is a very careful driver. Henri has been on that road many times too. He's an excellent driver."

"Mrs. Addey, the police will have the details. Mr. Lamarque's car was badly wrecked, I do know that."

*"We were forced off the road."*

The other's words came slowly. "I see."

"You don't believe me."

Carefully, the doctor said, "I don't disbelieve you."

"You think I'm in shock. I'm telling you—*a man in a pickup truck shot at us.*"

"All right. . . . You must tell the police."

*"I know what happened!"*

"Okay. All right. No doubt the police will be able to tell you more. . . . Right now, first things first. I'm going to give you a sedative. I want you to rest. . . . In the meantime, tell me, is there anybody we should get in touch with?"

Clara began to cry. As she remembered that too, tears began to pour down her cheeks.

"Yes. Oh yes. My father . . ." Her voice faltered. "You must call my father right away. . . . What time is it?"

"Seven P.M., Mrs. Addey."

"*Seven?* My God!"

"You've been unconscious a few hours. Mr. Lamarque is still unconscious . . ."

"Unconscious? But I'm awake." She wasn't making any sense and she knew it.

"Mr. Lamarque has a concussion. He took a bad hit. The steering wheel. The windshield . . ." The doctor paused. "He has a broken leg. Some ribs. We aren't sure yet."

"Oh . . . oh . . . my God."

"In Mr. Lamarque's wallet, there was a note, in case of accident to notify Clara Addey."

"Me."

"Are you next of kin? Are you related to Mr. Lamarque? Is there anybody else . . . ?"

Clara's throat seized up. A sob burst from her, like a bubble collapsed. Henri had no next of kin. She, Clara Addey, was the closest. "No. Not as far as I know." She stumbled on the next words. "I'm his fiancée. But tell me. I mean . . ." She couldn't go on. Dry tears ran down her cheeks. She reached to brush them aside. Her arms ached. But there was nothing there, no wetness.

The doctor put her hand on Clara's arm. "Not to worry. Mr. Lamarque is going to be okay."

Clara nodded, whimpering, "My neck hurts like hell."

"Whiplash. No surprise there. They said the car rolled over a couple of times."

"A hundred times . . ." She moved her toes. Her legs hurt. Her insides hurt. Her head hurt.

"As far as we can tell right now, nothing's broken. You're badly bruised. There could be internal injury. That's the bottom line. It's as if you'd fallen out of

an upstairs window. The momentum. The impact . . .
you understand?"

"Yes . . . yes. But my father . . . you must call . . ."
She recited the private Sonoma number. "His name
is Alberto Morelli. It's the vineyard . . ."

"I drink that wine!"

Clara tried to smile again. But she was crying too
hard to smile.

"Which one? The cabernet . . . merlot?"

She felt the prick of a needle in her left arm.

"You'll go to sleep now," the doctor said. "I'm going to call your father."

"Don't worry him, please. . . . Tell him I'm okay."

She *was* okay. She had survived a bad, bad car
crash. Henri had too. They were lucky. Very lucky
. . . let us hope, they would always be so . . .

# *twelve*

"THE NOSE ..."

Henri held the mirror in his right hand, moving it back and forth for different views of his battered face.

What he was looking at was not pretty.

A big sticky bandage covered most of his nose, another his right eyebrow. Two black eyes. A temporary cast on his right leg. His ribs had been taped. His hands were scratched. But he was alive and so was Clara. There was an incredible joyousness about merely being alive which she had never experienced before. Much else fell by the wayside.

"I am a disaster area," Henri hissed. "I will sue."

But he was taking it well, all things considered. "Oh, yes?" Clara asked. "Just who do you plan to sue?"

The morning after—but this was far worse than the worst hangover Clara had ever heard about. The slightest movement made her body not just ache— it rumbled with complaint. Even her skin felt swollen and cracked. Earlier, they'd wheeled her off for X rays. Finding nothing broken or out of place, Dr. Spelling declared Clara ambulatory and ordered her

up and around. As best she could, she'd hobbled to
Henri's room.

"Clarissima . . ." Henri put the mirror down on his
stomach. "Are you all right? Tell me. What did they
say? I have been praying that nothing bad happened
to your delectable limbs." He glanced at his own leg
and made an angry face. "Look at me! Those cretins!
Those unspeakable fascist thugs."

"It hurts every time I move . . . but I'm in one
piece."

"And a pretty piece it is! You are so brave! *Quelle
héroïne!*" The attempt at jocularity flopped, despite
his clown getup, the comical bandage across his
nose, and the black eyes. "I am so sorry. What a horrible jam I have gotten you into."

"Henri, you *saved* my life."

"Oh, no, no, I will never forgive myself. I should
have been paying better attention." He closed his
eyes, saying remorsefully, "I was so busy with the gab-
bing. If I had been paying proper attention, I
would've realized . . . I should have taken evasive action."

Clara dragged her chair closer, taking his
wounded left hand in both hers. "How could you
know? On a Sunday afternoon? In the middle of nowhere?"

The policeman who'd come to see her at break-
fasttime said they had been very lucky. He had never
known of better luck. The direction of roll had been
critical for, at a leveling dip in the hillside, the heavy
Jaguar had righted itself. The downhill rush had
been slowed, giving Henri a fighting chance to guide
the car through the speed-braking brush and into
one of the smaller trees . . . A police team was at the
crash site at this very moment. They'd be checking

skid marks, measuring things, inspecting the wreckage. Attentively, the policeman heard Clara out about the blond man with the gun, about the bullet hole in the windshield, nodding and shaking his head matter-of-factly as he jotted the details in his notebook. The problem was, he said, there wasn't any windshield anymore. In the course of the roll down the hill and final impact against the tree, the windshield had crumbled into a trillion pieces, so there wasn't any bullethole anymore either. It was just too bad Mrs. Addey hadn't gotten a look at the license-plate number on the truck.

When, later, Clara relayed this remark to Henri, he scoffed loudly. "Ridiculous! How were you supposed to see a license plate?"

Besides, she wouldn't have remembered anything except the gun. "I *did* see a gun. He *did* shoot the gun."

Henri responded with a slight movement of his shoulders, the best he could do this morning in the way of a Gallic shrug. "Even if there wasn't a gun—"

"But there was, Henri!"

"I know. I also heard the shot, my darling. I am saying that even if there had been no gun, those two were . . . making mischief." He glanced at her quickly. Would she accept such a mild interpretation?

The answer was *no!* Clara tried to laugh, gasping breathlessly as her rib cage protested. "*Making mischief?* Henri, please! Just tell me what you think . . ." This was no time to be shy. "*The Pinjattas?*"

Henri's eyes showed white. "No proof, Clarissima, no proof."

"And you don't want to talk about it."

"Not just now, no." Picking up the mirror again,

twisting his head to catch his profile, Henri filled in with a loud, self-pitying groan. He touched one finger gingerly to the bandage on his nose. "How it smarts!"

"Henri, your nose is broken."

"And flattened, like a pancake."

"Your nose will be better than ever," she promised, a little impatiently. "If need be, a plastic surgeon will fix it for you."

"All crooked, like a witch's beak."

"I've got news for you—it was crooked before. Maybe this'll straighten it out."

He smiled at her limply. "Clarissima, I *liked* my nose. I *loved* my nose."

"Henri, I like *all* your noses."

He refused to be soothed. But that was only for the record. He was feeling okay, his crotchetiness proved it. "Thank you for saying so. But what about *this* nose's *especial* talent? Genius, I say. Its fluted passages, its vaulted chambers taking up the aromas of fine wine? Savoring. Analyzing. Judging . . . now, all gone. The nose smells nothing. I detect no stink of hospital antiseptics, I smell no sour hospital cooking. And the taste buds? Paralyzed, Clarissima!" Tears welled up in his bloodshot eyes. "The smelling apparatus, Clarissima, the precious membranes battered, crippled beyond recovery. I am ruined."

"I doubt it," Clara said calmly, taking account of his peculiar mood, playful but deadly serious, Henri's way of dealing with a subject without discussing it directly, ironically and intensely at the same time. She tried to match his attitude. "Henri, *believe me,* the membranes are just stunned. Temporarily out of action. In a couple of days, they'll be back to normal. You'll smell better than ever."

"I smelled bad before?" Clara smiled. Bad joke. "I *did not* smell danger just around the corner."

"That's a different thing."

"Maybe, but a clever and alert nose should be able to detect danger—as well as fine wine. When those two *stupidos* pulled up so close behind us . . . *then,* I should have known. I should have speeded up. The Jag is quite capable. We could have outrun them." He shook his head despairingly. "But no, Lamarque was too busy talking, trying to impress the beauteous Clarissima—"

"Bull!"

"And I apologize! *Oh!*" A twinge of pain called him to order. "I have had better training and experience than this, I assure you, my love."

"Henri, you were a marvel."

"Surely?" He eyed her skeptically, then finally did get back to what was bothering her. "I don't want to mislead you, Clarissima. It is worrying. I am worried. For you. For me. I don't want to deceive you."

"The Pinjattas?"

He winced again at the name. "Possibly. But no certainty. We must consider the other, more obvious possibility, that it *was* two hooligans, taking a Sunday afternoon thrill. And think! Whatever it was all about, we are alive. Clarissima . . . so comforting. Sitting with you, I mean you are sitting, I am chained to this bed. Regard the sunshine . . . listen to me babble."

"The policeman said—"

"I know. Please, not to repeat it. I don't want to hear again about close shaves . . . I am not a barber."

"—that you must be a wonderful driver. Taking control of the car like that, halfway down that steep hill, guiding it . . . saving our lives."

"I *am* a very good driver," he agreed. "You don't know, I once drove in the Tour de France."

"That's a bicycle race, Henri."

"And *now* you tell me?" He winked, his black eyes the more dreadful for the attempt at gaiety. "Well, I hope your policeman is on the trail of those two sons of bitches . . . those miserable *miscreants.* I love that word."

"They've issued an all-points bulletin . . ."

"Good. Like a TV program. We are flattered. . . . Tell me, Alberto *was* here last night, no? What did I say? In my state, I might have blurted words. . . . How embarrassing."

"What words?"

"Who knows? Rash words. Unconsidered words. I may have asked for his daughter's hand in marriage." Henri tried to push himself up on his elbows. "Seriously, Clarissima, we *must* talk to Alberto. We must talk *seriously* to Alberto. How much does he know?"

"About us? Everything. That we were in Boonville together."

"*Mon Dieu!* But no, I mean about the accident . . . this attempt to . . ."

"I'm not sure what the doctor told him."

Henri sighed. "Today, for sure, he will find out. He will be furious with me. If it is some kind of plot, I am the target, not you, Clarissima, such an innocent bystander . . . oh, oh." His voice trailed off. "My dear, my dear friend . . . and more. Are you feeling well? I mean, in the mind, you are not depressed?"

"No, Henri. Not depressed. Angry. Furious. They say that's the best medicine."

"Exposure to such violence can play the devil with the spirit."

"No," she said, "I'm feeling very well. Aside from the whiplash. Somebody said there's nothing more invigorating than being shot at . . . and missed."

"Yes. Winston Churchill said that. Or somebody. Probably George Washington. Or John Paul Jonesy . . . he was referring to the time of the Boer War. Obviously, not a boring war for Winston Churchill . . ." One eyelid shuddered. "I hope this was not boring for you . . ."

Her throat tightened. "I'm never bored when I'm with you, in an accident or at home in—"

"If you are *ever* bored, Clarissima, I give you permission—"

"I told you. I'm not. Ever!"

Henri seemed to levitate. His body fairly hummed with delight. *"And we will be together? Yes?"*

"I think so. Yes."

His bleary eyes bubbled with tears. "You say *yes?*"

Nodding, Clara said, "After what happened; and us surviving it, yes, it doesn't seem like it should be otherwise."

Henri gasped. A labored grin twisted his mask of bandages and bruises. "Clara, please, kiss me. On the cheek only. My lips are very sore. I cut them with my teeth."

Clara hoisted herself up. Ignoring her own confusion of aches and pains, she bent down to put her lips to his hot face. Feeling the beard, ignoring the beard, she trailed the tip of her tongue across his wounded lips.

He shivered violently. "Take care. It would not be seemly . . ."

Clara dropped her hand to his thigh. "All seems well down in the engine room."

"God be thanked! Clara, we must celebrate. Champagne!"

*"Champagne?"* The word echoed, uttered by a starchy nurse who'd marched in behind them. "Who said champagne? Not just yet, my lad." Clara sat back down in her chair. "Mrs. Addey, I've been looking for you everywhere! You had a phone call from San Francisco." The nurse consulted a piece of paper. "Daisy Chaney, asking after you. She needs you to call her if you're up to it."

With a shock, Clara realized she hadn't even thought about the office, or Daisy, or anything to do with business. It seemed Alberto, assuming the same, had telephoned Daisy to advise her there had been an accident.

"You're . . . you're all right?" Daisy stuttered.

"I'm okay. Battered but bearing up." Before Daisy could ask, Clara said, "We went off the road."

"Then . . . you won't be in?"

"Obviously not."

"Yes," Daisy said, "obviously . . . I shouldn't bother you . . ."

"But?"

"Well, Mr. Tyler's been on the phone. He wanted to know if we'd received the drawings of the house. We did. They came Saturday. He's back in the Bay area today and tomorrow. He's inviting you to take a personal look at the project."

"No. Not today. Tomorrow either."

"I told him you couldn't. That it was impossible. I had to tell him you'd been in an accident . . . I don't know if you want it broadcast."

"You're right, I don't . . ." Clara didn't have to think about it. "Daisy, you go."

"Me?"

"Didn't we agree you were going to work with Tyler? Just go on over there. . . . If he asks about Henri, tell him Henri's been hurt but he's recovering."

"Clara!" Daisy cried worriedly. "That doesn't sound like a minor accident."

Clara interrupted with a laugh, painful though it was, at the same time thinking . . . what about Martha? Had Alberto called her too? Had he put a reassuring spin on it? She hoped so. She didn't want Martha, at once overcome by guilt feelings, to cut school and come rushing out to California.

"Daisy, I'm fine. But I wouldn't expect me back till . . . I don't know. A week from now. Maybe ten days. I'm going over to my father's for a few days." And, though she didn't say so, she couldn't leave Henri up here by himself. And when the time came she had to get him back to San Francisco. "Daisy . . . humor Mick Tyler. Okay? Compliment him. Admire his architectural daring. Flatter the view. You know how it's done."

"Yes. Well . . . but you *are* okay, Clara?"

"I am." How she yearned to tell Daisy the whole thing, to shock her, impress her, amaze her with the story of the murderous event on Route 128 and their great escape. But she dared not even hint at the gory details. One peep out of Daisy and Tyler would be on the case like a bulldog. Or? Maybe not. Going after two maniacs in a black pickup truck was a far cry from engaging in bloodless Wall Street battle.

ALBERTO KISSED HENRI on both cheeks, not bothering to conceal his deep emotion. He thanked Henri once, then again, and in a moment yet again for saving his daughter's life. The medal from a grateful family didn't materialize but Alberto gave Henri to understand that any reasonable reward was his for the asking. Holding her breath, Clara waited. Would Henri seize the moment? He glanced at her, then at Florence. He held tightly to Alberto's hand. But words failed him.

Then it was too late. Nurse Fuzzy-Wuzzy reappeared. It was time for a shot. Henri had been moved out of the trauma unit but he needed to rest. There was more work to be done on his leg and, as Henri had diligently reported, his sorry nose, that which had once been a nose. The doctor was also concerned about his internals, specifically a bruised kidney. "Nothing serious, but they wish for Lamarque to be available some more days."

Clara was being discharged, was going home with her father and Florence. But she would be back the next morning and again, however long Henri was in the hospital. And, after that, Alberto declared, Henri would come to Casa Morelli to finish recuperation.

"Until the *nose* is back in operating order," Clara added.

Nurse Fuzzy-Wuzzy interrupted. "You'd best be going. That policeman's here to see you again."

It was approximately five P.M., California Highway Patrol Officer Edgar Flange reporting. He bowed to Florence Rampling and shook Alberto's hand. "Mrs. Addey's father. How do you do, sir? Good. Well . . ." He cleared his throat. "The boys found that slug, Mrs. Addey."

*"Slug?"*

Low-voiced, Clara said, "One of them had a gun, Papa."

"*A gun?* Why didn't you tell me that before?"

That portion of Alberto's blood which was Sicilian

surfaced. He swore horribly and swept Clara into his arms. She began to cry, for the first time since the accident in earnest.

Florence's soprano cut loose. *"Somebody shot at them?"*

"Yes, ma'am. Any rate, the boys found a slug, ma'am." Officer Flange cleared his throat. "It was in the passenger door. *Imbedded*. Out of a big, heavy .45 revolver, looks of it . . ."

The words—big, heavy, revolver—fell like deadweights. Alberto's face changed color. His shoulders bulked. His eyes blanked. Clara had seen him angry before but never quite like this. The rage was so contained, controlled, so utterly lethal, like a ticking bomb.

Clara said, "I didn't want you to worry."

"Worry?" His voice was wet, heavy. "I didn't sleep a wink as it was." His eyes swung to the policeman. "I want those guys found. In jail. Behind bars . . . In the meantime, if they come anywhere near our place, I promise you . . ."

Red-faced, but very correct, Officer Flange said, "We want 'em too, sir. And believe me, we'll get 'em if they're still in the county."

Alberto's arm tightened around Clara's waist. He didn't know he was hurting her. More painful was the reminder of how much she meant to him. Clara was his child, his only child. If things on that hillside had gone differently . . .

Florence put her arms around both of them. "Alberto, easy now. Clara's okay."

He mumbled something, nodding, swabbing his eyes. He handed Clara his hankerchief.

"I am all right, Papa. I'm fine."

But he was not satisfied. Again, glaring at Officer

Flange, he demanded, "Why would somebody want to do that?"

What could Flange say? Nobody knew the answer to *why* questions. He pulled himself erect. "Can you think of anybody . . . any enemies? Bad blood? Any reason at all?"

*"Don't be crazy!"*

"It's an obvious question, Mr. Morelli."

"I grow grapes, for God's sake. I make wine. Not enemies. I've lived in Sonoma County all my life . . . the same for Clara."

"Most everybody's got an enemy or two, even if they don't know it."

Alberto shook his head bitterly, then nodded. "Of course. You're right."

"What about Mr. Henri Lamarque?" Officer Flange glanced apologetically at Clara.

What was he thinking, by any chance that Clara had a jealous husband? Not funny. Clara glanced at Alberto, wondering if *he'd* yet put two and two together and arrived at . . . the Pinjattas? No, all he knew was what she'd told him—that the Brothers Pinjatta and Henri Lamarque didn't think well of each other.

Clara replied as Henri would've wanted her to. "I don't know of anybody."

"Hell, Henri Lamarque's a wine critic, Officer," Alberto exclaimed. "You think somebody's out to get the wine critics?"

"Just a thought, Mr. Morelli."

"If so, we're all in big trouble."

"Well, if anything comes to mind . . ." Officer Flange had other information. "We're gonna try to match that slug up to a gun. There's also a long slash of black paint all down the side of the Jaguar. What we do is send a paint sample to the FBI lab. It's possible for them to pinpoint the manufacturer of the pickup, maybe even the model."

Alberto scowled. "But *not* where it was sold or who bought it."

"No, probably not," Flange admitted.

"Well," Alberto growled, "I'm getting my shotgun out tonight—"

*"Bold talk!"* With that derisory comment, Nurse Fuzzy-Wuzzy reappeared. Nearly falling out of her arms was a huge cellophane-wrapped flower arrangement. Elaborate, garish, it would've been suitable for sending off a Mafia don. "This just arrived. For Mrs. Clara Addey."

*"From?"*

"The card is right there."

Who else besides present company would know that Clara Addey could be found, more alive than dead, thank God, at a hospital in Santa Rosa? The card was looped around a bunch of long-stemmed red roses in the center of the flashy arrangement.

" 'Best wishes for a speedy recovery,' " Alberto read. He glanced swiftly at Clara. "It's signed Steve Pinjatta."

# *thirteen*

"N<small>O WONDER THE</small> Pinjattas and their friends
don't like you, Henri," Mick Tyler said admiringly, after he'd heard the story, now so familiar to
Clara, about the Case of the Bogus Gitane Flambé.
"Werner Flemming is close with them, you know. I
mentioned to him that I'd asked you about the late
Maurice Cumberbum's cellar and he started foaming at the mouth."

But Mick didn't know the half of it.

Henri smiled sardonically. "I am aghast, for I
think only the best of all of them."

Sitting with his bad leg propped up in the back of
Alberto's golf cart, parked just outside the winery
doors, he'd been entertaining with his rendition of
the Gitane Flambé "miracle," in which several tons
of the latter wine had been transformed by mere
labeling into vintage Château Montebanque . . . how
he had tipped over the applecart at the Hotel Pierre
tasting . . . how the Pinjattas had sought to defend
themselves with the absurd explanation that there
had been innocent misadventure at the vineyard. It
all sounded like such fun: *oops!* grubby Pin-

jatta fingers caught in the cookie jar, or wine barrel if that was a more suitable metaphor.

Henri was in what he called his fast recovery mode, up and around on level ground but not able to negotiate without a crutch. Bruises and black eyes had faded. His internals were okay. Although still bandaged, his ribs gave him less trouble every day. But his nervous energy wouldn't let him alone. The cast on his leg, he said, was a big pain in the neck. He fidgeted and squirmed. Invalidhood, even of the semisort, didn't suit him.

"My God, Henri, you've got . . . what do we call it? *Cajones?*" Tyler directed the question to Alberto.

That was all? Clara would've expected more of Mick. Even though he didn't know the details, how come Tyler's suspicious mind hadn't made the leap of logic from the Pierre to Flemming's Cellar to the "accident" on Route 128? Maybe, behind all the tall talk, Tyler after all was just plain naïve. On the other hand, even Henri, with all the facts at his disposal, was loath to go the whole way. He kept insisting they needed more solid evidence to implicate the Pinjattas.

Alberto had drawn glasses of new merlot out of a barrel. The wine hadn't yet clarified but nonetheless sent frothy bubbles up your nose on a fragrance of fresh roses. In a few weeks this, too, would adjust as the oak of the barrel brought out the best of the grape. In his glory—no, in heaven—Tyler gazed around the big shed like a boy in a bawdy house. Maybe that was why his suspicious mind wasn't connecting. Grinning, nodding, loving it, "Hey," he sang, "this stuff'll knock you on your keester, am I right?"

"New wine," Alberto nodded, "treat it with respect."

Henri smiled tolerantly at his prospective client. This being his first in-person experience of Mick's head-on enthusiasm, he wasn't sure what to make of it. "Mick, the new wine will produce the most horrible of all hangovers . . ."

"Not one glass," Mick cried. "Surely not!"

"Be warned." Alberto spoke gruffly. He hadn't decided about Tyler either. Impatiently, he turned back to Henri. "If Werner was foaming at the mouth," he said, "it was because of the Montebanque incident." They'd had to tell Tyler about that too. "Otherwise, what's it to Flemming? Why should he be interested in the Pinjattas' offer for this vineyard, or if we turn it down?"

*"Why?"* For Tyler, the answer appeared all too obvious. He swept his arm across the vineyard scene, at the blue sky and fast-moving clouds, the pieces of harvesting equipment scattered around outside the winery, the orderly ranks of south-facing cabernet marching up the hill in front of them. "Why? Because of all this, that's why. Flemming is down on Henri for the same reason the Pinjattas are. He's angry, and jealous of Henri's influence over you." Watching Alberto, he quickly amended himself. "I mean the influence he takes for granted, whether or not . . ."

"I get the point," Alberto said.

"They want your vineyard," Tyler went on, "and I don't blame them. What a place! This winery. All that stuff working away. The smell! I love it!"

The smell he mentioned, that fresh, clean, roundly fecund scent, more than scent, a powerful, warm smell of newly crushed grapes penetrated everything inside, even outside, the winery. The morning's crush of cabernet was resting in huge, open wooden tubs, precisely measured doses of yeast to be added during the afternoon, thus initiating the chemical process by which grape sugar would become twelve or twelve and half percent alcohol and eventually combine with fruit flavors and acids to give the cabernet its own, distinctive taste. The winery equipment and the floor had been hosed down and disinfected prior to the lunch break, adding an almost sanctified moistness to the rioting scents.

"All this you see"—Henri waved his hand too—"is the payoff for a whole year's sweat and tears. Wine drinkers . . . wine *collectors*," he said pointedly, "cannot understand the battles fought—against the weather, the bugs—"

"The creditors," Alberto interjected.

"And now," Henri went on, "grapes full and ripe and perfect, they are plucked from the vines, carried in here by all those men." He pointed toward Joe Alejandro's house where, under a big tent, the harvesting crew was having lunch. Loud voices, laughter came from that direction. "and so, to the wine."

"I know," Tyler said impatiently. "I appreciate all that. *I do.*" He faced Henri directly. "That's why I'm here. One reason anyway. Plus I wanted to meet you and Alberto." He'd gone straight to first names. "I've been looking into this Pinjatta gang a little bit myself. *You* got me very curious," he told Clara. "I've got friends and advisors . . . well, never mind. *You* ask about Flemming and *why*. Well, the rumor is the Pinjattas have extended Flemming a lot of, shall we say, financial help—"

"*A legal no-no,*" Henri interjected sharply.

"Right," Tyler nodded. "According to the federal

code, a distributor shalt not invest pennies in a retailer. That's deemed coercive. Own the retailing operation outright, or not at all."

Alberto to Henri: "Did we know about that?"

Henri shook his head sadly. "No. But, if so, it gives
them a grip on Werner's throat. Poor fellow."

Tyler reacted harshly. "That's how it is in the real
world, Henri. But there's more—the word in New
York, not that anybody there cares much, is that Bertram Hill is preparing an IPO. That's an initial public offering," he added in an aside, in case they
didn't recognize the code.

Alberto flushed. "Franco Pinjatta did *not* mention it."

Henri groaned dismally. "*And I, Lamarque, did not
know.* I am totally out of circulation. I am devas-
tated!" He smacked his leg cast with his crutch. "In-
tolerable! I *must* get back to work."

Smugly, Tyler said, "Well, now you do know.
That's confidential information, by the way."

Mick Tyler was continually surprising. He'd surprised them that morning. Telephoning first, he
asked if he might visit. He gave himself Sundays off
and this Sunday he just happened to be in town.
He'd heard from Daisy that Henri was at Casa Morelli—having been released from the hospital the
week before. Tyler said he'd invited Daisy to come
along . . . well, Clara could blame herself for that.
But never mind. Daisy couldn't make it.

Tyler's baby-blue Mercedes convertible was parked
up the hill in front of the house.

"*Valuable information,*" Alberto thanked him.

"You do understand," Tyler continued rapidly,
"why he didn't mention the IPO, don't you? He'd
want to assemble his California properties *first.*

Then, after a decent interval, when he does the offering, the price will leap on profit expectations . . . and Wall Street *will* care."

"And the Pinjattas cash in."

"Absolutely! They'll get their shares for, like, a nickel apiece and if the idea is to screw the market, they'll cash 'em in after the offering runs up to a buck or whatever. Nothing complicated about making money. Mr. and Mrs. America will supply it."

Grimly, Alberto moved toward the golf cart. "I suggest we adjourn to the tasting room. I want to hear more . . . I'll drive the invalid. Then we'll head back to the house for lunch." Florence and the cook, Mrs. Murphy, had given them an hour.

To the rear of the public tasting room, a modest place no match for many ornate tasting palaces, Alberto kept his own, private space in the Old Count's restored house. The back room was floored and paneled in weathered, then treated, wood from the estate's original, fallen-down barns. An antique poker table, hanging lamp, cushioned chairs furnished the room. In the corner, from a floor-to-ceiling wine cabinet, Alberto chose a bottle Clara recognized as one of his treasured reserves.

Opening it with little ceremony—so little that Henri actually looked pained—Alberto sniffed once and poured into the glasses. "A ninety-two, Mick. One of our best." He sat down and with an intent look at Henri said, "So now we know why the Pinjattas are so eager to get this thing done."

Henri agreed bleakly. *"Evidemment . . ."*

"This is *good* information," Alberto said, "and I'm grateful for it, Mick." Nevertheless, he hadn't stopped studying Tyler, obviously undecided how much to credit him, how much of what he said to discount. The brush-cut dynamo was a new species for Alberto. Clara wasn't sure he'd ever met a cyberman before. As for the cyberman himself, having dropped his bombshell, he'd given himself over to the wine. While Tyler had looked a little out of place in the winery—he was wearing a pair of tight black jeans, a white T-shirt, and a black leather bomber jacket—he was at home in the tasting room. Thank God, he'd removed his face-hugging black sunglasses which had obviously put Alberto off, but his eyes, revealed, were almost as disconcerting. Clara remembered pictures of James Dean. Tyler looked like James Dean with short hair and a little more heft. What a contrast they were, modish Mick Tyler and Alberto, who was dressed like a well-to-do hayseed, in red flannel shirt, blue thermal vest, suspendered corduroy pants, and work boots on his feet.

Dismally, Henri spoke again. "I should have surmised all this about the IPO. I failed you, Alberto. Esteemed Morelli Vineyards was to be used to better the financial situation of Bertram Hill—and you to be none the wiser."

Nodding vigorously, Tyler said Henri was *absolutely* right. "Frankly—I'm always frank, that's *my* business practice, not that I've been *practicing* so very long. Frankly now, after hearing about the Bordeaux scam, along with the Flemming stuff, there's a very bad smell blowing off these Pinjattas."

By his silence, Alberto agreed. He would be preparing a hell of his own for the Pinjattas. "If that was their plan," he finally growled, "it's failed." He touched his glass to Clara's. "So, my daughter, it's decided. Unless there's a radical . . . very radical . . . change of presentation, there's no way I'll—*we'll*—

do a deal with the Pinjattas. You agree, don't you, Henri?" he asked pointedly.

"Oh, yes. I think it would not be wise at all."

Tyler divided his attention among them, glancing at Henri, Alberto, then Clara. He seemed puzzled. No, he did not understand Henri's special relationship with Alberto. At that moment, Clara wondered if she did either. Then, she took account of the obvious: there had been some kind of a meeting of the minds while she'd been back in the city.

"A *good* decision," Tyler confirmed. He leaned forward, glancing at Clara as if to apprise her that something momentous was coming. "A *terrific* decision! Because it leaves the way open for Mick Tyler! Alberto," he said warmly, "*I'd* like to become an investor in Morelli Vineyards. I admire you guys so much . . . and I'd like an understanding that if you ever do decide to sell, I get first refusal . . ."

Ambush! Alberto had not expected this. He stumbled over his words, trying to get out of the way. "Mick . . . this is a surprise . . . a nice thought . . . but we don't have any outside investors."

"I know you don't need the money . . ."

"I'd *never* say that." Alberto continued to peer at Tyler as if searching for his motive.

An unlikely blush took over Tyler's square face. "I wouldn't interfere. That's a promise! I'd keep my nose out. I'd just like the privilege. Well, how can I say it? I'd love to be in bed with you guys!"

In bed? Business terminology. Indeed. But Clara wouldn't have it. *"To independence,"* she said, holding up her glass.

Yes, she did mean it and Alberto didn't disagree with her.

Chagrined, Tyler sighed. "Okay . . . but remember, I'm still a damn good friend. And if the day comes you change your mind . . ."

Henri hadn't intervened. Tyler's feelings and ambitions were not his business. A distant smile on his face, Henri stroked his nose, still very tender. Elbows on the table, he stared into his wine glass, as if embarrassed for Mick Tyler.

In a gesture that was almost formal, Alberto put his hand on Tyler's forearm. "And a damn good friend at that."

Not to be put down, or comforted, Tyler waved his glass grandly. "This stuff is wonderful! Henri, I *want* some of this ninety-two."

Henri gave himself time now, measuring Tyler a bit more haughtily than was absolutely necessary. Clara read his mind. Henri liked Tyler well enough but the man shouldn't take too much for granted. "You may want," he said tersely. "But there is not much available." Henri swung his leg around and cracked it again with the crutch. "This monster thing itches me."

Tyler took his irritability as partial answer. "Is that so, Alberto? There's not much ninety-two left?"

"Only a few cases."

*"Voilà! C'est ça!"* Henri exclaimed. "Storage space. I always preach that: *storage space*. More oak! Some of the Morelli vintages have the longevity for twenty, thirty years. Alberto is too modest of his winemaking skills."

"Now, Henri, I know all about storage space," Alberto fired back. "Do you know how much it costs to store a bottle of wine *per year*?"

Henri paid no attention. "Alberto makes light of the art, wanting it to be no more than a trade, like carpentry or plumbing . . ."

Alberto shook his head patiently. "I've been hearing nothing else for a week, Clara. Henri has been on me day and night. By now, I don't know what I'm doing right—or wrong." Oh yes, Henri would have made his presence felt. Clara was impressed that Alberto was so good-natured about it.

"You see . . ." Henri was trying to persuade Tyler, a businessman, one who should understand. "I must convince Alberto that it is also advantageous to *sit* for a while on the best of the vintages, thus to increase their value. My theory is that for every year a grand vintage is held back, it doubles its value. No secret—scarcity makes for bigger profit. Thus, am I not right, the investment in storage space is returned with a fabulous interest."

Trying to be a good guest, Tyler shrugged non-committally. "Makes sense."

"But this is against Alberto's philosophy of the wine."

"Not mine—the *Italian* philosophy!"

"And, at bottom," Henri went right on, "I do like Alberto's philosophy best. I swear it! Why *should* wine be kept too long just for price? Is wine so important? No. It is a beverage, something to be *imbibed*—I do like that word, it is the word I used for my magazine. *Imbiber!* Anyway . . . imbibed with the meals. It is not meant to be some noble, *ineffable* thing. It is no Star of India ruby or Fabergé egg, one of a kind. It is an agricultural product which renews itself every year—not something to make people psychotic, to be committed to *le booby hatch* screaming about shortages of good Bordeaux . . ." Henri paused, making sure of their attention, then proceeded. "You know what California wine lacks more than the age? It is the romance factor. A fine Bordeaux creates more romance than some kind of a Napa Valley blush. You say California wine to the uninformed and they think of the Golden Gate Bridge. . . . But when two people drink a wondrous Bordeaux, they fall directly in love . . ."

Alberto smiled at Tyler. "Maybe we should put a warning on the label."

Henri preened. The remark only provoked him— once let loose, he was unstoppable. "I think with the greatest disgust of all those cases of fine Bordeaux bought for investment and stored away in immaculate, climate-controlled cellars as the price goes up and up, men of great wealth hoarding the great years. They have never even seen the wine they have bought—much less will they ever drink it!"

"Greed," Tyler said confidently. "The motor of fraud. Greed is in those bottles."

"Exactly! The wine *scandale* I described, what was the biggest difference between that Gitane Flambé properly labeled and Gitane Flambé in a Montebanque bottle? Price. Fifteen dollars retail for the Gitane, twenty or twenty-five at the most . . . Montebanque of a quality year sold for five or six hundred or more—not for a case. Per bottle. Calculate the profit margin."

"Greed," Tyler repeated darkly.

*"Exactly."* Henri was in full flight, whether just sounding off or lecturing Mick Tyler, Clara couldn't say. "And this is the modern culture of the wine, its international structure, worldwide volume. Millions and millions of cases of wine are produced every year, shipped, exported, transferred from dealer to dealer and sold in every corner of the world—if our circular world can have corners."

Henri's harangue finally made Tyler uncomfortable. "I buy it for investment. But to drink too!"

"So you do," Henri responded. Right there, he might have dismissed the cyberman as a nouveau riche idiot. Rather, he seemed suddenly to perceive Tyler's better qualities. For one thing, Tyler seemed to have at least one worthwhile idea about what to do with his new wealth. "But my point . . . your point too. About the culture of the wine. Most people are honorable, I give you that . . . but it goes beyond honor, to mystique. Say, at auction, I buy a bottle of crusted old wine raised from the wreckage of the *Titanic.* I pay five thousand, ten thousand for it. Yes? Now, I take it home. Will I open it to share with friends Saturday night—or to taste, if there is any taste left? Or will I keep it corked, leaving the by-now rank contents unsampled? As Clara says, I will never know what's in that bottle." Henri smiled coolly. "And who knows, maybe it was rank even before the launching of the *Titanic,* never mind about the iceberg, Bordeaux on the rocks . . ."

Tyler shook his head doggedly, as if he didn't understand what all the fuss was about. "So much for the romance of the wine. Even filled with swill, the bottle from the *Titanic* is more valuable full than empty—well, *naturally!*"

Henri stared down his nose at him. "And for the simple reason that its capsule will be undisturbed. We *hope* it will be undisturbed, this piece of tightly wrapped foil at the neck of the bottle. If disturbed, noticeably disturbed, as if removed and replaced, for example . . . then no doubt the bottle would be worthless . . worthless, except as a souvenir."

"Chances are," Tyler said, "it'd also be a fake."

Henri chuckled. "And a *certifiable* fake. I recall a rather recent case, the discovery of a cache of Thomas Jefferson's personal Bordeaux, the bottles marked with his initials, from the late seventeen hundreds . . ." He laughed disparagingly. "One bottle was opened and analyzed. Within, it is said, was a wine from *this century* . . ."

"Nevertheless," said Tyler, "some of the stuff was sold for a lot of money at auction. So?"

Henri grimaced, "*Mystique,* my friend. So, therefore, I will sit on my cases of perfect Lafite or Montebanque until I can sell them for double my investment, or more. And so it goes, a business for *monkeys* . . . I think I will retire."

Clara laughed. "I've heard that one before."

Henri scowled at her. "I mean it! Ask Alberto! What is most distant from the vine? Making bricks. Driving a taxi. Maybe that is for me. I will become a long-distance truck driver. At truck stops, I have Cokes and greasy hamburgers and I leap up when they play the national anthem . . ."

"Go for it," Tyler drawled.

Making a face, Henri demanded, "This Mick Tyler, what does he want of me?"

"Simple. I'd like you to help me with my wine cellar."

"And you will not practice bad habits, my friend?"

"Henri, I *promise*! I'll taste every one of my Bordeaux futures."

Alberto emptied the ninety-two in Clara's glass and went back to the cabinet. "I think we have time for one more glass. A ninety-five? It's just beginning to express itself . . ." He hummed to himself, quite happily, but was this not a scene to suit Alberto Morelli? "We'll see what you think, Mick."

"I'm delighted to try . . . but what do *I* know?"

"And this cellar of yours," Henri asked, "it is to be

in a fantastic new house you are building in Belvedere, yes?"

"That's right. It's gonna be on three levels, dug into the hillside. We're starting at the bottom and working up . . ." Tyler performed another of his grand gestures. "The wine cellar is at the bottom, tucked into the hill. I look to have the place finished sometime next spring . . . so, if you could start thinking about it, Henri. If you would . . ."

Henri hesitated. "You must realize this is a whole new profession for Lamarque, the advising of electronic *whiz boys* in the ways of the grape—"

"That's *whiz kids,* Henri," Alberto corrected him.

Tyler wasn't bothered by the sort-of insult. "I hate to tell you, Henri, but there are quite a few of us around . . . we know the names of the wine. We know what we like, or think we do. But, after that . . ."

"There is a great difference in buying a few bottles here and there and assembling a famous cellar."

"I know. That's the point, *isn't it?*"

Henri was being just a little perverse. Was he, Clara wondered, taking it out on Tyler for having invited her to dinner?

"Yes, good, *good,*" Henri said. "I can advise. But what if I am wrong, and a year from now you disagree with me? I could make a wrong diagnosis. You know, it is best to remember that the business and art of wine is perception, fad, and fancy. Wine is like fashion. One year, fruity chardonnays are in vogue, the next big-busted Bordeaux, and after that, who knows? What if you run out of chardonnay and we have bought too much pinot noir? So, what is your intention, Mick Tyler? If to impress your friends with your new wine cellar, then conserve your funds—

buy second-rate years from first-rate châteaux, *not* first-rate years from second-rank châteaux. Or, simply, spend your money on what *you* like . . . for that, you don't need me."

"What I *want*," Tyler said earnestly, "is some good years of Pétrus and Lafite and Margaux and so on. Some prime Burgundies. A modicum of champagne and good Mosels . . . choosing, I'd have to leave it to you. Altogether, say, one, two, five hundred cases, of really great European stuff, if we can get our hands on it. And then I want to concentrate on *first-ranking Californians*—starting with Morelli reserve cabernet . . ."

"Bravo!" Henri waved his crutch. "A wine as good as any of the famous Bordeaux, blended by the master, a mixing of cabernet, a *soupçon* of merlot, and a solid percentile of cabernet franc, the exact dimensions we do not say, Alberto's rendering of the magical Bordeaux blend."

"Fine." Tyler's eyes gleamed.

"It is *so* good," Henri continued effusively, "we no longer compare it to the Bordeaux wines. We do not say *in the Bordeaux style* or *reminiscent of Bordeaux* or *Bordeaux-like*. We say it is a Sonoma Valley Morelli!"

Bemused, shaking his head, afraid that Henri was going too far, Alberto frowned at Clara. This Henri of hers was too much! If Henri was striving to make points with Alberto, he'd already reached the max.

"I'm with you," Tyler said. "Believe me! I'm in full agreement. And, for crissakes, let's get down to it!"

Still, Henri held back. "An ambitious project, it will cost a bit of money. It will entail buying at auctions or out of private cellars."

"I know that! I understand, Henri, believe me!

Like the cellar Flemming's offered me..." He waited for Henri's reaction.

Equably, never mind, of course, that Flemming foamed at the mouth at mention of his name, Henri said, "For the sake of the good old times, we could *try* to work with Werner."

"But I don't think we'd be very enthusiastic about it, would we?"

"Shall I tell you the utter truth?"

"Yes, I wish you would," Tyler said, "if we're going to work together."

"*Attends,* Mick. Without personal rancor, believe me, but for all the reasons we know, I *dis*-recommend Werner Flemming. As I have Bertram Hill and the Pinjatta brothers. To boot, when I was in Portland, Oregon, I have also heard that things are not well at the House of Flemming. My opinion, now seconded by your most excellent information, is ... *take care.*"

Tyler put wine glass to his mouth, drinking carefully, circling the wine with his lips, holding it for a moment before swallowing. All the while, he watched Henri. Finally, he laughed and said, "So I guess I'm passing on the Maurice Cumberbum cellar." With that, Tyler set his glass down and extended his hand across the table. "Do we have a deal?"

Looking the slightest bit amused, Henri said, "Remember, you will be a man amassing an art collection from scratch."

"I can handle it," Tyler said.

"Okay then..." Henri took Mick's hand. "We have a deal." Smiling broadly, he cried, *"Have nose. Will travel!"*

# *f o u r t e e n*

WERNER FLEMMING WAS on everybody's
mind.

For whatever his private interests or instincts, Mick
Tyler had taken it upon himself to tell Flemming
outright that Alberto was going to say no to the Pinjattas—and that *he* was saying no to the Maurice
Cumberbum cellar. Werner was on the telephone
immediately, complaining and pleading with Alberto
to change his mind, saying this was not a good time
for him, or Flemming's Cellar, even claiming that if
Alberto didn't relent he, Werner Flemming, was as
good as ruined.

"He whined and begged me to think it over," Alberto reported to Clara. "All I said was: what's it to
him if I say no to the Pinjattas? No answer. Just that
I shouldn't pay any attention to the little Pinjatta
whom Werner calls an arrogant and conceited little
son of a bitch. Not because of Victoria. He'd like to
break Steve Pinjatta's neck for other reasons. Business reasons. Steve is over his head, Werner says.
He's going to be loading cases of Rioja on the docks
of Bilbao, Spain."

"Serve him right . . ."

"But never mind that," Alberto went on. "My worry now is a bigger one. Werner says Franco Pinjatta is coming to San Francisco. He wants to see me personally, one-on-one. Werner implores me to stay open-minded until Franco makes his case . . . And he specifically asks that Henri not be present."

"I guess Henri wouldn't want to be there either."

"Franco will want to firm up that half-promise I made to consider selling them a couple thousand gallons of the cabernet." Clara heard a muffled curse. "Worse yet, it seems he wants to talk about the Italian Morellis, the Fratelli Morelli vineyard in Tuscany. Werner thinks it would be a *natural* to combine us—Morelli of California with Fratelli Morelli. Again, I ask him why he's so interested. Again, no answer. I got pretty blunt. I told him he's barking up the wrong tree. My cousins would *never* sell."

"And you're not going to either."

"That's right," he said firmly. "But I want to tell Franco no without turning this into some kind of hand-to-hand combat. I particularly don't want him over in Tuscany nosing around my cousins, telling them all sorts of crap, like Steve Pinjatta tried to offload on Oscar Bridges. . . . Our new friend Mick Tyler should've kept his mouth shut. He had no right—"

"I know," Clara said. "It's my fault. I'm the one who should have kept her mouth shut in the first place."

"Well . . ." Alberto wavered. "It's all coming out in the wash anyway. My idea is just to get them to go away . . . quietly. And don't worry—I'm going to be diplomatic. I'll figure something out before he gets here: thanks so very, very much, Franco, but no thanks . . ." He sighed. "Clara, I just don't like being bothered. It is, if I may say so, a big pain in the ass. *Punto!*" That said, he breathed deeply. "How's Henri doing?"

Henri was at her place, enjoying—if that was the word for one so fidgety—a last few days of peace and quiet before reentering the world sans crutch. The quiet, being out of circulation, was driving him crazy. "He's got to get back to work before he flips out."

"I can imagine . . ."

"Papa . . . stop brooding about the damn Pinjattas . . ."

"Clara," he said sharply, "I'm not brooding about them. I'm sitting here having a cup of coffee, talking to you, watching Joe and his boys. They're coming up the north hill, taking the last of the zinfandel. In a while, I've got to go down to the winery."

"Would you just remember, please, that you're not likely to be bamboozled by the likes of a Franco Pinjatta."

He sighed again. "I know. I know, Clara. It's just . . . like I said . . . a gigantic pain in the ass."

Flemming had been worrying Henri on the telephone too—her telephone, at home. About Mick Tyler. He accused Henri of stealing his client. Henri was saying bad things about him to Tyler. And Tyler! He'd begun asking so many questions. He was snooping into the affairs of Bertram Hill, the Pinjattas, even Werner Flemming. Why was he doing this? Was this Henri's idea? Was Henri on some kind of a crusade to destroy the Pinjattas and discredit Werner Flemming?

Henri had foreclosed. "I told Werner he was paranoid. I said he should perhaps consult a psychiatrist."

Then, Wednesday afternoon about four, Werner Flemming accosted Clara on Geary Street. She'd been over talking business with a set designer at the American Conservatory Theatre. Flemming marched up to her as she came out of the theatre, saying he'd just finished lunch at his club. He'd walk her down to Union Square. Coincidence? Clara had her doubts. Hadn't he spotted her going into the theatre, then waited? If he'd actually had lunch, it had been a long one, she would've said, for Flemming was drunk. His face, out in the daylight, was beyond its customary florid shade. Flemming was known to be a—at least—three-martini man. He trundled along beside her, a big man, even out in the open street. Broad shouldered, big-armed, big-bottomed, he wore a suit that seemed a couple of sizes too small for him. A little brown trilby perched precariously on his big head. But the shine on his big black shoes was impeccable.

"I'm glad I ran into you, Clara," he announced, false cordiality practically bleeping. "I've been talking to your father. And Henri. Maybe I can get *you* to see reason about the Bertram Hill offer. I know you were there when Henri and Alberto discussed it with Michael Tyler . . . I know because Michael told me."

She didn't deny it. "You mean Mick? So?"

"So I don't want to quarrel with you . . ." But he was already headed that way. And might even welcome a quarrel. He was in a foul mood by the look of his eyes. He'd taken her arm. His hand was heavy and reminded her immediately of what an autocratic, overbearing kind of person he was. Being dislikable was of no consequence to him. Give Werner Flemming *some* credit. He was not one to ask for understanding, tolerance, mercy . . . or a favor. Not if he could help it. "If *you'll* listen at least," he grumbled, "I'm here to *tell* you, to *inform* you, to *promise* you, that the Pinjattas are honorable men. And honest. I don't care what Henri Lamarque says to the contrary. I've been doing business with them for a number of years. I was one of the first to import their Chilean and Argentine wine. Then, when they moved to Spain, the Rioja. And, from France, Montebanque . . ."

"All right."

She tried to shake loose of him. His hand tightened. She was aware of the strength of his fingers.

"We do not sell bum wine, Clara."

"If you say so."

She walked briskly. He kept up. And didn't release her arm.

"When I told Franco Pinjatta about that magnum, you remember, at the Clift, he was *shocked*. Totally shocked. Horrified. You're aware of the history of bad blood between Lamarque and the Pinjattas?"

"I think so."

"You're aware that *Monsieur Lamarque . . .*" He couldn't suppress a sneer. "Monsieur Lamarque wanted to marry Maxey Pinjatta's daughter, her name is Carmen, but that the family rejected him? You knew that?"

"That's not quite how I heard it."

"The *truth* is the family forbade such a marriage . . . on religious grounds and on grounds Monsieur Lamarque was—and is—an adventurer."

"Okay." Clara halted, facing him. "I've heard you. Is there something else?"

Glaring steadily but, it occurred to her, rather blindly as in blind drunk, Flemming muttered, "I have nothing against you, Clara. Nothing personal. I wish you'd talk to your father about this." Jaw set, she turned stony cold. That didn't stop him either. "Lamarque's negative influence on the process has been . . . excessive. And I wouldn't want Alberto to miss the opportunity of a lifetime because of a man like Lamarque. *Would you?*"

Clara did not give an inch. "If that's all . . ."

She walked again, staring straight ahead. Her rejection finally seemed to sink in.

"I see you don't believe a thing I've said."

"I believe Henri had some kind of an affair with Carmen Pinjatta . . . I believe you want my father to talk to Franco Pinjatta. Otherwise . . ."

His voice thickened. "Don't you see, for God's sake, that your father will be missing a great opportunity? That he could become Bertram Hill's distinguished elder statesman? Their ambassador with wine portfolio?"

"No, I don't see it."

"And you don't see that the offer is very generous? That Alberto would become an instant millionaire, many times over?" He let the questions hang there. Then: "Can I buy you a drink?"

They were outside the St. Francis.

"No, thanks . . ." Clara shook her head. Then added, "Money isn't everything."

"No, not *everything*." His disdain fairly crackling, he grabbed her arm again. "Just ninety-five percent. It's the only measurement we have for success. Failure. Mediocrity. And now . . ." Flemming's cheeks flamed cholerically. "Now, *my* financial well-being is threatened. Because of Lamarque. Because of your stubbornness, your unreasonableness, not accepting a good thing when you see it! Stupid! All of you! Morons!"

Clara looked him in the eye, braving his fury. There were people on the street. She'd have witnesses if he went berserk.

*"Go to hell!"* That was mild but it would do. "Leave us alone! Don't think you can *bully* your way. I've already received all these messages from Steve Pinjatta, you know . . . in more polite form."

She turned and began to walk away. But mention of Steve's name had already done it. The gurgling noise made her look back. Werner appeared to be choking on his own anger. Unable to get words out, he stopped trying. He swayed, his eyes bugging. Forcibly, he inhaled, then exhaled noisily through his nostrils. A passing couple paused to stare. Then, deliberately, Werner loosened his shoulders, untensed his arms, shook out his fingers. He breathed in again . . . and out.

Clara had been about to ask whether he was all right. After all, she didn't want the man dropping dead in the street, not if she was standing next to him. He'd been to see a therapist, that was it, for lessons on rage control. Somebody had been trying to teach him how to relax, so as not to blow a coronary gasket.

Straining, he forced out his next words. "Steve Pinjatta is an interfering little—" His eyes were hot and wild. "You know very well the little son of a bitch has been having an affair . . . he has seduced my wife, Victoria. He is a . . . yet you mention his name in my presence!"

Undeterred, perhaps cruelly, Clara insisted, "But he says he's Bertram Hill's West Coast manager."

"In his dreams," Flemming almost shouted. "He's

out here . . . doing what? Trying to build himself a niche. He's got big ideas, including"—in a horrible whisper—"fucking my wife! He thinks if he hits a couple of home runs, they'll give him the job." He shook his head. "No way! The little peckerhead is going to Bilbao. After the consortium is set up, *I'm* going to be West Coast boss. Bertram Hill's gonna buy me out," Flemming cried hotly, recklessly, "and after that *I'm* gonna manage the West Coast consortium!"

Coldly, Clara responded, *"If there is one."*

Flemming's shoulders slumped. His heavy head dropped. When he spoke again, his voice was a low growl. "What the hell were you doing in that car with Henri Lamarque?"

A chill ran down her back. Clara did her best to keep her voice level. "Driving up to the Anderson Valley . . . and back . . . *why?*"

"Not the best place to be, was it?"

She didn't answer.

Flemming finally raised a mocking little laugh. "Well, if you won't join me . . ." He turned away indifferently, as if he'd forgotten she was there, as if they hadn't been together at all.

Clara watched him as he blundered up the front steps of the St. Francis. He disappeared inside and she continued on to Post Street. Thinking, Werner Flemming wasn't one to leave you laughing, was he? Shivering again, despite herself.

*f i f t e e n*

WHEN THE LITTLE Pinjatta barged unan-
nounced into the office Friday morning, the
day after her Flemming experience, Clara didn't
give him a chance. "What is this? I don't keep open
house—"

"I had to see you. It's *extremely* important."

"Really? Is it about your new appointment in
Spain? Are those your marching orders?" She
pointed at the brown envelope he was holding under his arm. He clutched it all the more tightly.

"This? No . . ." It pleased Clara to think his face
turned white. "Spain? News to me. Where'd you get
that idea? May I *please* sit down a minute?"

Clara looked at her watch. "One minute." She
waved him to the couch.

Once he was sitting, he announced pompously,
"My father, that's Franco Pinjatta, is coming out here
this weekend. He directed me to see you and arrange for a meeting with Alberto Morelli, regarding
our proposal."

Just as formally, Clara said, "I'll have to consult
with Alberto Morelli . . . I hope your father is not
making a special trip. Because—"

"Because, *nothing*, Clara," he exclaimed, suddenly agitated. "Now, you can't deny us . . . the old man's especially keen. It'd upset him if . . . you know, he always travels with a nurse, in case of paralytic seizure if he gets too excited. He's making a special trip, yes. They're gonna be staying in a suite at the Huntington Hotel which he *loves*. He says if it suits you and Alberto, you could all meet there for dinner—or at the most expensive restaurant in San Francisco, whichever you say."

"Short notice."

"*Jesus,*" Steve yelped, his voice somewhere between whine and snivel. "I can't help that. Just, you should, like, leave Saturday and Sunday kind of open? Huh?"

"*Huh?*"

He squirmed but didn't fight back. "Listen, Clara, please . . . there's something else I've got to ask you. *Please,* when you see the old man don't say anything about my problem with Werner Flemming." He edged forward on the couch, as if to get closer to her and more confidential. He started to put his envelope down, then changed his mind.

"I try *never* to talk about Werner Flemming."

"Me too, the miserable fuck . . . I can't make out if he's already complained."

"I doubt if I'll see your father anyway."

"Oh, yes, you must. The old man made a point of it." Steve's eyes drifted toward the outer office where Daisy was quietly working. And no doubt listening in. He lowered his voice. "Look, I'm just asking—don't bring it up, that's all."

"Why in the world would I?"

"Words slip out," he said. "And I've got some plans I don't wanna talk about."

Clara got up and went across the room and closed

the door. Coming back to her rocker, she asked, "So, since you bring it up, what's going on with Romeo and Juliet?"

"Nothing much," he replied sullenly.

"Not running off somewhere? Or have you ended it?"

He avoided her eyes. "Werner's threatened to quit buying from us."

"What a bad sport."

"Jesus, Clara! He's a big account, our best retail outlet in the West. You San Franciscans"—hard straits or not, he couldn't resist—"heap big boozers."

"My impression," she said contrarily, "is that Werner is going to be more involved than ever with Bertram Hill."

"Oh, yeah? Who you been talking to? *Werner?*" He crossed his skinny legs. "He's full of you-know-what."

Clara wanted to think he amused her. He certainly didn't frighten her. He was no Werner Flemming. "You know," she said, "you blew it. Don't blame anybody else. *You've* been reckless. Arranging assignations so Werner Flemming is sure to catch you doesn't make good sense."

"Catch is right," he agreed proudly. "He caught us in the hot tub."

"Where else? This *is* California."

"Don't rub it in, Clara, Jesus! It's kind of hard to think straight when you're in love."

Love? That, she doubted, and the remark didn't ring up any sympathy for Steve. For Victoria Flemming, yes, some. Clara let him brood for a few seconds—if brooding made noise, he'd be producing a racket. "What's happening with Victoria?"

"It's over. I've . . . we called it off. It's no good for

either one of us. I can't risk it. Neither can she. Werner?" He smirked. "He'll probably forgive her. A divorce would be expensive and right now old Werner doesn't have that kind of money." He licked his protruding lips. "He'd have to sell the business—which he ain't about to do . . ." He had one hand in his trouser pocket, rather openly, Clara would've said, playing pocket pool. Maybe he wanted her to see. "Being that he's in hock to us and we . . . might not like it."

She laughed, mocking him. "You're saying Bertram Hill won't let him sell—even if he wanted to? Unbelievable."

"What the hell does it matter?"

"It *doesn't* matter to me, not at all. Believe me." She stared at him unforgivingly. "Anyway, buck up. Werner's not going to cut your nuts off."

He yanked his hand out of his pocket.

"He told Alberto he didn't give a damn what you and Victoria got up to. The worst that can happen is you'll go to Spain."

"Clara, c'mon, where do you get that idea?"

She wouldn't tell him. Let him suffer. "By the way, I wanted to thank you for the flowers. I was going to send a card. But since you're here . . . how'd you know there was an accident? How'd you know where we were?"

"Daisy told me. I called to talk to you . . ." He tried a cocky smile. "The Pinjatta family is very big on flowers. Any occasion will do."

"Well," Clara said, "be sure to thank the Pinjatta family . . . for *everything*."

He didn't get it. Whatever had happened, or been arranged, she had to think, little Steve Pinjatta couldn't have been part of it. "You look fine," he mumbled. "Having accidents agrees with you."

Such a compliment. "Not really."

"The family sends Henri Lamarque all the best too."

"Really? I'll be sure to tell him."

"Listen, Clara, whatever you might think or *that guy* says, we've got the greatest respect for Henri Lamarque even though he really hurt our feelings a few years ago."

"How's that?"

"Well, if you must know"—his eyes rounded with spectacularly phony sincerity—"a few years back, he was involved in a plot to get us."

"You mean that wine scandal?"

"Yeah. That. He also made his best effort to seduce my poor cousin, Carmen Pinjatta. She's Maxey's daughter."

Clara laughed incredulously. "I don't know about your poor cousin, but the way I heard it about the wine, several full containers of mislabeled Château Montebanque were involved, six or eight hundred cases of wine. Sounds more like you *got* yourself."

"What?" He huffed. *"I am shocked."* And puffed, "Is that what Lamarque told you? Bullshit! Pure, unadulterated bullshit! I wasn't around then, I mean involved in the company, I was too young. But I know the story. After we bought Château Montebanque, a bunch of Frenchmen ganged up on us. They invented this thing about a wine scam. The idea was to force us out of Bordeaux. It didn't work."

"They invented a *whole shipment* of mislabeled wine?"

He whipped this way and that, not knowing how to answer. He tossed his precious envelope down on the couch to free his hands. He spread them wide.

"My God, Clara, it was *not* a whole goddamn shipment! Only a few bottles. Those French bastards! Lamarque worked for a Bordeaux grower when he was a boy. He's very close with them. We think they put a ringer in the winery and he turned the wrong knobs. Deliberately."

"Squirting Burnt Gypsy into Montebanque bottles?"

"Yeah, yeah! But the dirty tricks backfired when one of the ringleaders was killed in a winery accident. He was trying to sabotage a gas line and it blew up."

"You're serious? You're *not* serious."

He'd said too much, she could see it in his face. Backpedaling, he gasped, "Truthfully, *sweetheart,* at this point I dunno what I am. But I do know that anybody who got a bad bottle of Montebanque could bring it in and change it for the real thing."

"And how were they to know the real thing from a good fake?"

His eyes had started to water. "Don't say *fake*! It wasn't a fake, it was a mistake. *Whoa there, lady!*" He hunched over as if he had a stomachache. "I can tell you one thing—the old man's going to talk Alberto into the deal. We hear Alberto's having second thoughts—forget it! Wait till Franco Pinjatta goes to work on him. They'll be great friends. In fact, the old man wants Alberto and his chick to sit with us at the Masters of the Vine banquet in December. December the seventh, ain't it, Pearl Harbor Day . . ."

"He won't be here."

"We're planning to donate a huge *imperial* for the auction."

"I said, did you hear me, that he won't be here. He'll be in Italy."

"Well, you'll be there! By then, the pact will be finalized between Bertram Hill and Morelli Vineyards."

"I doubt it very much."

"See! See? There you go, prejudging. I'm telling you—the Pinjattas generally get what they go after," he declared, with the same wacky confidence. "Even so . . . Clara, you could make it a lot easier for us. We'd be ever so grateful to you. There are shares to be had—if you know what I mean."

Clara was jolted, even astonished. She'd figured there was nothing Steve Pinjatta could do or say which could surprise her. Yet . . . "Are you trying to bribe me?"

" 'Course not!"

"Shares?" She feigned ignorance. "Is Bertram Hill a public company? I had the impression—"

*"Who says?"* he demanded.

"You mentioned shares, didn't you?"

His eyes narrowed. "I mean *points*. You know, in the combined business." He waved one hand nonchalantly. "Anyway, look, you're not about to take over the vineyard, are you? No. So, what do you want, for the place to fall apart or to become the keystone of a wonderful new wine company?"

Calculatingly, Clara said, "I'm not sure that's the *only* choice."

"Oh no? Is your daughter gonna step in?"

"Martha? What do you know about her?"

"That's she's in school in New York. Columbia, isn't it?"

"I didn't tell you that."

"We know things. If we're gonna get involved with

a company, it's our practice to find out about the family, the principals. Anyway"—he was casual enough about it, the intrusion, the violation of privacy—"she's studying art or architecture and she's sure as hell not interested in making wine, no more than you are." He must have noticed her annoyance. His tone changed. Again, he was practically sniveling. "Listen . . . Clara . . . if this doesn't turn out, my ass is really mud."

"I thought Victoria was your big worry."

He shrugged. "I've had other girlfriends."

"So daddy wouldn't be very surprised to hear about Victoria after all?"

"Clara!" he sputtered. "You wouldn't! You said you wouldn't." He regarded her sullenly. "But Lamarque would. Just to cause trouble. You're *not* to bring him along," he ordered. "The old man doesn't want to see Henri Lamarque. Ever again!"

"But I thought you respected him so much. I thought all you Pinjattas sent him the very best . . ." Clara got him in her sights. "Listen, sonny boy, Henri wouldn't come anyway!"

"He's Alberto's advisor," he grunted.

Clara rapped her knuckle on the coffee table. "Henri is a friend. *Our* friend."

"Friend?" He laughed hollowly. "I'll say. You went up to the Anderson Valley with him. That's how you got in trouble."

Coldly, Clara said, "I don't think I'm in any trouble."

"I'm talking about the accident, not . . . all I mean is, if you hadn't been with him you wouldn't have been hurt, would you?"

By now, Clara was out of patience. "Tell me, where exactly is this conversation headed?" He stammered words, then stopped. "Steve . . ." Little lad, my boy, child. Gritting her teeth, Clara said, "Let me explain something to you. I trust Henri. It doesn't do you any good to run him down because you won't change my mind. Now, look, I'm trying to be nice. But don't push me. Your father is coming out here. *Maybe* Alberto will see him. *Do not push it.*"

Petulantly, he slung himself back on the couch, shoving the brown envelope out of his way. As he flopped one knee over the other, Clara noticed he was wearing those same long, rather effete silk hose. One wing tip swung loosely, as if too big for his foot. He put the foot down, pulling at the crotch of his pants.

"I don't have to push it. The old man is well known for his powers of persuasion"—his sallow face lengthened arrogantly, eyelids drooping for effects— "and all you gotta do is listen to him and quit listening so much to Henri Lamarque."

*"Okay, that's it."* Clara stood up.

Grinning foolishly, he made a calming motion with the palms of his hands. "Please. Clara, don't take me so seriously."

"You'd better get out of here before I really lose my temper." Her hand was on the doorknob. "I'm *very* serious."

"Okay, Okay . . ."

Taking his time, Steve pushed himself up off the couch. He checked the buttons and hang of his suit coat and fluffed out his tie. Narrow chin set cockily, he ambled toward her, saying, "You know, Victoria's very unhappy." The thought seemed to please him. "She's really crazy about me. She says I . . . you might be interested to know she says she could spend all day in bed with me, every day."

"Really? You're some kind of a fantastic lay? A skinny little lad such as yourself?"

Much to her satisfaction, he recoiled. "Jesus! For crissakes! The way you talk." His eyes blinked aggrievedly. "She's climbing the wall, if you want to know."

"Good-bye," Clara said.

"You're not interested. You don't care."

"I *said* good-bye."

"Okay . . ." He fumbled for words. "I'm going . . . I guess I'll see you with the old man."

"Don't count on it."

Her curtness hurt. He suddenly looked ready to cry. "I'm not as bad as you think I am, Clara."

He put out his hand. She did not take it. His doe eyes bled tears. Then, suddenly, desperately, words having failed, as if possessed by his own frustration, and before Clara could dodge him, he grabbed her around the waist, shoving his face at her, pushing her against the door. Mouth open, he sought her lips.

"C'mon . . . c'mon, Clara . . ."

Clara was dumbfounded. Horrified. He was psycho. And not as weak as he looked. She could do no more than gurgle. She couldn't move her head out of the way. He was strangling her. Summoning anger, the strength of outrage, she slammed both hands on his chest, trying to push him away.

"C'mon, Clara, you know I—"

She bashed him again. He hung on. "You're crazy! Lunatic! Cut it out!"

But he wouldn't. He fastened his lips to her neck like Count Dracula, the bloodthirsty Transylvanian night stalker. His hands flew, reaching for off-limits places.

Clara went slack. Sensing, wrongly, that she was giving in, he relaxed his grip. That was when she hauled off. The crack of skin solidly meeting skin was a delight to the ears. Then, Clara slapped him on the other cheek, just as mightily.

He cried out. He put his hand to his face. His eyes flooded. Both cheeks had turned bright red. He seemed to shrink within his double-breasted suit. "Clara, *Jesus* . . . that's a bitchy thing to do. That hurt like hell."

"You're just lucky I didn't hurt you worse."

"You would too, wouldn't you. *Ball-buster!* I oughta charge you with assault and harrassment."

She would have hit him again, was drawing back her hand to do so . . . at that moment, the door opened behind her. "Everything all right?"

"Fine." Clara felt wonderful, even though her hands were smarting.

Face flaming, from the slap, from the embarrassment—Daisy couldn't but know what had happened—Steve rushed past them, roughly pushing back the half-open door. When he was in the outer office and out of sight, he bawled, "Bitch on wheels! Fuck you!"

The other door slammed.

Clara grinned at Daisy. "So . . . good-bye, Steve Pinjatta."

Only when she turned did she realize that in the drama of the moment he'd forgotten his brown envelope. Clara picked it up. Why? She was certainly not going to run after him. And tossed it back on the couch. At which the flap opened and pieces of shiny paper slithered out.

Labels. Sheets of bright, new labels. But not only Barone Alberto Morelli labels. Others . . .

Ah. Truth dawned. At the same time, a rare opportunity knocked.

"Daisy, close the door. Go outside. When he comes back, stall him. Don't let him in here. Tell him I'm on the phone . . . I'll need a few minutes . . ."

# sixteen

"DID I DO the right thing?"

Reassuringly, Henri nodded up at the rearview mirror.

"Thank God for that fast copier," Clara said. "I made as many as I could before he came rushing back. He was in a god-awful panic."

"I am not surprised. In his stupidity, he has given the game away."

"For all he knows, the envelope was never opened. There's nothing he can say, even if he suspects."

"He would not dare say anything. . . ." Henri held up a sheet of elegant Lafite labels, crisp, like new money. "I wonder where they had them made." He shifted so she could see him better in the mirror. He was spread across the back seat of the BMW, his damaged leg on the cushion. "Probably somewhere in Europe. I think such counterfeits are expertly done in several capitals, and not-so-capital cities. You say—how many sheets of each?"

"A dozen. Maybe more. I didn't have time to count. I copied only a few."

Henri grinned into the mirror. "Lafite. Pétrus. Latour. Twin Bridges, Scudder of Napa . . . I see Barone Alberto Morelli. And there were *more?*"

"Yes. Many. I feel . . . a little guilty. I can't help it."

He reached to caress her shoulder. Clara felt the electricity; it penetrated her driving coat, reaching inside, making nerves jump in the pit of her stomach. "Bravo, Clarissima! You did the right thing. Your duty, no guilt attached." He ran his forefinger teasingly along the nape of her neck.

"Henri . . . careful . . . I'm driving."

It was only three P.M. but already hinting at dusk as this particular, sparkling November day played out. Aloft, as they were, in the middle of the Golden Gate Bridge, the weather had turned windy and cold. Far down below, the Narrows was steel blue going to black, whitecapped and irritable. They were bound for Sonoma but planned a stop in Belvedere to meet Mick Tyler at the construction site which in due course would become his new home. Or *newest.* According to Daisy, who had learned a lot in the last few weeks, Tyler also owned a deluxe A-frame up in the mountains near Tahoe and a New York pad to shelter him during those hurried trips in and out of Wall Street.

"Henri, please . . . you're driving me crazy."

"But *you* are at the wheel."

Yes, and she might just drive on, skip the Tiburon turnoff. Despite her better judgment, or whatever it was, maybe her unsettling feelings about Tyler, Clara had bowed to Daisy's enthusiastic urging, appeal, plea. They would take the Belvedere commission, yes, decorate Tyler's new house, buy furniture, drapes, doorknobs . . . and by the way, would Clara mind if she took three or four days off in the coming week? Mick was going to New York and he'd invited

Ms. Chaney along in his jet. Could Clara say no? Oh, yes, Daisy, anything Mick Tyler wanted.

A little jittery about driving so soon after what had happened on Route 128, Clara concentrated on the road, or tried to. With the weekend approaching, traffic was heavy, the outgoing three lanes of the bridge bumper to bumper at fifty miles an hour. The slightest slipup in such a clutter stopped bridge traffic for unseemly periods of time and humiliated the hell out of the offender. In other words, watch your step.

"If it was my duty to copy the labels," she muttered, barely glancing at him in the mirror, "then I should've taken my time and done more of them. Or just kept the lot. What could he do about it?"

"No, no," Henri said, "this is fine. Five sheets are as good as a hundred. They suggest *intent*." From behind, he stroked her cheek. "But what do they actually prove?" He caught her look of disappointment. "I think somebody must actually witness the culprit pouring the imposter in the bottle and decorating it with a Lafite or Pétrus label to make what is called an airtight case."

"But surely," Clara cried, "the suspicion itself . . . together with what we already know about them, that'd certainly be enough for the media."

"Enough for a big scoop, maybe, yes, in a wine journal. But Clarissima, you see, culprits so slippery could explain the labels away. They would say Bertram Hill is preparing a brochure or a promotional souvenir . . . anything."

"Oh no! Nothing that innocent. Not the way he came charging back to get his envelope."

"I agree, Clarissima, I do most emphatically agree with you. *We* know the young whippersnapper is not using the labels to wallpaper his *pissoir*. Nefarious? Yes. And worse. To violate the rules? Certainly, it would cast a large cloud of suspicion. But proof enough for the Appellation authorities to come down in France . . . or a fraud prosecution in this country? Alas, no. I think not . . . we need more . . ."

Always *more*. To Clara, the evidence seemed ample, overwhelming. *Why* would Steve Pinjatta be in possession of labels from vineyards with no connection whatsoever with Bertram Hill? California vineyards, okay, Scudder, Morelli, Twin Bridges, the argument might be made that Bertram Hill was using the labels as a recruiting device for its California consortium. But did BHill also have designs on those French châteaux which crowded the precious little strip of land northwest of the city of Bordeaux along the river Gironde? Not likely. Such an intention would've long since been revealed—there was nothing very secret within the wine trade, not prices, nor production figures. Wine was a commodity, not an art form. The only variables were the winemaking itself and the weather. There were tricks to the trade, yes, but no secrets. Winemakers worked with what they had: grapes. Some years, the harvest was good. Sometimes poor. Sometimes superb. It was how you rescued the mediocre that made the difference.

The Pinjattas were trying to leapfrog, to bypass the process . . . to cheat.

"We'll get more evidence," she promised, talking to herself. "You can count on it."

Henri didn't hear. Muttering unpleasantries in French—he always swore in French, such an expressive language, he said, for cursing and obscenities—he was repositioning his leg, in ill humor punching at the cast. He laughed at himself dismally. All well now except for the leg, he was fed up with crutch and cast.

Clara interrupted the blasphemous flow. "Anyway, for sure now, we've got enough to turn Alberto off."

"He had already determined not to accept."

"There was never any reason in the first place." Without thinking, she added moodily, "Except that I didn't give him a grandson. Somebody to take over."

"Clarissima!" Henri said softly. "Not to be hard on yourself. Besides . . . it is not too late. Is it?"

He was staring at her in the mirror. Goggle-eyed. Grinning. "No," she said matter-of-factly, "but we'll have to move fast."

"It is not for nothing I am called Speed Gonzalez!"

"That's *Speedy*. As in Speedy Alka-Seltzer . . ."

"Oh . . . this language," he wailed. "I admit defeat. It is the slang that kills, my dearest! But, in whatever language . . ." He let it hang, then added, "I am at your service!"

Clara laughed, a little self-consciously, she couldn't help it. "We'll leave that till later, Speedy . . ." She saw he had taken the labels out of the white envelope again. A necessary change of subject matter if she was to stay out of the ditch: "Anyway, Henri, you have no doubt they're counterfeits, whatever the endgame?"

"And good ones too. *Beautiful* . . . but they will need aging. Need to be antiqued. No problem. You rub some old attic dust on top of cat urine . . ."

"Ugh!"

Henri laughed gleefully. "Such is the price of such tomfoolery, my sweetness."

*Tomfoolery?* Surely, the evil act, or intent, demanded stronger language: fraud . . . deceit . . . criminal conspiracy. But Henri enjoyed words, more often using them for their texture, their sensuousness, than for their pinpoint accuracy.

"Having patinaed the labels," he continued, "we come to *corks*. To accompany these labels, one must use only the elitist, long corks, with distinctive vineyard brandings on the side. No huge deal, either, to have a stamping faked. *Or* to obtain the proper bottles . . . collect empty Pétrus or . . . connect with a complicit bottle factory. Easily managed by people who have had a great deal of experience in mischief-making . . . yes," he nodded, "I mean the Pinjattas."

"And they get away with it."

"Not always, as we know. It is not so easy to fool with pricey wine. Strangely enough, the wooden boxes in which come your Lafites, etcetera, are most difficult of all to duplicate." He shrugged. "Therefore, more convenient, perhaps, to counterfeit single bottles rather than full cases. A magnum here, a magnum there. Loose bottles, you see . . . and more. The foil capsule at the top of the bottle can be a giveaway. The knowledgeable can spot a new capsule on an old bottle. Also labels are now being coded to prevent just such counterfeiting. A complex fraud it would be."

"Who'd notice bar codes in a market of millions? You'd have to be watching for it."

"And thus," he agreed, "sheer volume conceals. For the unscrupulous, worth taking the chance. Money, Clarissima. Greed . . . but it is not over, take that from Lamarque. We wait. We watch. We listen. When the right occasion arises, then the explosion!"

Clara cast a warm look Henri's way. Too long a look. The BMW drifted.

"Please!" he cried. "Clarissima . . . please! *For cris-sake!* Eyes on the road! You are scaring the life out of me!"

Coming off the bridge, the highway swept in a wide curve to the right and a moment later entered the heart of darkness, the tunnel which emptied into Marin. Roaring traffic drowned out her voice. Cars thundered on the left. Somebody blew a horn. The noise echoed like a shriek. Seconds later, they reentered daylight. Down below was the jumbled, over-built so-called bohemia of Sausalito.

"Relax," she said. "It's under control."

"I will not look!" Henri put his head down. Then he began oohing and aahing, admiring the Pinjattas' work, which did not please her. "The vintages they have chosen, Clarissima. Nineteen hundred and seventy-five, a most excellent year, a classical year, a year of the century. Eighty-two. Eighty-four, I also see. We are not dealing with mediocre years here."

"We fake only the best . . ."

"Exactly. But remember, in the end, they are not selling *empty* bottles with pretty labels. There must be something inside—even swill, as Mick Tyler, you remember, noted."

"It's got to be better than swill to get somebody's thousand-dollar bill."

Henri's eyes danced in the mirror. "How about a nice five-year-old Morelli Reserve? A wonderful five-or seven-year-old Morelli might do the trick—if soft-ened a bit more at the edges, if warmed, then cooled again, then rested on silk for a few months to give it more dignity, *aplomb,* you could say." He smiled. "The bottle, the label, the mystique would do the rest. Only a fabulous nose"—he tweaked his own—"would mark the difference."

"Aplomb," she said, "that's nice."

\* \* \*

IN HER TIME, Clara had seen a good many Belvedere homes. Mainly, they were a mishmash of conflicting architectural styles, or fads—rancho California gone to Hollywood modern gone to redwood and hot tubs. She'd been wondering about Tyler's Frank Lloyd Wright. Perhaps to tweak Clara's curiosity, Daisy had reported merely that the Tyler house was big and long and "very interesting."

The first thing Clara noticed was the sheer power of the roofline. Low-pitched, eaves long and elegant, the roof gave the whole building a faintly oriental uplift. The house spoke of Mick Tyler, his self-confidence, his directness, his daring. There was nothing complacent about it. Or hearty. No cute detail or out-of-place balconies.

"Here it is, the Tyler palace."

"Unfinished palace." After a while, Henri murmured, "It does have a feeling of Frank Lloyd Wright."

Yes, with the emphatic, clean lines drawn against the sky, combined with heavy underpinnings, the effect was impressive, dramatic but soothing, reassuring. It would be a house you'd want to be inside. And, they were looking at a work in progress. The roof was covered but still not shingled. A big chimney had been framed, not yet finished. The raw walls were constructed of concrete blocks, window and door openings delineated by heavy, rough-cut timber. As he'd told her, Tyler was not into a lot of redwood.

Clara steered her car through the mess of construction—piles of lumber, a cement mixer, stacks of tile, bales of shingles, four Dumpsters of debris,

mud puddles, an electrician's truck—parking along-
side the familiar blue Mercedes 300. Nearby was a
yellow Volkswagen, one of the neo-Bugs. Tyler's car,
but who belonged to the Volkswagen?

Clara opened the back door of her BMW and
Henri hauled himself out. She passed him his
crutch. Just then, somebody walked spryly from under the overhanging entryway—Daisy Chaney, a cell
phone at her ear. So the new Beetle belonged to
her.

Somehow, Clara was not surprised. "Here's Daisy.
Can Mick be far behind?"

"Clara . . ." Henri put his hand against the pocket
where he'd placed the labels. "We say nothing of
this . . ."

Daisy was dressed in an open windbreaker, a heavy
sweater, blue jeans, and fur-lined boots which
seemed to come almost to her knees. Her short
black hair hidden under a long-billed cap, she
bounced toward them. Smiling, bright-eyed, she
closed the phone and shoved it in a pocket. Out of
the office, there could be no lingering doubt about
Daisy. She was a confident young woman, up to taking a risk. Which she would be doing with Mick Tyler.

"Where's the master of the house?"

"That was him, Clara. He's out in his boat. He
should be here in a little while. . . . Shall we go inside? The ground is a little rough right here, Mr.
Lamarque."

"*Henri.*"

Going slowly as Henri negotiated patches of mud,
Daisy led them into the front double-door opening
and what would be the foyer. Ahead was a beam-
framed archway. Clara smelled the tangy perfume of

curing cement, the sweet-sour odor of cut lumber bumping into the raw oyster scent of San Francisco Bay.

"This is one big slab," Daisy said informatively, "anchored into the hill with steel beams and piles, solid as the pyramids . . . Mick says." She gestured. "Through here, the living room. Big windows, all with a view of the bay. At the far end, that's the dining area, not a separate room, just broken up with bookcases or something. And in the back corner, a monster kitchen . . . do you want to take a look?"

"Sure . . . I see you've been over here a few times."

"More than a few," Daisy replied forthrightly. "But who's counting?"

Henri chuckled. He got the point. Daisy shot him a smile, apparently pleased with Henri's quick read. She led them into the large, open space, still all girders up above, and across to where the windows would be.

Henri whewed. "A hell of a view! *Formidable!*"

So it was, or would be. The living room, Clara estimated quickly, was about eighty feet long, thirty or forty wide, the whole expanse unsupported by pillar or post, somehow cantilevered off the weight of the slab. Daisy was right, there was a heap of decorating and yards of money in such a job. And this was only the top floor. There were two more of the same square footage down below.

"Mick's got the elevator going—in your honor, Henri."

"Elevator? *Bravo!* Only in America!"

It was closet-sized, in a shaft next to the stairwell in the foyer, but ample enough for three people. Daisy knew which of the unmarked buttons to press. "We go *down* to the second floor, bedrooms, baths.

Exercise room . . ." The elevator door slid open to a matching expanse broken up by the outlines of partitions. "See, it's all stepped down to the water . . . *Staged*, Mick says." They descended another twenty feet. The door opened again.

"Here we have Mick's playroom. His boathouse is the last level down but you have to walk it." Daisy glanced at Henri's leg. "We can skip that."

Clara looked around. "Daisy, this is a *big* job. Do you think we can handle it?" The question, she realized, was academic. Daisy was already handling it.

"Oh, sure. Mick's a very good client." Her stride became all the more purposeful as she steered Henri to the rear of the "playroom." "This area is to be the wine cellar. You see how it cuts deeper into the hill? Mick thinks that'll help climate control. The ceiling's going to be vaulted like a real *cave*. With a quarry-tile floor. Wooden racks and a big old oak table with a Tiffany lamp hanging over it . . ." Just like the Old Count's room, it occurred to Clara. "He's looking for the table right now—that's one of my missions. And the lamp."

Head well back, nose pointing, Henri peered around. After a bit, he muttered, "Perfect, I should think."

*"And now this."* The next stop was at a piece of smooth birch plywood laid across two sawhorses. Atop the makeshift table, four glasses and a bottle of something red, already opened, a white napkin tied around it to cover the label. The cork lay beside the bottle. "The first official drink in Mick's new house." So saying, Daisy went across to one of the window openings and peered into the dusk. "But where the hell is he? He said he'd be docked by the time we got down here."

"Then he will be." Clara went to stand next to Daisy, again vividly reminded of her daughter. Henri stayed behind, propped on his crutch. He'd already examined the cork. Now, he looked to the bottle itself. Without uncovering the label, he put his nose to the opening, then drew back, saying nothing.

"Well," Daisy asked Clara, "what do you think? Do you like what you see?"

"It'll be fabulous. No doubt. It must be . . . you and Mick seem to be getting along very well." Daisy half-turned but before she could answer, Clara said, "That's good. I approve. I was hoping you'd hit it off." Hit it off? That was putting it mildly.

Daisy's cell phone jingled. She snatched it out of her pocket, flipping it on. Instantly, her oval face pinched. Anxiety leapt, "What! Oh . . . my God! But you're . . ." Relief arrived. "Yes, yes. Okay . . . I will . . . thank God!"

Something had happened. Henri felt it too. Hastily, he swung across to them on his crutch. Clara put her hand on Daisy's arm. She was shivering. Holding the phone limply, Daisy mumbled, "Somebody rammed him. Just since he called before, somebody in a big power boat ran him down. That's against the law! Sailboats have the right of way. They didn't even stop to help."

In a hushed monotone, Henri repeated the words. "*Rammed him?* Is he sure? It was *deliberate?*"

"Of course he's sure! Of course it was deliberate! It had to be . . ." Daisy's voice dropped. "Sorry . . . the Coast Guard picked him up. . . . He was very lucky. The boat filled right up. He's got to do a report. He says"—Daisy gulped tearfully—"for us to go ahead with the wine."

"We will recork it. We will wait for him."

"No, Henri, please . . . Mick especially asked. Please, go ahead and pour. There's nothing we can do. I don't know how long it'll be. . . . They'll bring him to the dock." Daisy was rattled. But insistent. "I'll wait for him . . ."

"All right, if that is what he requires . . ." Henri hobbled back to the plywood table. "I *think* that Mick intended to test me, so therefore . . ." He lifted the bottle and poured a small measure into one glass, slipping readily into his wine taster's trance.

And so, here they were again. In this incomplete new house, with another disturbing "accident" to consider, at least for Clara to consider—for Henri was far away. This was like Kabuki theatre or *Swan Lake,* or croquet or poker, the players changing but not the play, as if this were the first production ever of a brand-new drama . . . like sex, always the same, give or take a few moves, but worth repeating.

Henri breathed in wine vapors, breathed out. Finally, he tasted, working the wine with his tongue, his lips . . . then swallowing. "*Excellent!* A Bordeaux . . ." Which was obvious from the shape of the bottle. Following through, he made himself look puzzled. Lines formed on his forehead. His lips searched for finish, the aftertaste or reminiscence of that just tasted. All at once, uncertainty cleared. "I think—from the left bank, *non?*"

Daisy looked at Clara. "How would we know?" Clara asked.

"I think . . . I think . . ." Henri tasted again. "I think what we have here is a Château Montebanque . . . a ninety-two?"

Daisy uncovered the bottle. She gasped. "Wait till I tell Mick! That's marvelous!"

Henri managed a quick wink for Clara. How had

he known? Obvious, Watson. This was the same year Werner Flemming had sent over to compensate for the questionable stuff at the Clift Hotel. Now it was soothing the Tyler temper? How did Houdini escape? He had his tricks too.

"And a very nice vintage indeed." Henri held up his glass. "I offer a toast to Mick's new house . . . *and to his safety*." He glanced at Clara. "We congratulate him on his escape. Tell him, Daisy—the house will be marvelous. And I am looking forward with great pleasure to helping him furnish his wine cellar."

*"I will tell him."* Daisy untensed. "He'll be pleased. You know, it's only a few years since Mick and his partner . . . now, all this . . ." Her eyes clouded again. "Success scares him and he worries, you know, that it might be bad luck, building such a big house. Like . . ." That this was unfamiliar territory for Daisy was clear from the trouble in her voice. "Like, he says, he's pulling the noses of the gods." She appealed to Henri. "Do you think so?"

"No, no!" Henri was very decided about such matters. "*Au contraire!* The gods are happy. Happy *for* you. The gods favor people who make the most of life, people who dream and build. . . ." His eyes found Clara's again. "The gods *protect* people who dream and love and love life."

# *seventeen*

ASSISTED BY THE oversized but wonderously named Astrid Wunderlick R.N. and leaning on a silver-headed cane, Franco Pinjatta had made it nimbly enough up the steps from their parked Cadillac.

He was a porky little man with a thin black moustache, bulging eyes, and puffy lips, and an expression, when unwary, which was anxious and scheming. Exercising her imagination, Clara detected the shadow of Steve Pinjatta within the bulk of his father—never mind what Steve said about being adopted.

Reaching the cover of the terrace, Franco whipped off a narrow-brimmed fedora, revealing a shiny baldness that gave way to little rolls of fat, like shock absorbers, at the back of his neck, and a tight-collared blue shirt and floral tie in front. A loud plaid suit was buttoned precariously across a bulging gut. He was not, in toto, a handsome man.

Aside from a slight breathlessness, however, Clara saw no obvious sign of his advertised paralytic disposition. He was certainly strong enough to grab a glass of cabernet, to hold it aloft for visual inspection.

Grinning like a gargoyle, he said, "Astrid, looka that stuff! I betcha this is the vino I told you about."

He reached for the bottle.

Alberto held it away from him. "It's my Reserve."

"I knew't!"

Henri had warned them about Franco, that the only language Franco truly understood was rebuff. With that, Henri had retreated down the hill to Clara's cottage, having no wish to see or be seen by the unwanted guest.

Having failed to keep them away, Alberto had become intensely curious about the gnomish Franco and his nurse. He poured another glass which he presented to Nurse Astrid. Accepting it in her big right hand, she first let down a large white bag, bigger than a pocketbook, smaller than a suitcase, bulging and heavy, Clara assumed, with an oxygen tank and pump . . . maybe a fibrillator, who knows, and a complete set of needles and bottles and other paraphernalia of her trade.

Astrid nodded a curt thanks. *"Primo,"* she muttered, guttural-voiced, an impressive figure, indeed, taller than anybody on the terrace, including Florence who was not a small woman. Broad-shouldered, narrow-waisted, with the hips and biceps of a weight lifter, she was also, evidently, an astringent personality, one who plainly would put up with no nonsense, whether from patient or anybody else. Astrid would've been about forty, Clara judged. She was dressed for her job in starchy white uniform, sheer white stockings, her hair blond enough to fly, sleek and smooth as a piece of metal. As unsociable as she seemed to be, Nurse Astrid provided perfect balance to Franco's bullheaded eagerness to please—and be pleased.

"I'm glad you like it," said Alberto.

"Heh, yeh . . ." Franco Pinjatta chortled. "*Like?* Astrid loves the wine. *Primo,* says *Wunderlick.*"

But wine wasn't what was on Alberto's mind. "Look, Mrs. Rampling and I . . ." He nodded at Florence, in case the introductions hadn't taken. "Mrs. Rampling and I are leaving for Europe in three days, you see, and I've got a lot to do in the meantime. And you know our decision. That's why—"

Pinjatta held up his hand. He would hear no more. The excuse, the explanation, given and repeated over the telephone the night before, hadn't been enough to deter him. Alberto had done his best to be hard-nosed about it, telling Franco that a trip up to Sonoma would be a waste of both their time. Without once mentioning the phony labels, sight of which had sent his blood pressure soaring, he'd told Franco that after hours of discussion, debate, consultation, even soul-searching, the Morelli clan had decided not to accept the Bertram Hill offer. If anything, the family had been reminded how much they valued their independence. Yes, thanks to the Pinjattas, Alberto went on, they'd decided to go ahead with some long-overdue expansion and modernization. Big money would be invested. New warehousing space and cellars built. The outdated shed of a tasting room at the bottom of the property spiffed up. Morelli Vineyards T-shirts were in the works. A hard-hitting advertising campaign was planned.

Listening to him, Clara wondered who Alberto had been talking to. Florence, of course. *And Henri.* Those few days of his recuperation at the Morelli villa had done wonders. Apparently, there had been a *lot* of talking behind Clara's back.

Driving the point home, Alberto told Franco Pinjatta he was looking to buy a few hundred more acres in order to increase production, to put greater emphasis on the Morelli Reserve. Which was like touching Franco's sciatic nerve.

Explanation. Apology. Excuse. None of it had any impact on the man. Franco was either too dense or too stubborn to comprehend simple rejection. He'd told Alberto he could resist until he was blue in the face and more, blue everywhere, and he, Franco Pinjatta, would not be put off. He insisted on seeing Alberto face-to-face. He wanted to hear Alberto's decision *mano-a-mano* was the way he put it, as if he were prepared to fight Alberto for possession of his own vineyard. Wasn't that why he'd flown to San Francisco sooner than expected, *diablos!*

But today, Franco wasn't in any hurry about it. He seemed content to stand on the terrace and drink some wine and have a look around. He loved the place. He loved the house. He would build one just like it. Alberto was going to give him—no, sell him—two acres. Franco was going to come here to die. "I know all about that, you have my word," he pledged. "I know all about time and the world and eternity."

"You're a religious man then, Mr. Pinjatta?"

"Sure." His closely spaced eyes barely acknowledged Clara's question. "Why not? Wine. Religion. The same. Eh?" He turned back to Alberto. "You two gonna get married in the old country, my boy told me that. Congratulations!"

"Thanks."

"My boy was to tell you, I come in Saturday instead of next week—just to see you." But there had not been a peep out of Franco's boy since the face-off Friday morning. "If you didn't notice, Astrid, she is my private nurse," Franco chattered on. "That is why it is all white. Stockings. Dress. Including the shoes. Also white underwear. White, from head to toes. *Correcto, Astrid?*"

"*Sí. Correcto.*"

The exchange seemed to enliven Nurse Astrid. As if Franco had kick-started her, she began to preen. Like shy Heidi of the Alps, she blushed, at least some telltale pink showed beneath layers of white powder. Eyeing Alberto as if he were the promised landlord, she followed through by dropping her eyes, then her hand to caress with fervor a heavy gold cross, displayed with its golden chain atop a definitely alabaster bosom, as firm as a shelf. The gesture evidently, Clara thought, thinking the worst, was meant to call Alberto's attention to a wickedly plunging cleavage. One thing was sure: a couple of more moves like that and Florence would be at Astrid's throat. Even her father, the naïve, the innocent Alberto, was embarrassed.

"Well," he said, "anyway, welcome to Morelli Vineyards, Mr. Pinjatta and Miss—"

"*Hey!*" Pinjatta shoved up close to him. "I'm Franco. I call you Alberto, okay, Alberto?" Franco's eyeballs spun with the effort of sincerity. He downed more wine. "Damn fine stuff you're growin' here, Alberto. What say, Astrid?"

She said nothing, merely touching the glass again to her pale lips.

"Astrid, believe it or not, she is a Brazilian," Franco said, as if that explained her peculiar character. "I myself Venezuelan, also with a French and

Spanish *pasaporte.* Astrid and me, around the world. Eh?"

Was Astrid completely immune to Franco's attentions, or intentions? Maybe she hadn't been listening. Or didn't fully understand what he was saying. Her momentary arousal past, she went limp, her eyes flat, dull, bored. She seemed more like a ghost from Valhalla than a life-preserving nurse.

Having done with Astrid, Franco whirled around to survey the vineyard to the south. "Damn beautiful!" Licking his lips avariciously, he went on. "Centerfold, like the crown jewel of the consortium, it shall be."

"Now, wait a minute," Alberto said impatiently. "Didn't you hear what I said?"

"But no espaliers. No, what you call . . . trellises? How come?"

"That particular acreage . . . is all head pruned," Alberto growled, "the old Italian way. That's how come."

Smoothly, Florence inserted herself between them. "We love this view," she declared very vocally, wrenching Franco's attention from Alberto. "We absolutely love it! And would part with it for nothing!"

"Yeh, yeh." Franco paid no attention. "What I love is opera. I tell you that! I am in love with opera and all sopranos. I seen you in New York at the Met."

As was his habit, a function of his aggressive nature, he sidled closer, his flat nose all but nudging Florence's also impressive bosom. Florence winked at Clara over the top of his head. He didn't notice . . . well, he couldn't see. But Nurse Astrid did. Her shoulder muscles rippled with resentment. Mockery of her master would not do.

Uneasily, Franco stepped back so he could look at

Florence without dislocating his neck. Doing so, hopping in reverse, his ingratiating grin intensified. His little eyes were crimped by a kind of joy. Clara noticed then, or thought she did, no, she would have *sworn* to it, Franco was wearing eye liner. Such a streak of black under his eyelid, could it be natural? His cupid lips, was it possible? Were they faintly rouged?

"If you saw me at the Met," Florence laughed, "that was years ago."

Franco laughed too. Laughing is good for you. It shakes up the body. Franco's tubby body shook. "Years ago, yeh, I was a little boy."

"And I an ingenue."

"*Correcto!* Can I call you Florence, or Firenze?"

"Make it Florence."

Franco didn't notice the haughty set of her lip. "So, here I am, me, Franco Pinjatta," he crowed, "speaking to the great Firenze Rampling, the greatest soprano. I am one horny sonufabeech, I kid you not!"

Clara cringed.

But there was hope—Franco might be on the verge of one of his seizures. He was surely excited. The prominent carotid arteries in his fat neck began to throb. His hand shook noticeably as he hoisted his wine glass to toast La Rampling. He wheezed a little. Clara heard a muffled fart.

If the latter was some signal of physical ill-being, Nurse Astrid took no notice. A Mona Lisa–like smile had carried her far away, as if back in time. Was that what the original Mona had been smirking about, an earlier, earthier Franco Pinjatta, definitely not a Renaisssance man? Nurse Astrid gave nothing away. She continued to finger her gold cross, the hand resting comfortably on her bosom, the locale the French called *le balcon,* upon which, in Astrid's opulent case, they would also have said, there were many people.

Franco's eyes flitted about, possibly looking for a dog he could blame for his uncouth eructation. Shuffling uncomfortably, he said, "Hey, Alberto . . . what say you and me take a little walk?"

Alberto's eyes went to the cane.

"Don't worry. I'm a rabbit. I gotta see your cabernet. That's the *main man* in this Reserve, right or wrong? All harvested now, right?"

"Yes. All done." Alberto shrugged. Clara knew what he was thinking. That he was stuck. And hated it. That life was too short. "The cabernet is down there," he said tersely, "if you're up to it."

"Hey! *No problema!*"

Franco handed Nurse Astrid his empty glass. He plunked his hat back on his head. Astrid passed him his cane. "Go, with care," she ordered. Under the white powder, like a masking cloud, her face was stormy. "Be cautious, *señor.* Take care!"

The three women watched them go, Franco side-stepping his way down the brick steps, limping past the Cadillac. Once on fairly level, albeit bumpy, ground, using his cane as a sort of fulcrum, he swung along like Short John Silver. Now, Clara told herself apprehensively, Alberto would have a full measure of Franco's great power of persuasion, about which Steve had boasted so. In fact, Franco was apparently already at it, stopping and starting as he and Alberto proceeded, stopping to wave the cane, to level an index finger at Alberto, speaking excitedly. Starting again, he stumbled through the grapevines, his screechy voice echoing up the hill.

He obviously aimed to talk Alberto into submission.

Well, they would see. Alberto had great power too, of stubbornness. This was evident in his walk, the steady, measured way in which he planted his feet on *his* ground, or kicked at stones and to uproot weeds, how he held his head, down, tucked in his shoulders, his whole posture only a shade less than fully belligerent.

There was, after all, the matter of those labels which, "just in case," Alberto had tucked in the pocket of his denim jacket, and the red-hot question of the Pinjattas' real intentions. Alberto wavered no longer. But, face it, Clara told herself, Alberto had known about the Pinjattas from the very beginning. He had never, really, been going to do a deal with them. Intuition had always been his strength.

Florence put her arm around Clara's waist. "Alberto's having his say now," she said.

Nurse Astrid hissed for silence. Riveted on Franco, her eyes shone adoringly.

The two men were in the middle of the oldest acre of Morelli cabernet, that first planted by Alberto's own mama and papa. The ancestors must be having their say too. And Franco didn't like what he was hearing. Shaking his head doggedly, he rocked back and forth, as if taking punches. When Alberto had finished dotting the *i*'s, he stuck his hands in his pockets and stood stolidly, waiting.

But Franco didn't respond, not immediately anyway. With an impatient, irritated rotation of his shoulders, he jerked himself around. His body rather scrunched up, reduced in size by disappointment, frustration, anger at not getting his way. Then, in sudden, wild fury, a spasm of insanity, he grabbed his cane by its ends and with a single powerful movement broke it over his knee. He threw down the two pieces. That done, in a final, hateful gesture he leaned over and spat at the ground, Alberto's ground, ground he would never own.

"My God!" Florence gasped, glancing at Astrid for her reaction. "He's . . ."

Astrid calmly nodded. "*Sí. Claro. El toro loco,* he is called."

Like a mad bull, a small and gimpy one to be sure, Franco blundered on down the hill, careless of the vines. He was drawing closer and closer to Clara's cottage. Did he have some inkling Henri Lamarque was also on the property this Sunday afternoon, that he was holed up down there with Joe Alejandro, waiting for the coast to clear?

Florence must have been thinking the same thing. Nervously, she asked Nurse Astrid if she wouldn't like to sit down for a while. Astrid stared at her disdainfully. "No! I must remain within full view of Señor Franco. I must at all times have him within the eye range."

"Is his health very delicate? Right now, I must say, he looks healthy enough."

"*Delicado? No!*" Astrid was focused on her master. "Who says such a thing?"

Clara answered. "Steve told me his father is sometimes . . . not well."

Which wasn't completely accurate. But she didn't want to repeat Steve's more specific suggestion that Franco suffered seizures.

Even with that, Astrid's nostrils flared. Another hiss, a bark of denial twisted her double chin. "Maybe that *Steve* is not so well!"

God knows what she meant by that. There was no chance to ask for from within the house came the sound of a ringing telephone. Joyfully, Florence cried, "I'll get it." And bounded inside.

Alberto had caught up to Franco only a few yards up the hill from the vegetable garden back of the cottage. They were talking again but it wasn't going well. Franco flung his arms around, wagging his fingers at Alberto, slapping his forehead in exasperation. Obviously, his great powers of persuasion had failed him.

Clara got the feeling the negotiation was over. "I hope Mr. Pinjatta is all right," she said to Nurse Astrid. "If he gets very tired, I can drive down there in the golf cart and get him."

Astrid shrugged.

Then, finally, out of patience himself with Franco's ranting, Alberto thrust one hand into his jacket pocket. Out came the labels. He waved them at Franco like garlic in the face of the Vampyre Sylas D'Entrail.

Franco responded violently. In a severe show of temper, he jumped back, tore off his fedora and hurled it down. He kicked it, stomped it. He threw his arms up as if appealing for help from the evil empire. Then, when Alberto was not instantly struck down by lightning, Franco flung his head back, baying, braying like an ass. Out of the noise, one word made sense.

*"Lamarque!"* And again. *"Lamarque!"*

Down below, the French doors at the back of the cottage swung open. There was no sign of a crutch. His cast concealed under his trouser leg, Henri took three steps into the garden. *"Hello, Franco."*

Clara shivered. Henri's voice was so deep, so distant, so close. It echoed inside of her. And worked magic on Franco.

He reeled, as if hit by a flying chunk of ectoplasm. He tripped on a rock and almost fell. No, he had definitely not expected to see Henri Lamarque. He covered his eyes, then ripped his hands away, the eyes swelling with terror, disbelief. It came to Clara—had Franco believed Henri Lamarque to be dead? Could he have been so misinformed? Had somebody . . .

"Yes, Franco! It is I, Lamarque. *And my health is good.*"

At that, Franco Pinjatta went completely off the tracks. Hopping up and down in a kind of war dance, bending over and rearing back, churning the earth, lameness forgotten, he shook his fists, screaming incoherently.

Nurse Astrid's fingers dug into Clara's arm. "Henri Lamarque?"

"Sure. That's him. He's here for the weekend."

*"Desastre!"*

Franco bawled up the hill, "Astrid! Astrid! Kill him now!"

What! Did she hear right? *Kill him now?* Clara turned. But Nurse Astrid had already bolted for her medical bag. Crouching down, her white uniform straining against her muscular buttocks, she started to unzip the bag, then stopped. She sucked air hoarsely, shaking her head in confusion, as if she'd been caught in the act. Quickly, she rezipped the bag.

Florence appeared at the door. Boisterously, she announced, "Telephone call for Franco Pinjatta. It's his son. He says there's grave news . . ."

Astrid's big eyes bucked. Which way to go, whether to keep her eye on the distraught Franco or—*"I come!"*

Grave news? Clara pointed down the hill.

Florence gasped theatrically. "Good heavens! Confrontation!"

Impassively, at least on the surface, Henri observed Franco's torment. But only for a moment or two. Then, aiming The Nose with deadly accuracy, he laughed, loudly and scornfully enough to alert the neighborhood if it hadn't already heard Franco's screaming. Enraged, recognizing that Henri was indeed alive, Franco spun around and around like a dervish, looking for something to throw, finally seizing a handful of dust which blew back in his face.

Henri turned and disappeared through the French doors.

Franco stared at the place where Henri had been. Then, wailing, he dropped to his knees and bashed his hands against Alberto's earth. Awful sounds burst from him.

Nurse Astrid stumbled back on the terrace. She flopped down in a chair. Moaning, all but ululating, giving the lie to those who might've said she was an unfeeling brute, she wailed, "Oh, exquisite Carmen . . . oh, the poor beautiful Carmen . . ."

"The beautiful . . . *who?*" Florence threw the question at Clara.

Clara shrugged. No, this was not Bizet's Carmen. "What's happened to her?"

"Carmen María Magdalena Pinjatta," the nurse wheezed, "who would have been Miss Venezuela. Then Miss World. So beautiful, like all the Venezuelan virgins . . . then ruined by . . . *Lamarque!*" She stopped, as if somebody had punched her off button.

*"Ruined?"*

Play. Astrid started up again. "Yes! It is true. Carmen would not listen. She fell in love with this Jew, this Austrian Frenchman Jew. He deceived her. She came to him in Paris. They were to marry. Then Lamarque tossed her to the side, as a man would a cigar butt. It is then too late for the beauty pageant . . . Carmen is lost. No Miss Venezuela . . . no Miss World. Carmen María Magdalena Pinjatta shall have . . . *revenge!*"

Astrid spit the word with a dozen or so exclamation points on its tail, the very venom driving her to her feet. At last, noticing what was happening on the hillside, she screamed: *"Caramba!"* And rushed down the steps. Stumbled down the hill. Alberto had gotten the dead weight of Franco on its feet. Roughly, Nurse Astrid pushed Alberto out of the way and, exhibiting an unlikely strength, swept Franco up in her arms. Wanting, needing, no help, she carried him up to the terrace and lowered him into a convenient wicker lounge.

No question Franco was in a bad way. Sweat poured down his round face, damming above his thin moustache, the runoff trickling past the corners of his mouth, mixing with drool, bypassing his pimpled chin, rolling down his fat neck into his shirt, the floral tie. Franco's legs twitched and jerked. Breath came in pants. His hands clutched at Nurse Astrid, pawing her. He pulled her down, burying his face in her bosom.

Astrid seemed accustomed to his symptoms, even welcoming them. But symptoms of what? Apoplexy? Epilepsy? Hypothermia? Astrid showed no sign of dismay or even, actually, great concern. Rather, as Franco grunted and squirmed and trembled and shook, Astrid opened her uniform. She unbuckled

the front closure of an industrial-strength white bras-
siere and popped out a large, freckled breast. Grim-
acing oddly, not exactly in a matronly way, she
poked a broad, red nipple into Franco's mouth.

*"Permiso,"* she murmured.

With an exclamation, Alberto strode to the other
end of the terrace.

Shaken too, Clara followed. If this was the whole
story, she thought, it didn't amount to much. But it
wouldn't be easy to take any of the Pinjattas seriously
after this. Also a blessing.

"Where's Florence?" Alberto asked worriedly. "Did
she go inside?" Florence? Not much. She was watching Franco and the nurse . . . fascinated. "My fault. I
had to show him the labels."

"No, Papa. Henri did him in. Franco Pinjatta can't
stand the sight of an honest man."

"Would seem so . . ." Alberto turned thoughtfully.
*"But do you love him, Clara?"* He looked surprised at
himself for asking.

Clara hardly paused. *"Sure I do."* And so, there, it
was said.

Alberto offered his arms. He hauled her in.
"That's what I wanted to hear. Our discussions with
the Pinjattas are officially over."

As if he'd heard, Franco's high-pitched voice
crackled. "Hey! Alberto!"

Alberto couldn't ignore him. "Well . . . feeling better?"

Franco pouted, his round face sullen. "I become
too agitated. You have not been *kind* to me, Alberto."

"Look, Franco, I gave you our answer. Isn't that
why you came up here—to hear it in person?"

"So you say. But you have not considered thoroughly . . . you will reconsider. *I know.*" Franco

didn't allow for rebuttal. He went on, unapologetically. "Madame . . . mesdames . . . please not to be *eshocked.* My treatment by Nurse Astrid, it is a famous therapy."

"Say no more." Alberto glanced apologetically at Florence who, in fact, wasn't bothered at all.

"Such therapy, it is recommended by the doctors, in Switzerland. It is a *Jungian* . . . a dream therapy. I shake. I have the fever. I dream. Astrid is dream object. Like that, you understand? It is about . . . it is the mother complex. Very complicated."

"Sounds more like Freud to me," Florence sang, almost gaily.

*"No! Jung!"* Nurse Astrid jumped up, taking offense. "Jung. *Si.* I tell you. I take my training from Jung . . ."

"Jung is dead. And so is Freud."

"The school of Jung!"

"Listen," Alberto said, "believe me, *it doesn't matter.*"

"Not matter?" Franco wheezed. "No! Franco will be a dead man in a few months. So what! Who cares for Franco?" Nurse Astrid did. She put her hand on his forehead. He brushed it away, whilst making a rejected lover's face at Alberto. "You, Alberto, my friend—no, *not* my friend—you say no to the Pinjattas. You accuse . . . you make me very sad. You listen to Henri Lamarque, our enemy, a traitor who makes slander about the Pinjattas. Lamarque, who spoils Carmen María Magdalena Pinjatta and does not marry her. Lamarque, who says bad things to the French Appellation about the *magnifique* Château Montebanque. Lamarque who—"

"Forget it!" Alberto's voice was strained. "What *is* the point?"

It took Franco a moment. He summoned strength. With Astrid's help, he struggled to his feet. She whispered something in his ear.

"Telephone call, *sí*, Astrid remembers me that she accepted a call from my boy . . . I must leave now." Franco's left eyelid leapt up and down. "From Steve, my boy, there is sorrowful word from Montebanque. An accident. René Renfrew is his name, one wine-maker at Montebanque. He does not know how to swimming and falls into one big tank of the first fermentation. René is drowned. *Mort! Merde!* A trag-edy. It is now not sure my brother Maxey may come to San Francisco for the Festivity of the Masters of the Vine."

The big benefit that Alberto and Florence would be missing. "I'm sorry," Alberto said.

"*You* are sorry. And we? We are not sorry too?" Sorry or not, Franco produced a broad smile. "But now? What do we discover in the afterbirth of this accident?" He stopped for effect. "I tell you! We dis-cover that Monsieur René Renfrew was a spy. Yes, *un espion . . .*"

"You mean," Florence interpreted, "he was selling your magic formulas to your competitors? That's not kosher, is it?"

"*No!* He was a spy for the Appellation Contrôlée, the wine policemen of France! They decree every-thing. Day of harvest, time of harvest, how many men to harvest, whether left-handed men or right-handed men, the temperature of the *crushing*, they order all. René Renfrew reports to them our smallest violation. It is no freedom!"

*Accident?* Yes, and Franco was eager to talk about it. "Sad, is it not? No loyalty. René . . ." He shook his head. "A member of the family. But this is not the most terrible of all accidents that may happen. Once, as we have heard, a man is falling into a great container of the molten glass . . . where they are, what you call it, making new bottles from the old."

*"Caramba!"* cried Nurse Astrid.

Franco grabbed his ribs. Was he trying not to cry? Not to laugh? Leading one to think . . . what? That he was making a joke? Or being very serious? "The man was, as you say, recycled!" He gasped. *"Sí.* Recycled. That is the word! *Le mot juste!"* Then he couldn't hold it in any longer. Giggles surged. Again, Clara heard the sound of a whistling fart. Franco was going that way again. "Yes! Yes! This man becomes a champagne bottle!" His elation was bloodcurdling. *"Oui . . . sí!* A champagne bottle for to hold a cheap Mongolian bubbly . . . like the yak pizz."

*"This is funny?"*

Franco's merry mood collapsed. "No. Not funny! *Tragique.* I look at you, young woman, Lamarque's such a good friend. Beware! I say, beware of Lamarque!" He put his right hand on Nurse Astrid's shoulder. "Come, Astrid Wunderlick, we go to San Francisco . . . I leave you now, Alberto, for the moment, only the moment, yes, my friend, if you are my friend and I think you are maybe not my friend despite that I want to be *your* friend . . ."

Alberto didn't blink. "Don't try to make too much of it, Franco."

"Best to remember René Renfrew. The wine business, it is sometimes a dangerous one, Alberto, best to remember."

Alberto's temper flashed. *"Meaning?"*

Franco bared his sharp white teeth. "Meaning . . . beware of bad friends . . . *my friend.*"

"Listen here . . ." Alberto was about to lay into him.

But at that moment, Franco let out a shriek and clutched his chest. His eyelids slammed shut. Then reopened. Unfocused, his eyes glared about with aimless anger. Clara heard another explosive fart. Franco began to sink down. But Nurse Astrid was nimble and she was quick. Before anybody else even thought to move, she had Franco in her arms again. Furiously, she flung him back in the wicker lounge chair. Locating a pulse, she tuned in. *"Hokay. Chust fainted."* She reached for her big, white bag.

From where Clara was standing, in back of the again recumbent Franco, she couldn't help glimpsing inside the bag as Astrid rummaged around, then found what she was looking for, a syringe, a small bottle of serum. Clara didn't mean to look. She was merely *there*.

You saw these guns in the movies or on TV all the time. But not ordinarily in a medical bag did you spot such a deadly but compact, rapid-firing automatic, an Uzi or the like, all obscene black metal and muzzle and stained-wood pistol grip. As Clara stood there, transfixed by the sight, Astrid rezipped the bag. Taking no notice of Clara, or anybody, she unsheathed the needle, pushing the tip into the little bottle, sucking up a few cc's of the contents. Then, in a single, determined movement, she plunged the needle into Franco's hairy belly. But she didn't push the plunger down, as one might have expected.

Instead, the reverse happened. Nurse Astrid loosened the top of the syringe. Clara became aware of a faint hissing noise. Air, or something perhaps lighter than air—hydrogen?—was escaping through the liquid in the syringe.

"We take *gaz*." Astrid murmured busily. "Too much *gaz* press on heart."

The odor of rottenness was instantly noticeable.

# *eighteen*

O FFICER EDGAR FLANGE of the California Highway Patrol had news. Early Monday morning, visiting with them in the Sonoma Valley, Flange explained in the minutest detail how a botched Sunday-night robbery of a Cloverdale service station had led to the arrest of a couple of bad men in a black pickup.

"Maybe the same one," Flange allowed. "I can tell you that one of the villains is blond. And there's a patch of green paint on the side of their truck."

"Then that's them!"

"Maybe."

What had happened, briefly, was that just as blondie had gone inside the station and stuck his gun in the attendant's face, a police car happened by. The patrolling officer spotted the idling truck revving in getaway mode and, at the same time, clear as a big billboard, the fellow with the gun. After radioing for help, the officer blocked the truck, then bravely leapt out, unholstering his own weapon. The driver gave up immediately. But blondie panicked. Blasting away, he ran out of the store. The officer fired one shot, taking him in the shoulder. Blondie dropped his gun and surrendered. Result, said Flange proudly, both villains in the hoosegow.

"*Hoosegow?*" Henri repeated the word.

"Jail," Clara translated.

Blondie, a twenty-five-year-old named Otis Cheroot, if they'd ever per chance heard the name, was a well-known local thug and, at the moment, he was under guard at Sutter Medical Center in Santa Rosa. The police were in possession of his .45-caliber pistol. Thus, Flange explained, the slug dug out of the upholstery in the door of Henri's Jaguar could be compared with one obtained in a test firing of the suspect's weapon. If there was a matchup, it seemed like they had their man.

Henri gasped admiringly. "*Mon Dieu,* that is a great accomplishment." Even as Flange spoke, he had opened a bottle of wine. "May I offer you—"

"Oh no, no sir," Flange said. "Way too early for me. Besides, I'm on duty."

Nevertheless, Henri poured a couple of fingers of Alberto's lighthearted—slightly reckless, he called it—sangiovese-cabernet blend for himself and Clara and just a touch in the bottom of a third glass. "At least, you can make a *smell-toast* . . . to the California Highway Patrol! A great victory!"

"Just luck." Modestly, a credit to his corps, Flange sniffed the wine, allowing himself to be swept up ever so slightly by Henri's cordiality. "Right. Okay then—to the patrol. Nice . . ."

"I want you to have a case of this," Henri said, "for yourself and that outstanding officer. It is called Morelli Tuscanoma, after Tuscan sangiovese and Sonoma cabernet . . ." Henri couldn't help lecturing. Officer Flange listened respectfully. "Now, tell me—

if this indeed is the man, the next step is to find out who hired him to kill us, *n'est-ce pas?*"

"You bet!" Inspired, Flange proceeded to the next order of business. "In that regard, I'll have some pictures to show you later today, for identification purposes. I have business at the hospital . . . if you could . . ."

That was easy, Clara said. They'd meet him at Sutter Medical on their way back to San Francisco. She explained that her parents were off to Italy in a few days and they had to say their goodbyes. Officer Flange said he fully understood.

"And Mrs. Addey will certainly remember," Henri promised. "She has the eye of an eagle. And by the way, you have my permission to torture this Cheroot if such is necessary . . ."

Flange chuckled nervously. He hoped Henri was kidding.

LUNCH WAS A lengthy affair. There was a good deal to talk about: Officer Flange's new information. Mick Tyler's boat mishap. On the telephone that morning, Mick had made an effort at nonchalance, even mentioning in a jocular way that his business rivals . . . no, that was a stupid joke. He was angry. Ten minutes in the icy water of San Francisco Bay was not a joking matter. Fortunately, another boat a half-mile away had come to his rescue and the Coast Guard hadn't been far behind. Aside from chattering teeth, a sore shoulder, and assorted cuts and bruises, Mick hadn't been hurt. But his boat was a write-off and he was damn well going to find out who was responsible. Somebody was going to pay.

Over espresso, Alberto asked the obvious. "Is there a connection?"

Whatever Henri thought, he wasn't saying. Clara took it upon herself. "I told you Flemming was complaining bitterly about Mick sniffing around Bertram Hill . . ." She didn't say what she really felt—that there was a direct, indisputable connection. She'd agreed with Henri earlier that they wouldn't needlessly alarm Alberto and Florence. Besides, Florence couldn't accept there was any danger from the Pinjattas, Franco being such a muddleheaded clown. They were more a laughing matter than a threat.

"Nevertheless . . ." Alberto turned to Florence. "We could postpone—"

Henri spoke up powerfully. "You must not. You must go. Even if all the dots do connect, which I doubt . . . no! You *must* leave as scheduled. The Pinjattas must understand once and for all that you have rejected them. That intimidation does not work, if such be the game. That there is no hope for them . . . you must not waver. You must go to Italy."

"All well and good," Alberto conceded. "But what if it's not over?"

"It *is* over, Alberto." Henri sounded very decided about it. "Listen, this man . . . Cheroot? Such a name! He is in the *hoosegow*. Apprehension of their villain must frighten those in command—*if* somebody is in command. They must fear—what if he talks? No," Henri repeated, "it will stop now."

Alberto gave in. He wanted to accept Henri's argument, for Italy was very much on his mind. "At the first sign of trouble . . ." He directed himself to Clara. "You let me know *immediately*."

"Yes, Papa."

"Now look," he went on, "I'm going to warn Joe

Alejandro to be on the alert. Have him keep three or four of the harvest crew on the property until we're back . . . they can patrol a little and keep their eyes open for strangers. I don't want any funny stuff . . . Joe will have all your phone numbers." To Henri: "You and Joe get along. I've watched you together."

"Yes, we're *simpatico*."

Alberto turned to Florence. "Shall I go on? Maybe it's not exactly the right time . . ."

"Honeychile! No time like the present! Now or never!"

Alberto knocked back his espresso, setting the cup down carefully. "Now, Clara . . ."

She recognized the tone of voice. Something was coming. "That's me."

"We expect . . . especially with all this going on, we're *counting* on you coming up here every weekend—until you leave for Italy. Just to keep an eye out. The Pinjattas . . ." He was silent for a moment. "Henri, you've said yourself they're totally unpredictable."

"Yes. That," Henri agreed, "for sure."

"I *can* count on you, then? Both of you?"

"Yes," Clara said, "on me, certainly. I can't speak for Henri."

She'd misspoken. Henri reacted passionately. "But Clarissima, you *can* speak for me. I give you permission to speak for me whenever you wish to." He laid his hand on his heart. "We will visit every weekend, Alberto. That is my promise."

"Good."

Clara caught the glimmer in his eye. She recognized the look. He was about to astonish her. "Now, wait a minute," she said, putting that moment off. "This very Friday night, Monsieur Lamarque is booked to be down in Los Angeles drinking Bordeaux—bad leg and all."

"That is so. I shall be at Le Dome restaurant on Sunset Boulevard for a Lynch-Bages vertical tasting. But Clarissima, I shall be back early Saturday morning. . . . At which time, we will drive to Sonoma," he added triumphantly.

He was so pleased with himself. And she saw that Alberto was pleased with him too. For a measurable moment, Clara experienced the uncomfortable, but perversely comforting, feeling that she was at their mercy, that Alberto and Henri, even Florence, were holding all the cards, that something, some decision, had been taken out of her hands. She looked to Florence. No help there. Florence was busily grinding more coffee beans. Clara sank back in her chair. "What are you grinning at?"

"Me? Grinning?" Henri became solemn as an owl.

*"Now, Clara . . ."* It was coming now. Alberto waited for Florence to finish with the coffee beans, to sit down again. "My idea is for you to give the vineyard more of your attention, don't you know that by now?"

"Papa! We've talked about this—"

"We've *never* talked about it. Not seriously."

"You know I have my business."

"I know that." His face gave it away. "What I'm *hoping* is that you and Henri, *together*, will give us some of your time. Lots of your time. But not *all* of your time."

He didn't have to say any more. It was very clear now that Henri and her father had been having some long and loaded conversations. Henri, *Monsieur Lamarque*, was sitting quietly, his game leg extended away from the table, hands on the arms of his chair, so composed she could have kicked his cast and made him howl.

"Alberto," he asked quietly, "are you absolutely *sure* this is what you want to do?"

"Yes. Absolutely."

"Want to do . . . *what?*" Clara burst out.

Florence smiled at her indulgently. Let them go on, she seemed to be saying, it's something men have to do. They get a kick out of it.

"You know we're *not* selling to the Pinjattas," said Alberto.

"By now, everybody knows that."

"Morelli Vineyards is going to stay in the family, at least for another couple of generations."

Generations? How to respond without being indiscreet, even indecent? Where did Alberto suppose these generations were coming from? Was Florence pregnant? Not without going into *The Guinness Book of Records*. And Clara?

Alberto reached for her hand. "I've heard from Martha."

Martha? Clara wasn't prepared for that. Weakly, she murmured, "You have? *I* haven't. What did she—"

"She wants to come back to California."

Clara was shaken, clear down to her toes. Family. Generations . . . what was he getting at? Small-voiced, she asked, "Is she . . . having trouble?"

"No. No. I called her at the time of your accident. I didn't make anything of it . . . just thought I'd better." He paused for a bit. "It's time you and Martha made up, Clara."

"Oh yes. I know." Probably so. Undoubtedly so. But still, was *this* the right time? Wasn't it more complicated now than before, with Henri in her life?

The situation called for lots of listening. "But it takes two."

"Yes—and Martha's ready to tango." Alberto grinned.

Henri was watching her, his eyes encouraging.

"Okay . . ." Clara took the plunge. "When is she coming back? You're saying she has made the decision? It's definite?"

"Yes. The end of the term. She's talking about transferring to Sonoma State. And she asked me to get some material from my friends at the University of California, at Davis . . ."

"*Davis?*" Clara was honestly stunned. "You're kidding! The wine school? I thought she wanted to do fine arts . . . architecture. That's amazing." She appealed to Henri. "That's where young Joe Alejandro goes . . . *isn't* that totally amazing?"

That worldly, surprised-at-nothing expression crossed his face. "Another nose? The world can always use another nose."

"Martha doesn't have a nose."

"Clara, in case you haven't noticed, *everybody* has a nose."

She frowned in mock exasperation. "I mean a *nose* nose."

"Clarissima," Henri laughed, "I would wager your daughter Martha has Alberto's nose. It is genetic."

"Poor girl . . ." Florence poured fresh espresso.

Thoroughly out of character, impulsively, Alberto grabbed Florence's free hand and brought it to his lips. Florence blushed extravagantly, right into the roots of her red hair . . . and Clara's throat caught. An instant memory of her mother flooded through her. But then something else, a contrary but complementary emotion, made her laugh, spontaneously, heartily. For just a second, a kind of embarrassment crossed Florence's face . . . and as quickly receded. She and Clara exchanged thoughts. It was okay. It was fine.

Alberto had caught the moment too. He waited for it to pass. Then, with a rush of words, he announced, "The point to all this is that I'm stepping back. *We're*—Florence and me—we're going to get out of the way."

"To *some extent* out of the way. That's what he means."

"But there's no way Martha could take over as soon as that. She'd still be at Davis."

"*Not Martha.* Not just yet anyway. You'll take over."

There it was. The impossible. The impractical. This was past Clara's ability, out of her time frame. She shook her head. "Papa, I cannot do it. I'm sorry. For one thing, I don't know enough about wine."

"You know more than you think you do. Much more!"

"No. You'd hope I do. But I don't. Besides, I have my business. I love my business! I can't just—"

"No, no, keep your business."

"But then how? I couldn't be responsible. *How?* Talk to Joe Alejandro on the telephone once or twice a week? It wouldn't work."

"All right." Alberto heard her. He nodded gently. "But what if *our friend* Henri Lamarque takes over as director of the vineyard? He would be working with Joe Alejandro on a daily basis and consulting *constantly* with you."

"Oh . . ."

"Yes, oh."

Even sitting down, Clara was reeling, speechless . . . yet surprised at her own lack of surprise. She'd seen it coming. They were in cahoots. They had it all figured out. Clara would fall into line. She and Henri . . . she remembered her thought about Henri and the poetic Cyrano. It seemed as though Alberto were playing Cyrano now for Henri.

Alberto dared her: "Tell me why it wouldn't work."

"Papa . . ." Clara felt more than a bit embarrassed. She couldn't look at Henri. "Henri is not going to agree to a deal like this."

Even as she said it, Henri spoke up. "Clarissima, I have already agreed. Undoubtedly, I will become interim nose-in-residence at Morelli Vineyards."

Alberto's laughter boomed. "And I shall be absentee winemaster!"

IN THE CAR, Clara drove for a while in complete silence, keeping her eyes on the tricky back roads, trying not to think about anything but the roads. Yet, it kept coming back. How easily everything had fallen into place. The mystery was why it hadn't happened long before. Now, just like that, with the snap of fickle fingers—more like a symphony of finger-snaps—her life was to be drastically changed. Or drastically corrected in midcourse. She saw that it had always been an inevitability. She *would* be going home again.

Quite serenely, given what had transpired, Henri was sitting beside her, the passenger seat pushed back as far as it would go, his leg extended under the dashboard. Confronting her quiet with his own, he'd been looking out the window at the passing vineyards, the farmhouses, the intensive rural scene. What he saw seemed to please him, for he was humming to himself. Second thoughts? It did not seem so.

"Somehow," Clara said, "I have trouble seeing you in work boots."

"And straw hat."

"You won't shave anymore. You'll look like Joe Alejandro."

"My darling," he chuckled, "Joe shaves every fourth day, surely often enough for any civilized *vigneron.*"

Clara drove another mile before assembling her next set of thoughts. "Well, we know what he's counting on, don't we? With your help, he's figured it all out. He wants us married . . . and Martha makes three."

Henri pulled off a perfect shrug, as delicate as a ballet step and not easy in the sitting position. "Is that so shocking?"

"You two guys think you're mighty clever, don't you? You're just like him . . ." He nodded, muttering that he hoped so. "Henri, you know, it's just possible I might not *want* to be in the wine business."

"Clarissima—"

"Stop calling me Clarissima."

"Mrs. Addey—"

"Or that!"

"Okay. *Ms. Morelli.* And *please* not to protest so much. You are not forced! If you don't want . . . okay. Alberto proposes to give the vineyard to you anyway, I know that, for he has told me so. Marriage"—he faltered—"or not. We do *not* have to be married. But I take the job. I become director. I shall be your hired hand!"

"Oh . . . you know better."

"I do *not* know better! In my long career in wine,

never have I had the opportunity to *manage* a vineyard, to grow the grapes which become the wine"—he touched her shoulder, a peace gesture—"to apply *the nose* to blending it, not just sniffing and tasting and spitting in a bucket. This is a different thing . . . Ms. Morelli."

Well, she admitted to herself, it would *probably* work. But she wasn't going to say so. She didn't intend to be as easy as that. But she was almost argued out. "You guys plotted behind my back." This was her final, nonnegotiable complaint, touching the vital matter of her independence, her integrity, her self-esteem. "*You* bartered me away."

"Plotted? Bartered?" Henri was cross. "No! Alberto discussed it with me while you were in San Francisco those days after our accident. He needed to know if I would consider such an offer. After all . . . the nose has its needs too."

"The nose! I'm surprised the nose accepted. . . . What about the column in *The Imbiber,* what about that?"

Henri said he wasn't worried. If he continued the column, it would take on a different flavor, treating the subject of wine from an entirely different vantage point, that of the grower, the competitor.

"And what makes you so sure you'd be happy? You think growing grapes is where the action is? *You'd be bored!*"

"Clarissima . . ." She knew what he was going to say before he said it. "If I am ever bored, I give you permission . . . no, I require you—"

*"Shut up!"*

He was laughing to himself. She could see him, making no noise, just laughing. Finally, solemnly, he said, "Dearest beloved, I considered Alberto's proposition very carefully. In the end, I decided to take a chance. It is *my* career. Whatever happens, *my* life. I said yes to adventure. And to the challenge: to produce the perfect bottle of California cabernet, to out-Bordeaux Bordeaux!"

"And *my* career? My life?" she demanded testily.

"Easy," Henri said. "You maintain your office in San Francisco but you also work from Sonoma by phone, fax, and e-mail. You are in contact with the city but accessible to Sonoma and Napa counties. Clarissima, your business will grow, it will grow like tipsy."

*"Topsy."*

"At the same time," he continued, "Ms. Morelli would be active in the wine business, not passive, like now."

"I am not passive!"

Henri stroked her shoulder. *"I do know that."* He squeezed her thigh. "We will start tonight. For Alberto, I would do anything."

"I knew it would come to this!" Reaching a bit of straightaway, Clara hit the gas, so as to get his undivided attention. "One last thing, *beloved.* Before we *start* anything, I want to know *everything* about Carmen Pinjatta."

He was terrified, not by the question. "Please . . . Ms. Morelli, *lentement.* Yes, okay, *I'll talk!* Slow down, please! Did I not tell you of Carmen?"

"You did not tell me about Carmen María Magdalena Pinjatta. About to be Miss Venezuela. Almost Miss World. Whom you threw aside . . . like a soggy cigar butt."

*"Who says?"*

"Franco's nurse. She knows the whole story."

"Not the whole story . . ."

"Tell me the whole story then. Why was Franco so bothered by you and Carmen? She's not *his* daughter . . ."

"No. Maxey's." He shifted his leg uneasily, not really wanting to talk about it. "But one might well ask such a question. Does Lamarque sound cynical? I can tell you that Carmen was no Miss Venezuela when Lamarque first met her. She was already married. Did Nurse Astrid tell you that? At age sixteen Carmen did an elopement with some Fidelista Cuban madman. Two years later, when she came to Paris, the family was struggling to extricate her. Beautiful she was, she could maybe be a contender. But she was *not* a miss. And she was also demented . . . no surprise there, if you see the rest of the Pinjattas."

The memory must be very unpleasant. Henri's face had fallen into deep *tristesse*. Attending to the road, Clara gave him time. There *was* time. Behind the scenes in old Sonoma, every once in a while, around the next bend, one came upon one of those small Victorian gingerbread farmhouses, renovated these days, repainted, prettified. This one was red with white trim and a white picket fence. There was, naturally, a vineyard attached to it. "So beautiful," Henri murmured. Then, abruptly, "Clara, you *must* believe me about this."

"I do. But the plot's a lot thicker than I expected."

"Thicker than water, for sure. . . . In Paris, oh now, how many years ago, twenty? I was young . . . a novice in the wine-tasting world. We met at such a one. Carmen arrived with Franco Pinjatta. Uncle and niece. At first it did not occur to me. But then I realized something was going on between them. I asked Carmen but she would never say. I think it was too awful and decadent a thing, even for her."

In all this, Clara reminded him, "Nobody mentions the Pinjatta wives, except Steve said his mother ran away with a Greek."

"Maxey's too. Both wives of the twin brothers ran away with Greek distillers. One is an ouzo king, the other is large in retsina."

"Can this be true?"

"Yes, madness but true, my dear. At the time of Lamarque meeting Carmen, the Pinjatta brothers had just invaded the Rioja district in Spain. Not yet were they in Bordeaux. Yes, Carmen was *always* with Franco." Henri pulled at his nose. "We became acquainted. Carmen would slip away from Franco. She came to my ugly rented room near the Gare de l'Est. I was so poor then, Clara. I had nothing. And I tell you, with shame, yes, Carmen gave herself to me. More. More than *gave*, she forced me to accept . . ."

"Poor you. But you were a young man . . . younger, I mean."

"Yes, with the raging hormones, it is true."

"Did Carmen want you to marry her?"

"No, maybe just worship her—that was enough for Carmen. She was a narcissist, I can tell you, if anything in love with her mirror. It went on a bit like this. Until Franco discovered she was deceiving him, coming to me in my dingy lodging."

"So *that's* really why he hates you. The rest is subterfuge."

"Franco never forgave me. Of course, after the affair with the wine, his hate only deepened." Henri hooted contemptuously. "Not that I care a single *whit*. Anyway, by then, when he discovered us, Carmen was divorced from the Fidelista and the Vatican had graciously granted an annulment. Ergo . . . such a pretty word . . . *ergo,* the marriage had never taken place. Carmen was declared a virgin reborn. Very humorous, my darling, a second chance at virginity. You know, being partly aborigine, these Pinjattas are very superstitious. They believe in such things."

"Except . . ." How was it? "She deflowered herself again right away, with you."

"Sadly, yes," he confessed, "and continued to do so with Franco. But who was to know? She returned to Caracas. She entered the Miss Venezuela competition."

"And didn't win."

"How did you know?"

"It wouldn't have been poetically justified."

"*Vero!* Truly *vero!* That was the moment when Carmen tried the first time to kill herself—*so it was said.* But not because of me. Out of self-hate, for she did not win the crown of Miss Venezuela. She did it with cocaine, from Colombia. Soon, she blessemed—"

"Blossomed."

"Into a horrible addict. She involved herself in terrible affairs. Once, even, she fought a duel over a Peruvian movie star and now bears a saber scar on one cheek. No more Miss Venezuela for Carmen Pinjatta. So it went on. In the following months, she lost weight. She came back to France, thin like a cadaver and facially disfigured. I did not recognize her. By now, the Pinjatta clan is eager for me to take over the burden of this neurotic beauty contest has-been. But Lamarque has grown up a little bit. He has heard stories about the Pinjattas and he has it in his mind to steer well clear of these people. Including . . ."

Carmen María Magdalena Pinjatta.

"They blamed you for everything, didn't they?"

"Exclusively! For want of a better scapegoat. They said her loss of the Miss Venezuela title was due to the way she walked during the competition. It seems, so it is argued, that virgins do not walk like girls who regularly boom-boom. It is something to do with the tightness of the buttocks . . ."

It was a good thing Clara was old and mature enough to suffer only a kind of secondhand jealousy. In his Parisian days, she hadn't even known Henri existed. And now, history, as far away as a story out of the *Decameron* by Boccaccio or whoever.

"Henri . . . one last question. Was Carmen in love with you?"

"I suppose, in her way."

"But you rejected her."

"I ran, Clarissima. I fled to New York. She was crazy with drugs and so I escaped and I resolved to stay away from the Pinjattas. And they have never forgiven me for that either."

Henri was just finishing the story as they rolled off the side road from Sonoma and onto the freeway, Highway 101. Santa Rosa was about a half hour to the south.


THEIR BUSINESS AT the hospital didn't take long. Officer Flange was sitting in his police car in the parking lot, waiting for them. He escorted Clara and Henri upstairs to a waiting room on the second or third floor. Inside, alone, he took a number of pictures out of a big folder—mug shots, they were called—and spread them on a table. "Have a look, please. Tell me if you recognize—"

Clara spotted him immediately. That face, light-skinned, the shock of dirty-looking blond hair, the nutty eyes.

"That one," she said, pointing. "Is he here? Is he the one you've got?"

Flange hesitated. "You've made an identification," he said. "And I've duly noted it and you sign here, that you saw the pictures . . . and so on." Clara did so. "I've got to go by the book here," Officer Flange added. "There're legal procedures to be followed."

"I understand," Clara said. "All I'm asking is if he's the one you've got."

Flange didn't reply. He put the pictures back in his folder. Then, he motioned for them to follow him. He walked them down the corridor to where a cop was sitting outside a door.

"One moment, please," he muttered. "Wait here, will you? I've got to check something inside here."

Flange nodded to the guard and opened the door. Leaving it ajar, he stepped into the room. There, in front of her, a man was stretched out in a hospital bed, his left arm and shoulder caught in some sort of cast and traction. Startled, more than she'd expected, by grim reality, Clara caught her breath. The man named Otis Cheroot stared back at her for a second. A sneer developed across his mouth. Even if Clara hadn't recognized him, he sure as hell knew her. His loose-lipped ugliness was as frightening in this controlled environment as it had been on Route 128. Clara turned around, hating the face.

Flange's voice interrupted. "Sorry about that. I left a notebook in there."

Silently, they went downstairs.

As they were saying good-bye, Henri muttered, "That man there, he is a nasty-looking rogue!"

"Nasty as they come," Flange agreed.

"Is he the kind to cooperate?"

"He hasn't so far. I doubt he'll tell us anything helpful."

"And the other fellow, the driver?"

Flange shook his head. "Maybe. Right now, he's just confused. Doesn't seem to understand much. He's Mexican, or some kind of Hispanic. The interpreter's having trouble."

"Thumbscrews," Henri suggested. "For the blond one, the rack . . ."

# *nineteen*

"LISTEN, CHILD . . ." MINA paused and
Clara heard Hugo's voice. "Ah, Hugo's
brought me a cup of tea. Isn't that nice? Thank you,
Hugo . . ." *Another* cup of tea, one of a steady stream
of cups in and out of Mina's parlor, all day long.
Mina must have world-class kidneys and a bladder to
match. Mina went on, "What was I saying, oh yes,
your father called me last week with some news . . ."
Which obviously pleased her. "Then *again* on Friday
as they were going out the door, just to make sure
Hugo and I were still coming. . . . They must be in
Rome by now."

"They've been there since Saturday morning,
Grandma. Today is Wednesday . . ."

Mina's teacup rattled. "You seem to be in a
naughty humor, dear."

"Not naughty. Just tired. And a little confused. Has
Alberto told you his plan?"

Mina would be concerned about that. Her wish
was for everybody to be at least satisfied, if not totally
happy, with their lot. But that was not why she'd
called. She was concerned about the weather in San
Gimignano in late December. Was it going to be very

cold? How were they going to get from Rome up to
Tuscany? Clara advised she bring her fur. No, as far
as she knew, the Italians were not particularly concerned about the animal rights thing.

"Yes," Mina said. "He did mention he had a plan.
And Martha's coming home. It'll be all right now,
don't you think?"

"I hope."

"And Henri's going to Italy with you. That's definite?"

"Yes, Grandma."

Pause, the telltale pause. "Well?"

"Well . . . what?"

"I *like* Henri. I guess you must like him too."

"I do."

"*Well?*"

Again, as in: well, what're you waiting for?

"Not just yet, Grandma." Clara had a good mind
to say how much she liked Hugo and . . . *well?*

Mina had forgotten her other question, about
ground transportation. "I think it's very romantic,"
she said. "Don't you?"

"Oh yes."

"It is what Henri wants, isn't it?"

Clara sighed. "Henri says . . . *he claims* . . . that's
what he wants. He might be sorry."

"He told Alberto so—how many times do you have
to hear it? And it's what you want too, isn't it?"

"Is it?"

"Of course it is! You'll still be able to practice your
own profession . . . and Martha is sure to like Henri,
once she knows him."

"The wine'll take over. I know it will."

Mina was shocked. "Is *that* what you're worried

about? My God! Clara, making wine is not exactly an ignoble occupation."

"I know, Grandma. But after a few years, what's the diff—selling wine . . . selling buttons?"

Of course, there was a difference. You couldn't smell buttons or taste them. Buttons were inert things. Wine, well—she'd heard Henri on the subject often enough. Wine had personality, character. First, it was young. It aged. Matured. Then it died, if nobody had drunk it in time . . . and its soul went to . . . ?

Mina didn't say anything for a bit. Then, in measured tones, "I remember, when your mother married Alberto—that was long before you were born of course—"

"No kidding . . ."

"Clara, please! I remember I had the same misgivings. Had I raised my daughter to become some kind of a peasant woman stomping grapes with her bare feet? To live on a *farm* far from the city and all its culture?"

"You never told me that."

"I've never had to tell you. Then, I met Alberto and his father and I knew your mother would be happy. And she was. And that's what counted. That's what always counts, Clara."

"Yes, all right . . ."

"So that's the question you've got to ask yourself," Mina concluded. "What's going to make you happiest, your business or a life?"

"The way you put it . . ."

Suddenly, Mina said, "We've got to talk about this. You'd better come to me this afternoon."

"*This* afternoon? I'm alone in the office. My assis-

tant's run away with a client. I've got a lunch date
. . . tons of work."

"Get here *before* four."

"Grandma!"

She couldn't just haul ass out of the office at the
drop of a hat. Daisy was across the Bay—again—
measuring walls and room layouts. And probably being measured by Mick Tyler. The whiz boy, as Henri
called him, had interior designs on Daisy. And had
most likely already implemented them. But that was
fair enough because Daisy felt the same way about
Mick Tyler.

"No arguments!" Mina decreed. "There's a gentleman coming to call at four. At least, Hugo and I
assume he's a gentleman, though Hugo says he
didn't sound much like one on the telephone. He
told Hugo he wants to talk to me about selling my
share of Morelli Vineyards. He has a very generous
offer to make me."

"What? *What!*"

"I thought that'd catch your attention."

"*Who?* Did he say who he was?"

"Well, of course he did. Otherwise . . . well, Clara,
that's self-evident, isn't it . . . an impressive name,
dear. Here, I have it written down."

Clara heard the teacup and saucer being shoved
to the side, then the rustling of paper. On that table
next to her chair, along with her teacups, Mina kept
all her files—names, phone numbers, invitations,
business correspondence. . . . It was a miracle she
could find anything in such a mess or didn't spill tea
all over the lot of it.

"*Maximilian.*" The old lady's voice crackled. "Maximilian, that's the first name. The other is compli-

cated. Hugo tells me it's a Latin name of some sort. Pin . . . Pin—"

*"Pinjatta."*

"Yes, something like that. I'll spell it."

"No, no, don't bother, Grandma."

Distressing news. So Maxey Pinjatta had come to town after all, the reportedly tragic event at Montebanque apparently put to rest. Where Franco had failed, *Maximilian* would try. Would they never be rid of these Pinjattas? Clara would've welcomed some fast backup counsel. But Alberto wasn't available. He and the brilliant Florence would already be out to dinner in Rome or having aperitifs there with friends, the latter plentiful enough from Florence's opera days and Alberto's wine connections. And Henri was up in Sonoma, actually in a car with Joe Alejandro on his way to a winegrower's meeting in Healdsburg, getting his feet wet, he said. There was no way Clara could reach him before four P.M. And what could he tell her anyway, except to ride with it?

"Grandma, how could these people possibly know you own a piece of Morelli Vineyards?"

"I've discussed that with Hugo, dear, and we cannot figure it out. Have I *ever* talked about it, even with Alberto? No, I've *never* brought it up because I know how much it rankled Alberto to have to come to me. No, I've never breathed a word of it. I don't want anybody else to know."

"How then?"

"A mystery, dear . . . And I do love a mystery . . . *don't we, Hugo?* Perhaps they read about it in some dusty legal document we filed with the state or the county. Well! My intention is to send this fellow

away. I'll deny I own even one share. What I have of
the vineyard really belongs to you."

"Grandma . . ."

"Clara, I want you here with me."

BEFORE TROTTING AROUND the corner to
meet Victoria Flemming, Clara took a chance and
called the Hassler Hotel in Rome. Their time, it
would be just about eight-thirty P.M. As she'd expected, Alberto and Florence were out. And just as
well. Why bother Alberto? She could handle Maximilian Pinjatta. If he was Franco's twin brother, what
was there to worry about? Yes, there was a good deal
of bluster in her mood but just now—as co-boss-to-
be of Morelli Vineyards—Clara was quite looking
forward to an encounter with the third Pinjatta.

She'd call Alberto afterward. Her report was all
but predictable: the Brothers Pinjatta rejected again.

Clara did as much useful work as she could in the
next fifteen minutes, then locked up and headed for
the St. Francis Hotel. She was feeling very much on
top of things as she turned down the hill on Sutter
toward Union Square. Wearing a plaid wool poncho
against the lingering morning chill and her beret set
at a rakish angle over her thick hair, curly in this
kind of weather, she sauntered along like a guards-
man, or a bold entrepreneur at the very least. Above,
a good sign, sunshine was beginning to make a
patchy breakthrough. The afternoon might just turn
out to be glorious.

The talk with her grandmother had finally
wiped away all lingering doubt. She, Clara Morelli,
was going to take over the family vineyard. Well,
*take over* was a little strong. She was going to give it

more of her time, a lot of her time. She and Henri, yes, *they* were taking it over. Together, the Morelli-Lamarques.

That would be her name. Morelli-Lamarque. Drop the Addey. People would love the sound of her new name, Clara Morelli-Lamarque, the sheer elegance, the way it would roll off the tongue—the poetry of the sound. The name might be anything, Venetian, Tuscan, Spanish, who knows, a name of substance, cosmopolitan and strong.

Lightheartedly, Clara skipped over a crack in the sidewalk. And this was precisely when she spotted the red Porsche, with a too familiar face above the wheel. Steve Pinjatta. He was driving up Sutter straight at her. The top of the car was down.

He saw Clara at the same time. His gypsyish face twisted into a scowl-sneer. Drawing abreast of her, he lifted his left hand, shooting her the finger. Then, with a final show of incisors, he accelerated and was gone.

VICTORIA FLEMMING DIDN'T look nearly as bold and adventurous as Clara felt—had felt, that is, before seeing Steve Pinjatta. Victoria was waiting for Clara in the upper-lobby café, a short glass of something hard and strong in front of her, a vodka martini on the rocks, as Clara soon discovered.

"Hello, Vicky."

She sat down opposite, noting Victoria's peevish expression and, worth mentioning at once, a bluish bruise on her jaw, half covered by one of her blond tresses. Victoria was wearing a high-necked white blouse under a lined black leather trenchcoat. Her legs were hidden inside black wool gabardine slacks.

Very high-heeled black patent-leather shoes completed the ensemble. They'd give her a couple of extra inches in height but not much class. "I've got lots to tell you," she muttered. "You'd better have a drink."

Clara ordered a strawberry kir, a drink Henri didn't especially favor, an Algerian lady's drink he called it. Hopefully, it would brighten up what looked like becoming a dire occasion.

"Are you all right?" she asked Victoria.

"Whatayouthink?"

"I think you don't look so good."

Victoria put one finger to the bruise mark. "A little love tap."

"Who? *Steve?*"

" 'Course not. *Werner.* A week ago. You should of seen me then." Suddenly, giddily, laughed. "I kicked him in the pearls."

"Was it about Steve?"

Victoria half nodded, her eyes scorching. "It's about the Pinjattas, period. Steve and Franco and Maxey."

"I just saw Steve in his Porsche."

"Yeah, he was here. He drove me down."

"You're still at it? I thought—"

"Yeah, still playing around," Victoria confirmed airily, glancing at her wristwatch. "As of an hour ago anyway."

"I thought it was over."

"That was the idea. But Stevie . . . you know. He says if he doesn't have sex every day, he's got to . . . you know . . . he gets very nervous." Victoria barked another laugh. "These Pinjattas, they're really something. Franco's still here. And he's giving Stevie hell . . ."

"Because?"

"Because of the way he's fucked things up. *Those labels* for one thing . . ." Victoria was curious, at the same time accusatory. "He blames you. Says he forgot 'em at your office and you took some."

"I copied some, if you want to know."

"He says they're not what you think."

"Oh, yeah?"

"Werner found out about the labels too. He's *really* sore."

"Who's he sore at? *Me?* I didn't have counterfeit labels made."

"Counterfeit? Werner said they were just, like, *extras.* Whatever, he'd like to toast Stevie on a bonfire. This could make them look awful bad, Clara, if your side makes a stink."

"Did Werner say that? Is he worried?"

Victoria nodded happily. "You bet. And it's nice to watch too. . . . He's hoping you'll lay off."

"Did he tell you to say that to me, Victoria?"

"Oh no, Christ, he wouldn't tell me to do anything. He thinks I'm the dumbest bunny in California, maybe the lower forty-eight. But so what, what do I care?" Victoria tossed her narrow shoulders. "And now, to complete the menagerie, Maxey's here too. They've got a bigger suite now at the Huntington. Those guys better count the silver! Pinjattas everywhere, Clara. I can tell you without fear of slander that Maxey's the ugliest of the bunch, a skyscraper of hair and dirty ears. Stevie must take after his mother, you know about her, she's famous? Madame Lattice Sububris." Victoria snickered, reveling in spite. "Maxey's also the most vicious of the family. Luckily, he's forgotten what I look like since a few years ago in Vegas."

That didn't sound very promising for her afternoon. Clara didn't tell Victoria she'd soon be meeting this same Maximillian Pinjatta. "Franco said he didn't think Maxey could get away from France because of an accident at Château Montebanque—"

"*Accident?* My God! Don't you know what happened?"

"A man fell in a wine vat, according to Franco."

"Don't you know who the guy was? *My God!* Maxey's son-in-law, married to Maxey's daughter. Her name is Carmen . . ."

"I . . . knew he had a daughter named Carmen."

"Holy cow, Clara! Carmen's been arrested! From what Werner leaks out, even though he doesn't want to talk to me but can't help it when he gets all excited and starts cursing the butterfingered Pinjattas . . . *apparently* Carmen is accused of pushing the poor guy. He was drowning and she wouldn't throw him a rope." Victoria's heavily made-up eyes winked and blinked. This was big news. Hot news. Bad news for the Pinjattas. And it didn't seem to worry her at all. In fact, the reverse.

"Then how come Maxey's here?"

"Ha!" Victoria cried. "He wants to get some kilometers between him and Carmen."

"Leave his own daughter in the lurch?"

"Sure! It's a *huge* stink. Maxey doesn't want any part of it. Carmen is on her own. Anyway, Werner says Maxey needs to be here because they're pushing ahead with this California scheme of theirs . . ." Victoria eyed Clara inquisitively. "They're buying three or four wineries."

"Not Morelli, I can tell you."

"I *know.* And that's a sticking point," Victoria confided. "They won't give up, you know."

"Won't do any good, I promise you." And Victoria could tell Werner Flemming so.

Victoria looked doubtful. "The idea is to wrap the announcement of their California company into the winemasters' benefit next month. Werner said they're going to be *big* California players."

Well, if Werner still believed it, good luck. "So who *are* they hijacking into their consortium?"

Victoria shrugged. "What do I know? Or care? You probably know better than me. All I hear is what Werner lets slip—if, *by chance.* I happen to be listening." Victoria glared into her martini. "I'm *not* going to that party, you'll be interested to know. There's no room for me at the Bertram Hill table. *Werner says.* 'Course not. Franco and his fuckin' nurse have got seats, and Maxey and Steve—that's if Werner hasn't killed all the fuckin' Pinjattas by then."

"Victoria! *What* is going on? You'd better tell me."

The question was like opening a gate. A loud sob burst out of tiny Mrs. Flemming's generous chest. "It's not just what Werner drops when he's too drunk to care. I hear him talking in his sleep. . . . We're not even in the same bed these days, so I listen at the door. I *have* to. He mutters and tosses around and sometimes yells out loud. I dared . . . I asked him the other day what was bothering him— and this is what I got for caring." She pointed at her face. "And all the rest, underneath, body punches mainly."

"That's why you're wearing that old-fashioned blouse?"

"For God's sake, why else, do you think?" Victoria goggled at Clara. "I guess you're not as worldly as I thought. Batterers always hit where it won't show, for crissake."

"Werner is a batterer? It never occurred to me." But now that Victoria mentioned it . . .

"It's all the stuff with the goddamn Pinjattas. It's driving him crazy."

"*What stuff*? What *does* he say in his sleep?" Clara needed to know. "*C'mon*, Victoria . . ."

"Oh, hell . . ." Victoria looked tearful but also glad to have an attentive ear. "The poor bastard, he's cornered. It seems like he owes the Pinjattas a ton of money. I can hear him yelping in his sleep about fuckin' bloodsuckers, all of a sudden yelling out that he's gonna get 'em . . . he's gonna kill 'em all . . ."

"Meaning . . . the Pinjattas?"

"Sure, the Pinjattas. Clara," Victoria said earnestly, "you know they hate Henri Lamarque, don't you? Well . . . you should warn your Henri to be very careful."

"Careful of what? Another *accident*?"

"Maybe," she whispered. "Werner—and he wasn't asleep this time—when I mentioned to him I was sorry to hear about your accident, he just burst out, 'Accident!' Then laughed like a maniac."

"When was this?"

"I dunno. Right afterward, I guess."

"It's important, Victoria."

Victoria tossed down another ounce or so of vodka martini. "I'm telling you, a couple of days later. Maybe the next day. Hell, I think maybe it was actually Werner who told me about the accident in the first place."

Which would've been some time before the arrest of Blondie and his accomplice. Not that Werner should know anything, unless he'd been involved in staging the accident. Clara touched the kir to her lips. "Victoria, why do you think it's so important this consortium, this *wine scheme*, gets done so fast? Surely, if they took their time about it, didn't push people around ..."

Victoria cast her a knowing look. "Money, Clara, of course. Their plan is for this humongous, world-wide booze company. Werner's in on it. I suppose that's how the Pinjattas are gonna get their pound of flesh. And Werner says he'll make money at the same time. The klutz. He believes them."

Clara shook her head, feeling very sorry for both the Flemmings. Even for Werner. What kind of a man was he? "He hates them—and he goes right along with them. Victoria, that doesn't seem right ... or bright."

Victoria shrugged. "Greedy ... greed ... green. Right. But look at it this way, Clara—maybe he doesn't have any choice." She looked at her watch. "Me? I've got an appointment with a lawyer." Mocking herself. "That's right. I'm bailing ..."

AﬀTER SEEING VICTORIA into a cab which would take her downtown to the offices of Smith, Smith, and Jones, Clara went back to Addey and Company and immediately placed a call to New York. This was a mother worrying about her daughter. Be careful on the street. Make sure to lock your door. But first things first.

"Martha? This is your mother speaking. Clara Addey, that's right. I'm glad I caught you. We've got a lot to talk about. ... Do you remember Henri Lamarque?"

# *t w e n t y*

WITH THE SWAGGER of the late Benito Mussolini, Maximilian Pinjatta entered Mina's sitting room, a short man trying to look tall. He was not alone. Behind him trailed the bulky and desperate person of Werner Flemming. It might well be true that the Pinjattas owned Werner, and that he feared them. But, more than fright—pure disdain was evident. He didn't want to be here. His face was ruddier than ever, livid with embarrassment at just being seen with the ugly little man. Maxey Pinjatta, of course, was oblivious to extraneous emotion. Like a hairy mole, he bored into the room.

*"Good afternoon,"* he announced himself, his voice formless, unmusical. "I am happy to be here."

Flabbergasted, though she'd seen it all, Mina glanced at Hugo. Both of them turned to stare at Clara, as if she were responsible.

Franco and Maximilian Pinjatta, twins though they might be, with overstuffed, short-torsoed little bodies, were not identical. Whereas Franco's cranium would have been a near-perfect bowling ball, his twin had hair for a dozen people, a mass of it, a six- or eight-inch-high hillock of wavy, jet black hair, thick as a mink's coat, fine and oily, presuming to the altitude of Louis Quatorze in a powdered wig. The hair bounced when he walked. It swayed. A taller man might've been thrown off balance or put at the mercy of a high wind. The impressive hair narrowed to a pronounced widow's peak on his sloping fore-head, reaching like a black wedge almost to the bridge of his nose.

"Thank you for receiving me, Madame Caboot." Maxey bowed stiffly at the waist, coming forward with his hand outstretched.

"*Cabott,*" Hugo corrected him.

"Madame *Caboite.*"

Mina waved it away. "My granddaughter, Clara Morelli Addey."

"And Grandma, this is Werner Flemming. I don't think you've ever met him. He owns Flemming's Cellar here in the city."

Werner's only acknowledgment of Clara had been a curt nod. Oh, yes, goddamn batterer—and harasser of women on the street. He was not pleased to see her. Obviously, they had hoped not to find Clara at Mina's side. How simpleminded. What had they aimed to do, these two, catch the old lady on her own?

"Oh, yes," Mina said, "the wine merchant."

A tradesman, in other words. Mina had not forgotten how to be snooty, when it suited her. Flemming rolled with the put-down. For Maxey's information, he muttered, "Mrs. Addey is Alberto Morelli's daughter."

"And I'd like you to meet *my associate,*" Mina went on, "Hugo Wanamaker."

"Charmed," Maxey murmured.

Which was a laugh in itself. Imagine Maxey Pinjatta being charmed. He screamed Neanderthal. In every detail, he was a throwback. Short arms and legs, the sloping brow, the deeply recessed eye sockets behind the craggy bone structure of the forehead, the prognathous thrust of the jaw: *Neanderthal*! And the hair of course, insulation against those arctic-frigid northern European winters during the winding down of the Ice Age.

Maxey's eyes leapfrogged Hugo and landed back on Clara. Flemming must have briefed him. He scowled like a peptic ape. Why? Because of the way they'd treated Franco? Because of Steve and the labels? Then, on second thought, Maxey went for a less hostile approach. "Alberto Morelli's daughter, yes? A *pleasure* . . ." Such a pleasure, Clara told herself, like he'd stepped in a turd. "To meet you too."

Responding in kind, thinking why not, Clara said, "We understand there was a terrible accident at your winery in France. My father was so sorry to hear that."

"Which winery do you speak of?"

"Château Montebanque."

"Oh. *Sí.*"

Maxey's hair trembled. He reached up to steady it, then, crying out angrily, yanked his fingers away. There was blood on his thumb, which he stuck in his mouth, sucking. Had he struck a hairpin, barbed wire . . . ?

"What happened?" Mina cried.

"Somebody is falling in a fermentation. And *drowneding.*"

"Drowning? Oh, my heavens!" Mina would be sympathetic. "I hope that doesn't occur very often. . . . No, your finger, I mean. You've cut it."

Sepulchrally, Werner Flemming broke in. "It's

rare. But it happens. Unfortunately. Usually when
the workers are drunk."

"Yes, yes," Maxey agreed, "an accident. The workers sampling too much of the good thing." If Victoria was to be believed, this was a barefaced lie.
Maxey's son-in-law had been shoved into a vat of
must. Carmen had been arrested. But Maxey skated
right over it. Nursing his thumb, he said, "It is not
to worry about."

Mina gestured at the pair of chubby Victorian
chairs on the other side of a round, linen-covered
table upon which Hugo had set a big silver tea service in preparation for the visitation.

"Please sit down. Hugo, sit here."

She patted a chair at her left, on the other side of
her catchall table. Saying not a word, Hugo sat, plac-
ing his hands on his knees. This was obviously not
the first time he'd taken his place at Mina's left.
They made a handsome little pair.

After another ineffectual swipe at his engorged
and glistening pompadour which this time left the
palm of his hand so wet he wiped it surreptitiously
on the tablecloth, Maxey had a good look around
Mina's parlor. Glittery, yes, feral eyes inventoried
Mina's excellent furniture, the polished, glass-
fronted cabinetry, her Empire desk, a horsehair-
stuffed sofa by the door, family pictures, potted
plants, crystal chandelier cut in Bohemia, brocaded
drapes at the bay window, and finally an old oriental
carpet.

"I love this place," he declared, as if he'd decided
to buy it. "It is . . . what you call . . . old San Francisco, no?"

"*Old?*" Loftily, though she was not much taller
than Maxey and both were sitting down, Mina stud-

ied him. "No, just plain San Francisco."

"But not many such houses like this one are remaining. No?"

"Well, I suppose that's true . . . Hugo?"

"No. Not many."

"Very few, in fact," Flemming interjected. "This one is a marvel, Mrs. Cabott." His smile was oily and false. He obviously calculated Mina would like him a little bit better for the flattery. She didn't notice.

"Tea?" Mina never offered drinks to strangers. Anyway, it was too early. "Clara will pour."

Clara sat down next to Maxey at the table. "Milk?" she asked Werner. "Or lemon?"

"Neither," he grunted. "I don't care for any tea, thank you."

Maxey also declined. Mina might have offered him rum, maybe a rum and Coke, and Flemming a scotch perhaps. But she didn't.

Clara handed Hugo tea with milk. The same for Mina. Clara took a half cup, straight up. Then, she waited. They waited. Flemming seemed determined to remain mute. He sat like a burgher, his florid face blank, thumbs hooked in the pockets of his vest, his mood stretching between indifference and impatience. Brooding, heavy-browed, Maxey studied Mina, then Hugo, frankly cooking them in a glassy-eyed stare. Neanderthal . . . supposedly, Clara remembered from college, the strain had bled into the early *Homo sapiens*, then, as an integral species, died out. But, obviously, vestiges of the Neanderthals' genetic strain lingered on. She could even imagine Maxey as a missing link. But he had not passed any of his physical ugliness on to his daughter who, by all accounts, was, or at least had been, tall and slim and beautiful—though neurotic and murderous.

Perhaps the latter were the real marks of the Neanderthal.

Finally, Maxey grunted, "We hope we all can be the fastest friends."

Mina didn't respond. Friends, that'll be the day. "I believe *you* are also in the wine business," she stated.

"Yes! So! The profession of the vine." Not sure where to go next, Maxey looked at Flemming. "Bertram Hill is our company. We are associates of Werner's Cellar."

"No!" Werner leapt in anxiously. "No, Max. *Suppliers.*" His mouth set sourly. "I buy from Bertram Hill. Our association is *only* of buyer to seller, don't you see?"

Maxey stared at Werner for a moment, then waved his hand regally. "No matter. We sell other drink products as well, you should understand. It is not only the wine. The wine is a smaller part, thirty percentiles, *más o menos.* But yes, we have vines in the Americas, in Europe—Spain, Portugal, France. Soon, we hope, in Italy, and . . . I hope we can be friends . . . California."

Hugo, solemnly: *"To what end?"*

His lips hardly moved. Like a ventriloquist, Hugo projected. His voice seemed to come from over near the door. Maxey's head jerked around. But Flemming hadn't spoken. Who then? He glared at Hugo. "To what end, you ask?"

"Yes."

It was the sort of query which demanded an answer but, in a way, was unanswerable. Stalling, Maxey coughed and hawked phlegm. There was no place to spit so he swallowed it.

"Well, well . . ." Again, he glanced at Werner Flemming for help. Receiving none, he stammered, "The fraternity! We are all of the fraternity of the vine. I tell you something . . ." He put his thumb to his mouth again, shoving the nail between his big, white, widely spaced front teeth, picking at something foreign, or maybe just the annoying thought that they were being unfriendly. "Flying down to San Francisco, I must tell you, I bring with me a big bottle of wine. *An imperial of Château Montebanque!* That is *six full liters,* eight bottles, Madame Caboot, of the glorious, priceless year nineteen seventy-five. Given by Bertram Hill to be auctioned at the winemasters' banquet. . . . You know about this?" he demanded of Clara.

"I know about the dinner. It's a benefit for retired sommeliers," she told Mina. Then to Werner, "I didn't know about your wine."

"Not mine! Bertram Hill's."

*"Indeed! Ours!"* Maxey cried boastfully. "The wine came with me from the Montebanque estate in France to New York City on an airplane and then on to California. Yes! We reserve one whole seat for this bottle of wine, yes! First class. We fastened such a safety belt around the wine, with cushions for the vibration. They said it would make *primo* publicity, with the mayor of San Francisco at the *aeropuerto* and pictures. . . . *Nothing!* No mayor. No pictures. No nothing! *A catastrophe!*"

Maxey's eyes flapped. Without looking at Flemming, he was assigning him the blame.

"The mayor was busy. Otherwise engaged. We never promised—"

*"Forgeddit!* No mind. I bring this wine for honoring my older brother Franco. He is born four minutes,

twanty *segundos* before me. Franco is not well, you see?"

Not well? Who would have guessed it? Clara offered the thought that, indeed, Franco had seemed a bit off-color. "But Nurse Astrid seems to take good care of him." She was thinking of the bosom. The needle. The Uzi . . .

Maxey nodded, working his thumbnail at his teeth. "See? Should I tell?" he asked Flemming. "You see, *somebody* is slowly killing Franco with poison . . ."

Not Nurse Astrid surely?

*"Arsenic!"* Mina said. "I've read about that, haven't we, Hugo? You feed the victim a little each day, until the cumulative amount . . ."

Clara shook her head at Mina, warning her away, not believing this herself, not for a second. Why would a man allow himself to be poisoned? Like he was a good sport or something? How could such bad men be so comical and ridiculous?

"No, no," Maxey said, "the poison, you see, it is too far. One day soon, my brother Franco will become yellow skinned like a Chinaman and he will turn to dust and blow away. . . . *Ha! Ha!*" These twin brothers, they had wonderful senses of humor. "You understand, Miss Clara Morelli?"

"Understand *what*?" She didn't understand this any better than she did Maxey's son-in-law falling into a tub of fermenting *vin rouge*.

"That we give—*donate*, the word—this imperial of Château Montebanque in honor of the *coming death* of Franco Pinjatta. Memoriam in advance. It is also our good-faith gift to the wine industry of California which Bertram Hill, our umbrella, will soon become of such a big, big part . . . BHill will also help in building such a home for the retired California sommeliers. For our imperial," Maxey predicted, "you will have ten thousand at least in auction."

Mina burst out, "I have never heard of such a thing. What next? I know about homes for unwed mothers and old actors—but sommeliers? What *ever* next?"

Clara explained. "When their noses give out they can't work anymore and they get very depressed . . . they need to be among their own."

"Yes, yes," Maxey said. "Madame Caboot, you must realize it is the nose which is so much more *importante* than the mouth . . ."

"The taste buds," Clara said.

"Yes, *mucho más importante!*" Maxey pressed on. "A good, a *skilledful* sommelier employs his *nose* more than the tasty boods for choosing the good, the better, the best wine. You see?"

Hugo slurped tea. "What's that got to do with the price of beans?" he demanded.

As if stung to the bone, Maxey Pinjatta inflated his chin and got down to business. He reached inside the tight jacket of his chalk-striped black suit, double-breasted and obviously designed to put maximum height underneath his mound of hair. He hauled out several sheets of legal paper and unfolded them on the table.

"Here, Madame Caboot, I got an agreement with a neighbor of Morelli Vineyards to become partner in Bertram Hill California Consortium . . ."

"And *which* neighbor might that be?" Clara asked.

His craggy face intent, Maxey replied, "This! Madame Francine Dumaurier Shingles of the winery called Los Shingles, producer of huge cabernets—"

"*Huge?*" Clara said disparagingly. "She's got less than fifty acres."

"He means huge-nosed . . . *obviously*," Flemming growled.

"Yes. Please, Clara Morelli!" Maxey admonished. "Château Montebanque itself of Bordeaux is no more bigger. Less bigger than fifty acres. Maybe twanty *hectares*, that is forty-four acres. And I say cabernets of *huge* flavor with bounteous aromas of berries and flowers! *Like Maison Morelli, next door, the same!*"

Sure. Sure. But nobody was going to be impressed with Bertram Hill's buy of the minuscule Shingles Winery. The vineyard was little more than a hobby for Francey Shingles. For a long time, she hadn't even bothered to make her own wine and still sold a considerable tonnage of grapes to Alberto Morelli. Fortunately, Francey didn't depend on the vineyard for her bread and butter. A trust fund provided for that.

"Yes, it is so," Maxey conceded. "Madame Shingles is small. But . . . a little bit by a little bit and the consortium will grow and grow. And that is why we prayed for Alberto Morelli, your father, to join with us, so not to be isolated and alone in the county of Sonoma."

"Alone? Isolated? I don't think so, Mr. Pinjatta," said Clara. Nonetheless, she knew there would be repercussions if Francey Shingles did join BHill. First, there would be the proximity of the enemy. And then Morelli Vineyards would be deprived of its regular portion of the Shingles cabernet harvest, particularly important in bad years.

But, okay, they'd just buy someplace else. It was surprising, she thought, that Francey would've agreed to the Bertram Hill proposal without discussing it first with Alberto, neighbor and friend. Also that she'd agreed to sell to a big combine, for she made much of being an organic grower and an experimentalist. Most recently, and this had gotten people talking, Francey had taken up the practice of performing her crush while in the nude, something to do with the psychic relationship of Man and the Earth. Skin on skins. Joe Alejandro kept his crew well out of the way when Francey Shingles was stamping her grapes down the road at Los Shingles.

Maxey smoothed the document down on the table. "So, Madame Caboot, it now arises for you to give your percentile of Morelli Vineyards into the BHill group as we are sure you will, as a brilliant woman who says hello to money in a friendly way . . ." He stopped to look at Clara. "And we hope Alberto Morelli will understand the wisdom of making the same . . ."

Then, to Mina's evident amazement, he reached into his hair and found a ballpoint pen. Jumping up, he glided across the room. With an—almost—gallant flourish, he handed Mina the pen, fluttering another document before her.

"My," Mina said, "it says '*Avec Compliments, Château Montebanque.*' Look, Hugo."

Hugo looked.

Maxey grinned crazily.

Mina played the scene for all it was worth. "Well, how much are you offering, Mr. Pinjatta?"

"Ah, good lady!" Maxey glanced at Werner Flemming who listlessly arched his eyebrows, all but declaring the exercise futile, so sure was he that Mina would never agree. "Well," Maxey said nevertheless, "Bertram Hill will pay for your interest in Morelli Vineyards the sum of three million American dollars."

"Three million . . ." Mina counted on her fingers. "That means the whole place is worth something like thirty or forty million. Is that correct?"

Alarmed, Maxey shook his head. Flemming sneered. *"Más o menos."* Maxey muttered. "More or less."

"Señor . . ." Mina made the most of the big moment. "What in the world makes you think I'd do such a thing?"

Maxey's eager smile flickered. "But madame, it is all done but for you."

Clara leapt in again. "All done? What do you mean?"

*"Qué?"*

"Furthermore," Mina said, "what makes you think I own a share of Morelli Vineyards anyway?" She handed him back his pen.

*"Qué?"* Caught there, as if in the headlights of his own dismay, Maxey stared at Mina blankly. Then, understanding, he whirled around, grumbling intemperately, and scooted back to the tea table. He sat down on the edge of his chair, grinding his teeth noisily.

"As I . . ." Werner began to say something to Maxey, then turned on Clara. "Mr. Pinjatta was led to believe Alberto had agreed to the terms."

"What . . . are you *crazy*?" Clara heard Flemming's knuckles crack. "You know damn well Alberto agreed to *nothing*! We sent Franco Pinjatta away."

He knew all right. "Impossible, stubborn people!"

Maxey interrupted with a single word: *"Lamarque!"* Maybe they were not meant to hear. With a sickly grin, he began again. "I am sorry, Madame Caboot, I do not understand, it was decided, the papers are drawn up, Franco completed everything, and now *where* is Alberto Morelli and what are we to do?"

"Alberto Morelli did not agree to anything and *Mr. Flemming* knows that."

"But . . . but you *must* sell this vineyard to us," Maxey stammered. "It is decided. That is the plan! The money, it is not enough?"

"Nothing to do with the money."

Maxey's face changed. It darkened but for splotchy patches across his forehead and under his cheekbones. Thwarted. His lower jaw jutted forward, into overbite. Clara half expected him to pull a club out of his beehive. "It is a last chance. Last offer . . . we do not take no for answer."

*"No."*

Blustering, Flemming said, "Alberto agreed to sell a couple of tons of his cabernet to Bertram Hill. . . . When's he delivering?"

"He's not. It was never agreed. You're misinformed. He considered it. That's all."

Flemming's face swelled with outrage. "Unheard of. Breaking a contract . . . we'll sue!"

"*You?* You're not Bertram Hill."

"They'll sue!"

"Let them! Just let them go ahead and sue. Let it *all* come out," Clara declared.

Flemming pushed his chair away from the table. Luckily, the legs held against his weight. His heavy body was shaking with anger—and anxiety because he understood very well what she was saying . . . threatening. "That damned Henri Lamarque," he thundered. "He poisons the well. I am *very irritated* at *Monsieur Lamarque.* He's interfered in my affairs once too often. I don't appreciate it. Not at all . . ."

Clara sat rigidly, giving him back his stare.

"Deliberately, over and over, Henri Lamarque undermines me. My Cellar. Bertram Hill, with whom I am associated. Monsieur Lamarque misuses his function as critic. He is vindictive and unfair—"

"Not so."

"Oh no? What about Michael Tyler? This could cost me!" Flemming banged both fists down on the table. Cups, saucers, silverware, teapot, and all the rest jumped and jangled. The milk pitcher fell over. Not deterred, he slammed one fist down again. "I am *not* letting Henri Lamarque run over me! He's going to be goddamn sorry! *I promise you.*"

Mina glanced at Hugo. Hugo was waiting for orders. Clara jumped to her feet. If Mina didn't order Flemming and Pinjatta out of her house, she would.

Maxey Pinjatta leapt up too, his hair set to swaying. Facing Clara furiously, his pointed face like a weapon itself, he croaked, "Lamarque! You say this name and Maximilian Pinjatta grows weak with outrage. *Lamarque,* such a terrible *rascal,* he has said to Alberto to say no! Because why? Because Henri Lamarque hates us, the Pinjattas, we, honorable family to be dragged in the dirt by Lamarque, who despoiled our daughter Carmen. Who tells everybody Château Montebanque is blended with such Algerian camel pizz."

"He never called it Algerian camel piss!"

Mina gasped.

"Oh no? Oh no? We have many witnesses to that very thing! Why do you not understand, Clara Morelli, it is around and about Morelli Vineyards that we must build our group? *Dios mío! Solo mío! Mío mío!* Morelli is like the stone . . . in the harch—"

"*Arch.*" Flemming yelled. "He means keystone in the arch. That without Morelli, there can be no arch." He stared at her, suddenly broken. "So, then,

the answer is really no. All right. You've written the
*end* of Flemming's California Cellar. I hope you're
happy. I hope you and Lamarque are *very* pleased
with the work you've done."

Maxey Pinjatta shook his pudgy fists. "And the
curses of the Pinjattas upon you! For this *humilia-
tioning,* I tell you, will you pay very costly a price! You
too . . . *old lady Caboot!*"

"Hugo, ask these people to leave my house."

Without fear or hesitation, Hugo advanced on
Maxey, as if to take him by the arm.

Maxey stepped back. "No touch! A warning, there
will be great trouble for the Morellis."

"I think you'd better leave, Werner," Clara said.

Flemming did his best with a dogged sort of smile,
the smirk of the undefeated. His jowly face quivered.
Eyes glistened behind his shiny spectacles. Hefty
shoulders tensed, he seemed ready to advance upon
her. But Clara stood her ground, ready to scream, if
it came to that. *Batterer!*

After a moment, Flemming muttered, "Come
along, Max. It's no use."

"Madame Caboot, it is you who is responsible now
for whatever bad things befall on the house of
Caboot-Morelli."

Hugo turned Maxey politely but firmly toward the
door. Suddenly, treacherously, thinking to take
Hugo by surprise, Maxey whipped around, lunging,
both arms and hands flailing. Beating at air, as it
happened, for Hugo had pirouetted to the side.
So fast one didn't even see it, one foot flew up,
taking Maxey smartly in the midriff. With a *whoosh,*
the third Pinjatta buckled forward. Hugo was just
preparing to deliver a disabling chop to Maxey's

shoulder when . . . out of his disarranged hair flew a small bird.

A miniature canary it might have been. No, it was a tiny golden finch.

"Coo-coo! Coo-coo!"

Or did Clara imagine this?

The bird flew into Mina's Bohemian crystal chandelier. "Coo-coo." Scarcely landed, it loosed a gob of birdshit on the rug. "Coo-coo," it sang—its last coo-coo. For coolly, very coolly, Hugo picked up a newspaper from Mina's crowded table, folded it once, and swatted the bird senseless.

Maxey Pinjatta eeked. He sank down in a chair. Rusty tears came to his eyes, those of a true man of the Iron Age.

After a very long moment, Mina said, "Mr. Pinjatta, I think you'd better leave. Mr. Flemming too."

# *twenty-one*

IT WAS THE end of a full-blooded autumn day by the time she and Henri arrived at the vineyard. There had been last-minute business ahead of the long weekend, an afternoon appointment, telephone calls, one from Alberto—he and Florence had just arrived in Lucaterra—then from Mick Tyler, reminding them of the Masters of the Vine benefit that Sunday night. They were to be at his table. Mick had heard the Bertram Hill bunch would be there *en masse*. The Pinjattas had bought two tables. Whether they'd fill them and with whom . . . that was something else . . .

Then, they'd been delayed picking up the car Henri had rented, a heavy but nondescript maroon Ford which seemed twice the size of hers and was big and heavy to drive. As well, perhaps, Henri said, for them not to be needlessly conspicuous in her near-classic BMW. And finally, they'd been held up on the bridge due to a spillage of a truckload of tomato paste all over the inside lane—like half-coagulated blood it looked, Henri remarked cheerfully as they passed by.

The car was parked down below, out of sight in one of the garages, across the road from Joe Alejandro's big frame house.

Joe's wife had invited them to join the family for Thanksgiving dinner the next day. Clara knew they were welcome. But she said no, they didn't want to butt in and besides . . . she didn't have to explain. Perhaps they'd have a meal together or some drinks later in the weekend. Henri certainly had business with Joe. They planned to tramp around the vineyard, Henri's leg permitting. Big Joe had a whole list of things he wanted to discuss—he'd taken to the new arrangement with gusto. And Little Joe wanted to listen in. Clara enjoyed the Alejandros. At this point in the history of Morelli Vineyards, there was no question they were family . . . but there'd be plenty of time for family in the years to come. Soon, well, she didn't say so . . . Clara and Henri would *soon* be on the premises, sort of permanently and then Martha would be coming for Thanksgiving too.

Anyway, they'd brought their own Thanksgiving provisions—*the bird,* a twelve-pounder, a couple of dozen oysters, yams, cranberries . . . etcetera, etcetera. Henri had seen to it all—and, by the way, he was going to cook the meal. Yes, the nose was also a chef.

It was nearly dark by the time they'd put all the stuff away, except for the turkey. Let it thaw. Next, Henri laid a fire to warm the cottage. Then in the rising wind, dressed in woolly stuff and heavy footgear, feeling like country people indeed, going slowly, they walked up the hill to Casa Morelli.

There, they turned on all the lights and revved up
the heat and took a little wine out of an open bottle
of cabernet. It looked like rain. With dusk had come
heavy clouds. To the west there was a crack of thunder, a flash of lightning. The wind picked up. Whip-
like, it blew through the vineyard, ripping at the last
of the leaves. It made lonely, preachy noises in the
roof and whistled through the Mexican tiles over the
terraces.

"Stormy weather." Henri sighed happily. "Soon
comes the rain. And winter. Clarissima . . . I'm going
to have fun here."

"Me too."

*I'm home,* she was thinking, and after that there
wasn't a lot more to be said. Anyway, the weather,
the time of day, didn't encourage conversation. Indeed, the weather laid down the mood. Of quiet.
Inner thought. If you prayed . . . maybe prayer. It
was one of those times when the sound of Alberto's
grandfather clock ticking was like time itself saying
pay attention because I'm flitting by . . .

Not really the right moment to think about the
Pinjattas. But Clara couldn't help it. She couldn't
forget Maxey's parting words. Having been presented the cocktail-napkin-wrapped corpse of his
tiny bird, Maxey Pinjatta had flown into a hysterical
rage. He didn't stop babbling about revenge, even
as a glowering and shamed Werner Flemming
dragged him away. But, such lurid threats as he had
made, could they be taken seriously? Henri didn't
think so. He laughed them off. Nonetheless, Clara
thought, he'd hired an anonymous car for the weekend. Nonetheless, he was brooding about it, she
knew it. Who did he think he was fooling? Watching
him, the lonesome face, the eyes, as he stared out

the window at the gathering storm, Clara understood Henri better than she ever had before and loved him the better for it. He was maddeningly stubborn, no question. But not always unreasonable. Sometimes, it seemed as if he actually forced himself *not* to think the worst of people or to expect the worst of them: i.e., the Pinjattas. Negative feelings, he kept saying, were *counterproductive,* a term he loved, more damaging to him who indulged than to the recipient. What Henri *hated,* if anything, was the thought that there were people who might actually hate him and wish him great harm. Perhaps, she thought, he believed he was not important enough to hate.

Clara broke the silence. "I think we should take Alberto's shotgun down below with us."

"Oh, Clarissima . . ."

"For my peace of mind."

"You will have peace of mind with a shotgun under your bed? Guns do not give me any peace of mind."

"Henri, don't argue. You know as well as I do what's been going on. Our little accident. Then Mick's. Don't coddle me. I can face a few facts. And the facts are that the Pinjattas hate *both of us* now, not just you."

For a second or two impassive, Henri gazed at her. Then, he stood up. "Okay. We will borrow Alberto's shotgun."

The .20-gauge double-barrel was in Alberto's study, locked in a gun cabinet. Clara consulted her keys and opened it. "That one," she said, pointing at the weapon Alberto always used when he went after a destructive red fox, now and then to scare off bothersome deer.

"Beautiful," Henri said, turning the gun over and over in his hands. "Handmade . . . Italian."

"You know about these things?"

"Yes," he said simply, "I know."

"It belonged to my grandfather."

Henri placed the gun on his shoulder, then presented arms like a soldier boy. "Now we are armed . . . and ammunition, Clara, don't forget that. The gun is useless without ammo."

She got out a box of shells.

"Ah, ammunition for an army."

"Let's go, smart guy. It's going to rain any minute. We'd best get home to our castle. . . ."

"Clarissima, home is where the heart is."

They turned the lights off and locked the house up again. Outside, the wind was howling. Clara flicked on the flashlight. Holding each other up, laughing, hugging, they tramped down the hill and, just as it began to rain, regained the cottage. Henri's fire was blazing. The big room was warm. Clara turned on a couple of table lamps.

"Hungry?"

"Not yet," he said. "First, some drinks. I prescribe chilled martinis . . ."

"Then what?"

"An 'amburger. *'Amburger américain.* A pickle. Some ketchup. A glass of something or other red."

Expertly—was there anything he didn't know how to do?—Henri stirred Beefeater gin martinis on ice cubes, precisely enough for two drinks apiece. He garnished each glass with a crisp twist of lemon. They spread out—the perfect description, spread out—on the sofa in front of the fireplace.

"To you, Clarissima."

"To you, Henri."

Naturally, no sooner had he landed than Henri hopped up. He went back to the door, shutting and locking it again. He'd put the shotgun on the breakfast table with the ammunition. Now, he cracked open the gun, had a look down the barrels, then slammed a shell into each chamber. No question, Clara noted, a little surprised, Henri knew about shotguns too. Then, he came back to her, situating the gun on the floor next to his end of the sofa.

"Not too close to the fire, eh, Clarissima," he said lightly. "It might go pop-pop before we want it to."

"Be prepared, Henri, that's the Boy Scout marching song."

"Clarissima, no! Were you one?"

"A Boy Scout? No, Henri. I wasn't a Girl Scout either."

"You would have been such a pretty little Girl Scout . . . Clarissima, you would've won all the races. Were you long-legged and tall as a girl, tell me?"

"Yes," she said, "and well developed too. But I wasn't a joiner, you know. I was moody, a loner, I guess a lot like Martha. And I didn't need the Girl Scouts to be exposed to the Great Outdoors."

"And were you interested in the little boys?"

Yes, but she didn't have to answer. The telephone sounded.

"For you," Henri said drolly. "The evil empire calling."

There was nothing evil about the reassuring voice of Officer Edgar Flange of the California Highway Patrol. He had telephoned the office in the city. Getting only the answering service, he'd tried her home, then taken a chance and rung this number. He'd wanted to reach Ms. Addey before the weekend.

"Some news," he said, "which you should know about."

"A moment," Clara said, "I want Mr. Lamarque to get on the other line . . ." She motioned for Henri to go pick up the kitchen extension. "What's happening?"

Flange was a superior example of politeness, and a credit to the force, as they had so often said. He waited for Henri, then announced, "Several things to tell you. First, we couldn't make a match of the .45 slugs. Which doesn't mean they didn't come out of the same weapon. The slug we dug out of your car was just too badly marred. Secondly, Otis Cheroot was arraigned this morning, but only on the gas station charges. The other, attempted murder, is harder to make."

"I don't know why," Clara said. "I saw him, the son of a bitch."

"Yes, yes . . . we're doing this much so we can hold him. Bail was set at one hundred thousand . . ."

"You're not going to tell us he made the bail?"

"No. He made some phone calls. But to no avail. No bail."

"So he stays in jail?"

To no avail. No bail. He stays in jail. A rap song.

"For the time being anyway. Which is to the good." Flange dropped into one of his weighted silences. Then, "In the course of investigation, searching criminal records and the like, we were able to establish one very interesting fact. Which is that at a certain time three years ago, Cheroot was in the employ of a San Francisco company called Flemming's California Cellar . . ."

"*Merde!*"

Steadily, Clara said, "We *know* Flemming very well.

My father does business with Flemming's Cellar."

"Yes, so I understand. According to Werner Flemming, Cheroot was fired for brawling in the warehouse where he was employed as heavy labor. He was arrested at the time and charged with assault."

"Flemming fired him?" Henri asked.

"Not personally. Flemming himself doesn't remember ever seeing Otis Cheroot. Cheroot was only one of a couple dozen employees . . . those kind of jobs, they come and go."

Nevertheless, the information was stunning. If ever so circumstantially, it connected Flemming with the man who'd tried to kill them.

"Three years ago, that is a long time," Henri mused. Would he take this as another of those coincidences which meant nothing? "And not so long either."

"Mr. Lamarque," said Officer Flange, "I'd like to know about *your* relationship with Werner Flemming. Are you a friend of Flemming's? In your work, I would think you'd see a lot of him."

"Not friends, no. I would not say that—"

"And, lately," Clara cut in, "not good relations either. Not good at all."

Officer Flange was politely curious. "Why's that?"

She'd tell, even if Henri wouldn't. "Henri had some critical things to say about some of Flemming's wine."

"Yes . . . well, Flemming told us about that too," Flange reported. "He said you'd had a quarrel about a bottle of French wine, that he'd been very annoyed with you. But that he'd gotten over it. He said he's a grown boy—"

"Did he? Did he say that?" Henri chuckled. "A grown boy? How interesting . . . Officer Flange, if I may, what we need to know is if this Cheroot creature still has connections in San Francisco . . . *and who with.*"

"Sure, that's right." Taking his time, Flange asked, "So, Mr. Lamarque, *is* Werner Flemming a grown boy? There's no hard feelings? Would it surprise you if . . ." He didn't want to suggest it outright, that Flemming might have had something to do with the *incident* near Cloverdale.

Henri was quick. "Do I suspect him? Officer Flange, I suspect *everybody.* This is my nature."

"Including Werner Flemming?"

"Not excluding Werner Flemming."

"I see . . . well, so far, we've drawn a blank. We can't make any current connection of Otis Cheroot with Flemming's Cellar." His voice hurried. Maybe somebody had come into the room. "And that's all I have to tell you at the moment. If you have any new information of your own, please keep me informed. . . . In the meantime, we wish you a happy turkey-day . . ." With that, Flange hung up.

*"Turkey-day!"* said Henri disgustedly. "I wish they would not! I hate that expression. Why not merely wish *Happy Thanksgiving?* Is that not the holiday? Does one say Happy Noodles on Chinese New Year?" He sat down beside her again, complaining that the martinis had gone warm. "Why, next it will be Saint Turkey, patron saint of giving thanks for all our blessings. And we have so many." Henri hugged her. "And the police could not match the bullets, bah! But Clarissima, not to worry. They are in full retreat. The low-life Cheroot is in the *clink!* And stays there. The others will be keeping their heads hidden."

"Cheroot may be in jail. But they can always find another one."

"All right!" Henri dropped all pretense. "Of course. I'd be a fool if I thought otherwise." He picked up the shotgun and caressed its patinaed stock. "I will tell you what I think. *Yes*, the Pinjattas arranged the attempt upon us. Yes, I think they sank Mick's boat." He jumped up to pull the drapes at the windows on each side of the fireplace. In the breakfast area, he adjusted the blinds so they shut out the night. "But we cannot worry ourselves into a state, Clarissima. Come, let's have our 'amburgers."

This was true. They had to eat. "At least," she said, "we have Flange, even if he seems kind of plodding."

"But Officer Flange is not standing outside, is he, on guard?" He laughed lightly, trying again to jolly her. "But I, Henri Lamarque, will protect you, Clarissima, have no fear. I was once a champion skate shooter."

"I think that's *skeet*."

"Skeet? Skate?"

"A skate is a big jellyfish thing. A stingray."

"Not a bird?" He mugged. "On second thought, I think I was fishing."

". . . pulling my leg . . ."

"Your long and shapely leg. *Gams*. A word from the movies . . . if only."

The rain came again. Without warning, suddenly, it lashed the roof. Gusts of wind hurled it against the windows. Then, a few minutes later, just as suddenly it quit. The night became eerily silent. Henri opened a bottle of Alberto's most rambunctious zinfandel. The sound of the pulled cork echoed like a cannon shot. Henri poured: Niagara Falls. Wordlessly, as if suspended, they toasted each other. Without speaking, they finished eating. Leaving the plates on the table, they went back to the sofa. Henri set the open

wine bottle on the coffee table. Saying nothing, he
turned off all but one table lamp. He added fresh
oak to the fire. It hissed, like a cornered animal.

"It's so *goddamn* quiet," Clara whispered.

Henri fell back and against her, kissing her neck,
slipping one hand under her heavy sweater, caressing her into a state of drowsy desire. "I love it like
this," he murmured. "Just us. In the silence. *Dead*
silence of the groaning, creaking universe. In the
middle of nowhere. Of somewhere. We *rusticate.*
Which means not what you think, that we rust like
old tools, but that we wallow in simplicity here in the
countryside, like the peasants we really are. Or
should be. Or wish to be."

"The peasant you'll *never* be . . ."

"So you say, Clarissima, but it will not be for want
of trying. Lamarque is fed up with being a sophisti-
cate. He is bored as a man of the world. He yawns
ennui at the cosmopolitans. He sneers at the effete
. . . Heavens! *More wine!*"

Reaching out for the bottle, in one of those sudden, unplanned movements of his, Henri jerked to
the side, falling half over her, brushing his face
against her legs . . . rubbing her knee with his beard
. . . grabbing for the bottle.

The shots rang out . . .

Not a single shot, or sound. A *brrrt.* And another,
like somebody running a spoon down a washboard
and back. But louder, something ripping. Metal
drumming, as if there'd been a lightning strike directly on the building. Then came the horrifying,
very personal sound of shattering glass, the rattling
and splintering of the slatted-wood blinds in the
back window. Storm. No. The end of the world.

Before the first brief rip of noise had died away,

there was another burst. Fireplace bricks blew apart. Sparks flew. A vase disintegrated on the mantel.

Henri had already moved. He had tumbled to the side, knocking over the end table and the lamp, pulling her after him. Without knowing how it had happened, she found herself flat against the cold tile floor between the sofa and the coffee table.

"You okay?" he hissed, knowing she was. "Don't move! Stay down!"

The room was black, save for the nervously flickering fireplace.

Clara heard him grunting, slipping along the floor for the shotgun. The faint click as he pushed off the safety. Clara heard every sound now acutely. It came to her brilliantly, frighteningly, that somebody was still outside, at the window. Waiting. Thinking they had hit their target but not sure, waiting for some confirmation, a moan, a groan of pain. Another shard of glass hit the floor. Somebody was out there! She heard a movement, feet, a rustling of clothes, whispers. A low-pitched, urgent voice. Would they come inside to finish the job.?

Breathing shallowly beside her, Henri was also waiting. Waiting with the shotgun. Clara made herself one with the tiles.

Then came the voice. *"Hey! Up there! Everything okay?"*

Joe Alejandro.

Outside, a shuffle of feet.

Simultaneously, from right beside her, deafeningly, the shotgun blasted. Henri had fired one barrel. He scrambled up. In the firelight, Clara saw him fire again, from the hip, at the outline of the window.

Clara heard a gasp from outside, then a cry of

pain, a guttural exclamation. And a single word, *spit out.* Then the sound of squeaky shoes on the patio tiles.

Henri was cursing, slowly, in detail, describing the enemy in fragrant terms. He was at the table, reloading, then rushing out the kitchen door. His voice came back at her. "Don't turn on any lights!" In a moment, there was a thunderous double blast as he fired both barrels of the shotgun. Then his voice, hoarse and angry. "Joe. Come up. Be careful. Some *bastard* is out there."

"You okay, Mr. Lamarque?" That would be Little Joe.

Panting loudly, the elder Alejandro also made the hill. His loud voice boomed again. "I got my .22, Henri, come on, we catch 'em. *Joe!*" To his son. "Run up there! See if you can see 'em!"

"No, no!" Henri knew better. "They have some kind of automatic. Not in the dark . . . too dangerous. I think I hit one of them . . . Clara," he shouted, "open the back door."

They came inside, Big Joe still breathing hard, his son red-faced and excited. Henri turned on the one small light over the stove in the kitchen.

*"Wow!"* Little Joe said it all. "What a mess!"

Clara began to see what had happened to her house. The back window was gone. The wooden blind was shredded. There were pieces of glass, chunks of fireplace brick everywhere. The back of the sofa was in pieces. The stucco wall next to the fireplace was pitted with bullet holes. And the smell, the stench of burnt powder and spilt wine . . .

Big Joe Alejandro crossed himself. "Holy Mother! Are you okay, Clara? What the hell happened here?

Man, automatic is right. They musta put about thirty rounds in that fireplace."

"Did you see anything?"

"Not me," said Big Joe. "What about you?" To his son. "You were up the hill before me."

"Nothing very clear. I think there were two people. I saw two figures just before they got to the top of the hill. One looked big, the other smaller. Sorry . . . then they were gone, down the other side."

"I am certain," Henri said, "that one at least was hit." He pointed at the shattered sofa. "Right there, Lamarque was sitting. I feel even now the heat of the bullet . . ." The back of his sweater had a burn mark across it. "Had Lamarque not reached for the wine—"

"Henri . . ." Clara began to cry. She was more than shaky. She was trembling, shaking like a leaf. Admit it! Somebody had tried again! She was cold, very cold.

Henri knelt beside her. He put his arms around her. "Come, come. Clarissima . . . we are okay."

"You were almost killed, you idiot!" She pushed him away. "And I'm mad as hell!"

Henri began to laugh. Unsteadily. His eyes filled with tears. "Me too! Look." He jumped to his feet, still laughing raucously. Clara, believe it not, joined in. "Mad as hell—*and alive!*" He danced an awkward little jig. "We're both alive!"

Joe Alejandro looked at his son. "And a little bit loco . . ."

# twenty-two

L ET THE FESTIVITIES continue.
   More than a little drunk, the eccentric Francey Shingles had taken—seized, grabbed, stolen—the stage. With the help of the "society strings" of Duke Dever and his Red Devils, she was belting out her version of Sinatra's signature song, "My Way." Francey, naturally, had reworked the lyrics for purposes of the evening:

> *When it comes to the crush,*
> *I'm not in any rush . . .*
> *So call me a lush.*
> *I wouldn't make a fuss,*
> *Becuss . . .*
> *I did it my way!*

And so on, to thunderous applause from the sold-out and unruly crowd in the Fairmont Hotel Grand Ballroom, fifty tables of ten, all winemakers, distributors, retailers . . . wine lovers, wine drinkers . . . *all* with much to celebrate. A nearly perfect harvest had run its course. The weather had held until mid-November . . . the magical days of first fermentation were nearly over. The muck of the crush had become clean, honest wine. There would be product, something to sell, something to drink. The year's yield having been moderate, the winemakers were expecting a quality vintage. And prices would hold. The whole wine community could be happy, proud of itself. And relieved. The growers would survive another year, pay back a few loans, contract new ones . . .

This was the winemaker's night out. *His* night to be celebrated. And, at five thousand a table, the evening's take would also, incidentally, add a good bit to the retired-sommelier building fund. After expenses, Mick Tyler calculated, the take would probably be in the neighborhood of two hundred thousand dollars. And well deserved, according to the evening's master of ceremonies, Jerry Moscatar, proprietor of Mosca Vista Vineyards.

The dancers left the floor. Jerry had taken back the stage: who recommends the wine? Who pours the wine? Who *loves* the wine? Our sommelier, without whom . . . our unsung heroes . . . tonight we sing *your* song! Jerry wouldn't shut up. At the top of his voice, struggling to be heard, he was going on about the benefactors of the evening . . . the auction which was to commence in just a few minutes, that is, *before* dinner so as to outwit the clowns among us who would eat and run . . .

Paying no attention to Moscatar, Henri was studying the menu and the auction lots. Mick and his digitally oriented friends had ceased listening. Daisy Chaney was holding Mick's hand. Clara had been trying to talk to cousin Cabott Root's bad-tempered wife, Nan. Fortunately, Francey Shingles stumbled by. She kissed Clara sloppily on the cheek, demanding boozily, "Tell me, honey, what the hell I'm doing with that gang over there . . . the whosis . . . Pinjattas?"

Clara smiled. "Aren't they buying your vineyard?"

"What?" Francy laughed roundly. "Those little men are buying Los Shingles? I've never heard of anything so crazy!" But maybe Francey didn't remember. Still, it wasn't something a person would likely forget, sober . . . or drunk. "*Bullshit* and *balderdash!* Werner Flemming and I talked about it . . . hypothetically. The very idea! They're saying *that*?" Briefly, Francey was disturbed. Only briefly. "Where is Werner anyway? I've got the little bald one next to me. But the furry one is worse . . ." She straightened up, pulling at the neck of her ill-fitting dress, gazing balefully around the room. "Not much in the way of decor, is it? Old grape leaves and leftover Halloween cum harvest ball . . ." The pastel shades of autumn, at each table? Not ostentatious but suitable enough, Clara thought. "Doesn't matter though," Francey said, "we're just here for the wine." She stooped down again, asking loudly, "That's your cousin, ain't it? Cabott? Square Root?"

Cabby heard. "At your service," he bellowed heartily.

Francey ogled him, ignoring the unlovely Nan. "I could do with a little of that service," she yelled back, sort of man-to-man.

Cabby whooped. He would. With a final leer, declaring she had no intention of returning to her table, Francey loped away, leaving Cabby stroking his wine glass contemplatively. Surely not, surely her cousin wouldn't even think of making a fool of himself with the horsey Madame Shingles. But Cabby's reputation not only preceded him; it followed him everywhere. Just now, he'd been working his charm on Daisy Chaney. Getting nowhere, he wisely realized Mick didn't care for his effort, and turned his attention to Mick's other four guests, two colleagues—whiz boys, in Henri's terminology, with similar Silicon Valley credentials, fast money and large position, and their sleek wives. Clara hadn't caught any names, or they hers, she presumed. No business there. Cabby was off and running about his think tank, not beating around the bush, and how it was the responsibility of *new money* to promote and support social and scientific research. Yes, indeed, *indeed,* such outfits as his Pacific Rim Research Center, so hard at work on technology for the new millenium.

Mick grinned at him fixedly. He was holding fast to Daisy's hand, neither of them making any secret that they were mutually, jointly, entirely smitten. Clara thought she might soon be looking for another assistant.

"Hey, Cabby! Cab!" Mick finally interrupted. "We're here for the wine. Cabott Root is a demon," he warned the others. "But tonight I'm taking gravity for granted. Henri"—putting the lid firmly on Cabby's sales pitch—"what do you think of the wine?"

All but dozing with boredom, Henri revived. "Outstanding! Very consumable. As we know." They were drinking Alberto's reserve. Mick could've had anything he wished on the table. In order to flatter, maybe to prove a point to his two friends, he'd chosen the Morelli. More than ever, it looked as though Mick wanted in on the Morelli operation. Their task, Clara told herself glumly, would be to hold him off.

Mick held up his glass. "Right! This is maybe the

greatest California cabernet being made today. Unfortunately, Alberto Morelli isn't with us tonight—he's in Italy getting married." Squeezing Daisy's hand. "But Clara here is the daughter of the man who makes it. Here's my toast . . . I give you: Alberto!"

Clara had to say something. Over the din, she managed to make herself heard. "Alberto thanks you. He's sorry not to be here. This is the first year—" Clara stopped, suddenly conscious of Steve Pinjatta. He was watching her, glaring from the other side of the dance floor, accusation and grievous hurt in his eyes. "This is the first year my father has missed the party. But, as Mick says, he had a prior engagement."

"Bravo." Henri grabbed her hand and put it to his lips. "Alberto has an *engagement* to be married. *Bravo.* Well put, Clarissima!"

Yes, all the Pinjattas were there: bald Franco, hairy Maxey, and young Steve. Nurse Astrid was seated on Franco's right. On her right, Maxey. A brassy-looking tootsie had the spot between Maxey and Steve. Whose date was she? Maxey's? She looked his type. Or Steve's, not impossible. Next, a couple of empty chairs: Francey's, Werner Flemming's. Then, two unknowns who partially filled out the first of the Bertram Hill tables—heavyset men with flat faces and nervous hands.

Having gotten Clara's attention, Steve Pinjatta began to process a whole series of dirty looks for Tyler's table. Mick was bound to notice and he did. "What's bugging that little freak? Is he one of the Pinjattas?"

Clara hoped Steve could lip-read. "Yes, that little freak is Steve Pinjatta."

Mick waved. "Hi, there, Stevie!"

Steve stiffened. Turning away angrily, he muttered something to Maxey's date. She looked over, making a cutie-pie face.

If the evening had been planned as the Pinjattas' grand introduction to California, so far they were a dismal flop and the Brothers Pinjatta looked as gloomy as if they'd already read the reviews. This should have been a golden opportunity for them to meet top people in California wine. But Werner Flemming, unaccountably, was not there to introduce them around. Maybe it was too late anyway. The word was out, Henri said. California growers were not of the extreme xenophobic nature which prevailed in Bordeaux—even so, nobody volunteered to break the ice. Nobody made an effort to welcome the Brothers Pinjatta to the fold. It wasn't as though people didn't know who they were. Not like they were inconspicuous.

An adjoining table, also paid for by Bertram Hill, was pure desolation, save for another of the heavies and a lonely-looking redhead who might or might not have been with him. Surely, young Steve could've done better, even if he'd gone out to the hotel lobby and given away tickets. It had to be said: as an advance man, Steve was in full retreat. Now and then, Maxey turned in his chair and glared at Steve, his lips forming nasty words.

"It is worse than failure," Henri murmured out of the side of his mouth. "It is *catastrophe,* veritable *catastrophe.*"

"But they're too dumb to know it. Look at them, sitting there like little toads."

Sounding much too sympathetic, Henri murmured, "No, it is not going well *chez* Bertram Hill.

If Los Shingles is not accepting their bid . . . then who is?"

*Poor* Pinjattas. Ha! Clara couldn't keep her eyes away. If Steve looked at her again, she'd freeze him solid. "Did you notice Maxey's hair?" Somebody had been taming it. The beehive was not as bulky as it had been the other day but it still gleamed like oil on water. "I wonder if he's adopted another bird."

But Henri had a different interest. "*Regards!* Franco's nurse! Clarissima, *look* . . ."

Nurse Astrid had gotten up, awkwardly, it would be said, gripping the edge of the table for balance, by no means her normally agile self. She made no effort to move on to the ladies' room or—an unlikely possibility—drag Franco out on the dance floor, for the Red Devils were back, pouring out a forties big-band number. No, Astrid just stood there like a post, towering over the Bertram Hill table, indeed over the whole proceeding. Slowly, she began to flex her broad shoulders. She stretched her arms, shifting her weight from one foot to the other . . . thankfully, making no attempt to look their way. Nurse Astrid had put aside her white uniform. She was wearing a looser cut black evening suit which, if the truth be known, was at least as severe as the uniform. There was nothing she could do to soften the military cut of her hairdo.

Now, carefully, as if nobody was supposed to notice, she reached behind and began gently to knead her buttocks, gingerly caressing, smoothing her skirt . . . then, unshyly, tugging panties or a girdle or both into more easeful position. Astrid still took great care not to look at them. She seemed to make a point of their knowing, if they happened to be watching, that she was absolutely not favoring them with her attention. Gazing attentively, as if appreciating the music, toward the bandstand, at the opposite wall, and, over her other shoulder, at the exit, she continued to run both hands over her buttocks.

Suddenly, she dropped her hands. Her body jerked. The side of Nurse Astrid's face they could see tensed and twisted. Her lips parted, as with a suppressed gasp. A spasm? Of pain? Of shock? At once, she wrapped her arms around her waist, hugging herself, rocking back and forth. Then, after a moment, carefully, almost surreptitiously, she put her hands behind her again, pulling at her skirt, yanking at her elastic underthings.

*"Regards!"* Henri whispered gleefully. "Nurse Astrid's ass is hurting her!"

Hurting or not, Nurse Astrid was forced to sit down again, lowering herself very carefully, as Master of Ceremonies Moscatar went to the mike to announce that the auction was about to commence. Therefore, he would introduce the auctioneer, a man, he claimed, who had once made his living in the tobacco barns, whose name was Wendell Hack. Hack was a fast-talking character. True to his name, he coughed a lot but moved it right along. Bidding was spirited, fast-paced—hell, people were hungry.

A vacation trip for two at a luxury hotel on the beach in Oahu, including transportation, went for six thousand. A catered banquet for fifty at Le Tourniquet in San Francisco, ten thousand. Next New Year's Eve in Paris at the renowned Ritz Hotel, twelve thousand. A case of 1975 Pétrus out of the cellar of the late financier Maurice Cumberbum (Clara remembered the name. So did Mick Tyler. This was the cellar Flemming had offered him exclusively.) A Cartier diamond necklace recently recovered from a jewelery heist in San Remo, twenty-five thousand. A weekend at the Peau Rouge Golf Resort in Palm Springs, fifteen hundred. A weekend at the Cricket Club in Tijuana, Mexico, five hundred. A weekend at the Waldorf in New York, three thousand. A weekend in Newark, New Jersey, one hundred and fifty. Two first-class tickets from San Francisco to Paris and return, seven thousand. Six bottles of Cristal champagne, eleven hundred. A round trip on the Concorde, weekend in Champagne country, including limo from Paris, gourmet meals, twenty-five thousand (Mick Tyler bid for this lot and got it. Lucky Daisy!) Five pounds of Beluga caviar, five thousand. A ten-day cruise to choice Mediterranean troublespots, twenty thousand. A case of Mouton Rothschild, five thousand . . .

But the Pinjattas were becoming restless. Queries danced in their hooded eyes. Where was the imperial of Montebanque? God forbid—had somebody smashed it backstage? Maxey leaned across Nurse Astrid to speak to Franco. Maxey stood up. Sat down again. Astrid squirmed, shifting from ham to ham, trying in vain to get comfortable. Franco fidgeted. Astrid opened her big black pocketbook. She passed him a pill . . . and took one herself.

The auction continued.

Then—Clara wasn't sure when it registered—she became aware of Victoria Flemming.

Victoria did look a wraith of God. Pale-faced, very short—her feet were bare—her platinum blond hair frizzed, she floated into the back of the room. A long, filmy, flimsy white dress flowed and ballooned behind her. Speaking to no one, making no sound, she wafted through the tables. She seemed dazed. What an entrance! Auctioneer Wendell Hack coughed and went silent. So did the room. People sensed something was terribly wrong. Victoria's eyes were so large . . . round . . . spooked. She saw Clara and didn't see her. But she wasn't vague about where she was going. She made straight for the Bertram Hill table. She sat down in Werner's chair. Cupping her hands, she blew Steve Pinjatta a puckery-lipped kiss.

Steve? He was terrified. "Vick . . . what . . ." His voice was squeaky with anxiety. He made as if to get up, then sank back down, as low as he could get.

*"Caramba!"*

Franco's pudgy face hardened. Only the deaf would've missed his words: *"Where is Werner?"*

"Werner . . ." Victoria spoke faintly, but so sweetly that the sound echoed like a high soprano. "Werner couldn't make it."

"Couldn't . . . what you mean, *couldn't*?"

But Victoria's attention had already drifted. Not knowing any better, and being a kind of gent, one of the Bertram Hill heavies poured wine in her glass. She held it up, thanking him with feeling. One would've thought this was the kindest thing anybody had ever done for her.

"Well . . . well . . ." Stuttering, Jerry Moscatar attempted to regain control of his show. "Let's get on with it now! On with the auction! Welcome to Mrs. Flemming. Better late than never. . . . Here's hoping Werner will feel better in the morning . . ."

Did anybody else notice that Victoria was shaking her head?

"So, to lot fifty-three," Jerry shouted in the mike. "Which is . . . a very fine imperial of Château Montebanque donated by the wine *negotiante* and distributor Bertram Hill, *it says here* (he didn't know any better than anybody else), of New York, Paris, and San Francisco . . . and founder of the new California Consortium, fine western wines for the moti- vated . . ." A slogan Steve Pinjatta must have in- vented. "And over to you, Mr. Hack . . ."

Franco and Maxey Pinjatta applauded, making as much noise as they could. . . . The rest of the room was noisily . . . *silent.* Maxey and Franco exchanged looks. Then both glared at Steve. Steve was out of it, staring blindly at Victoria. *Victoria,* what was she do- ing here? What was her game?

Then, all at once, another distraction, a low and agonized whimper.

*Astrid!* Red in the face, she was rocking from side to side, shaking her head in distress, biting her lip.

Meanwhile, two wine interns in short purple dresses had carried the Pinjattas' imperial out of the wings. They set it down on the auctioneer's prop, a velvet-covered table. It looked . . . how should one describe it? It looked imperial.

Wendell Hack began to chant. The bidding had begun.

"Henri, watch me . . ." Mick Tyler raised his hand. And again. In seconds, they heard ten thousand. His hand flew up. Eleven. Again. Twelve . . . thirteen . . . fourteen thousand . . . once more.

*Fifteen.*

"Going . . . going . . . gone! Mr. Mick Tyler . . ."

Fifteen thousand was a lot of money for less than a case—in fact, eight bottles—of even the very best of Bordeaux. The Pinjatta twins should've been happy and proud of themselves, as the proprietors of the château. But they were not happy. Applause rippled. They sat on their hands. Most people in the room didn't know Mick Tyler from Adam, except he was the same guy who'd just bought the trip to France. But the Pinjattas did. As the auctioneer's assistant carried the important bottle to the Tyler table, Franco Pinjatta jumped up.

A squat, lone figure, his baldness by now legion, he crossed the dance floor to confront Tyler. "You paid fifteen. I give you sixteen thousand for the wine."

"Nope. Sorry."

"Seventeen . . ."

Mick looked Franco up and down. "Who are you anyway?"

As if he didn't know. This made Franco all the more irate. He wheeled on Henri and Clara. "Ask Lamarque. He knows . . ."

"Mick . . ." By now, who wasn't listening? "May I introduce Franco Pinjatta. He and his brother own Château Montebanque."

Tyler pretended astonishment. "You want to buy back your own wine? I do not believe it! No, no, thanks. We're going to drink it. Right now, with the meal. Yes, sir! I've heard a lot about Montebanque. Let's see if it's as good as they crack it up to be—"

*"Twenty thousand!"*

"Mr. Pinjatta," Mick said, "I do not want your money!" He reached in a jacket pocket. "I've even brought along my own corkscrew . . . Henri, would you mind?"

Shrugging like an existentialist hero, one of Sartre's own, Henri got up. He couldn't refuse. The time demanded it of him. People were standing up in the back, crowding around the Tyler table for a better view of the face-off. How strange this must have seemed to Franco. He was sweating profusely. He was shaking, staring at Henri wildly. He could have retreated but he didn't. He couldn't move. Henri ignored him, busying himself with the bottle. First, he folded out the little knife at the business end of Mick's corkscrew and cut away the foil capsule at the top of the bottle, carefully brushing debris off the exposed cork.

Franco cried out. "No! I say no! You must not drink it now, in these, such circumstances, giving him no chance to catch his breath—"

Mick cut him off rudely. "No! Keep quiet! Go on, Henri. Open the goddamn bottle! Stick around, Mr. Pinjatta. We'll taste it together. . . ."

Clara began to wonder if Mick knew something they didn't. He was so sure of himself. Franco's face had turned pasty white. He swayed, reaching for the back of a chair! At that ominous signal, like a wounded Valkyrie, Astrid bounded across the dance floor. She grabbed Franco's arm to steady him, casting dirty looks in every direction. At Henri, her gaze halted. *"Du . . . verdammter Kerl."*

Obviously not a compliment. Henri's reply was a long, cold look of inquiry and so effective Nurse Astrid blinked. She sagged, all but cringed before Henri's eyes. He didn't have to say it out loud. He knew: Astrid had been at the cottage three nights ago. *She* had fired the shots. And she was carrying Henri's birdshot in her ass.

Astrid whimpered again. Her forehead furrowed. Pain? Guilt?

But, as for now, Henri Lamarque would open a bottle of wine. Judgment would again be passed on a Château Montebanque. What had Henri said about the theatre of the wine?

He probed the soft center of the cork. Meticulously, he inserted the point of the corkscrew. Holding the bottle firmly by its neck, he wound the medieval instrument into the giving cork. Reaching the moment of truth, he folded down the pronged lever and placed it over the lip of the bottle. Tugging steadily, he began the extraction.

"It . . . it gives very nicely," he reported. "Firm. But supple, this cork."

With a faint pop, the cork came free. Henri breathed more easily. So did they all. With the napkin, he wiped the lip of the bottle. He held the cork to his nose. Clara was thrilled, impressed. There were tears in her eyes. How many times, how many, had she seen him do this? Many, many times was the answer. But never quite as dramatically as this, never with this kind of an audience. This was Henri's greatest performance. After this, he could reasonably retire.

"Bravo!" somebody shouted.

But not Franco Pinjatta. Nor the other Pinjattas. Franco was leaning against Nurse Astrid who bore his weight stoically, save for her own fearful shaking. She was holding a handkerchief to her nose, her mouth, biting on it to override the pain. A faint smell of antiseptic came to Clara's nose. What else? A scent, she thought, of festering bandage.

Henri wasn't finished. He leaned forward to sniff, his nose working furiously, all the passages, Clara remembered, the vaulted chambers, the foyers and anterooms he talked about, all taking note and cognizance of the wine as it paraded. Cognizance. But making no judgment as to character or worth.

He arranged three glasses. Taking the neck of the bottle in one hand, the bottom in the other, he lifted it gently and made ready to pour.

"Clarissima . . ." he whispered to her. "Please hold

the glasses steady . . . ah, there, good." He poured a tasting portion in the first glass. Then the next. And the third.

"For Mick . . . For Franco . . ."

"And yourself, Henri," Tyler said. "So, gentle-men . . ." He held up his glass, twisting it, making the wine swirl. He nosed it. Then waited for the others.

Franco Pinjatta dealt with the wine swiftly. Clutch-ing Nurse Astrid's arm, in extremis, he tasted once and swallowed. "Excellent! *Perfecto!*"

Now, Henri. He stared at the wine. He put his nose to the bouquet. Clara held her breath. He was not impressed. Finally, he took a tiny bite of the Montebanque. He held it on his tongue, washed his palate. Swallowed. Said nothing.

Mick went last. He took a mouthful of the wine. He coughed. Made a face. Spit wine back in the glass. Gasped. "Awful! Gone. Over the hill. Corked! It tastes like . . ."

*Horse piss,* Clara thought, please don't say horse piss!

Franco tottered. "No!" he screamed.

Mick was merciless. "Mr. Pinjatta, it's off . . . *way off!*"

"*Caramba!*" Forgetting herself, Nurse Astrid loosed a high-pitched cry, a Valkyrie indeed. The exclama-tion. That voice . . . wasn't it the same Clara had heard from the other side of the shattered window at the cottage? Astrid delivered again: "*Estúpido!*" she yelled at Mick Tyler.

Franco was gone. His body began shaking. Head fell back as if the neck muscles had failed. He dropped like a sack. Nurse Astrid managed to get an arm around him.

"Astrid!" Henri pushed a chair forward, bumping her cruelly. *"Voilà!"*

*"Fool!"* she screamed. *"Take care!"* Nurse Astrid dumped Franco on the chair and eased herself down beside him, with one arm over his shoulder, holding him. She made as if to open the top of her black suit . . . oh, my God, Clara thought. Then was thrown awry by her suffering buns. She reached . . . stopped . . . reached . . . wanting, yearning to comfort herself. But she was afraid to give it away.

"Astrid . . ." Clara had to do it. She banged her hip against Astrid's chair.

*"Idiot! Caramba!"* With a screech, Astrid leapt up. Clara thought she would attack. Instead, Astrid grabbed a glass of water off the table and poured it unceremoniously over Franco's palpitating skull. He seemed to stir. He lifted his head.

"What have you done to yourself, Astrid?"

*"Nossing!* It is *nossing.*" Then, unable to resist, she shoved her hand up under her skirt. Not caring now that Clara was watching, Astrid got her fingers underneath the elastic of her panties. She yanked on them, whining with discomfort, pulling at them and shaking them, as if to separate the fabric from the painful, sticky, suppurating skin . . . and, for a second, succeeded for she sighed with relief.

At that moment, Clara heard a curious rattling, a rattling sound, like pearls, perhaps, from a broken strand. With all the noise, for things were getting out of hand, it was surprising they heard at all. Light broke in Henri's eyes. Quickly, carefully, he got down on one knee. In a moment he was on his feet again, grinning, holding out his hand. In the palm, three, four, five, maybe six rusty . . . they looked like BBs.

"Buckshot!" Henri thrust his hand at Nurse Astrid. "Out of your panties, Nurse Astrid! *Voilà! C'est ça!*"

She staggered backward. *"Scheisskerl!"*

"What the hell's going on?" Mick Tyler roared.

*"Verdammte Idioten!"* Astrid was in some kind of a mood.

"Is he okay?" Franco had slipped out of the chair and lay crumpled on the floor. "Do we need a doctor?"

"Better call the police."

"I did *nossing*!" Astrid bleated. "I deny . . ."

Too late. A shrill voice rose from the Bertram Hill table. "Victoria . . . *Vicky! Jesus . . . Vick!*" Steve Pinjatta's voice broke in a wretched sob. "Vick! Jesus! What're you doing?"

Doing? Victoria was not doing anything. She had slumped face-forward on the table. Her eyes were bright, unseeing. One of Bertram Hill's mystery guests put a big, fat index finger to her throat. He shook his head. "I think the little lady's dead."

When they turned around again, Nurse Astrid was gone.

# *twenty-three*

So was Werner Flemming. Gone, that is. Dead. He'd been knifed in the gut, then apparently staggered out on his deck where he'd been shot, once, in the back of the head.

Victoria, on the other hand, had died of poisoning. An empty vial of strychnine was found in her purse. The assumption—maybe stretching it a bit for the sake of forensic convenience—was that she'd done for Werner, then determined to take her own life in a last dramatic gesture. In the state she'd presumably been in, the miracle was that she'd found her way from Tiburon to the city, thence to the hotel, to carry it off.

The poison vial was in her purse. Her fingerprints were on the knife. But there was no sign of a gun. Maybe she'd thrown it off the bridge. Then, in the confusion, during the dramatic tasting and noisy rejection of the Château Montebanque, she'd dumped the poison in her wine and quickly, quietly died. But in sudden, awful pain . . .

The cruel joked that Victoria had made herself the death of the party. Pure San Francisco. The kinder opined that Werner and Victoria had surely

been a star-crossed couple from the word go. Which
they'd never passed. At least, Victoria hadn't. She'd
never collected her two hundred dollars.

It was sad. Clara thought it was *very* sad. Victoria,
whatever her past, and now it began to come out
that her past had been kind of shady . . . anyway,
wherever she'd come from, Victoria hadn't been a
*bad* person. Not really bad, in the sense of spiteful
or hurtful or vengeful—except, evidently, in the case
of Werner Flemming.

"You know," Clara told Henri, "he used to beat
her up."

*"Le Werner."* he nodded, "he was no angel, for
sure. He was on the brink of bankruptcy and was
not going down quietly. Then he made mistakes—"

"Getting mixed up with the Pinjattas!"

"Yes. Bad news . . ."

"Officer Flange believes the Pinjattas forced Werner to hire that miserable Cheroot. I think he's
right. Werner never would've done such a thing on
his own . . ."

"We will never know," Henri said.

"And you're not even interested anymore . . ."

"Not today, Clarissima. Today . . . I enjoy. Up and
away!" Henri levered his seat back. "A most comfortable aircraft, is it not? Why do people complain
so? *Alitalia*. Rome-bound, could anything be finer?"
He sought her hand. In that most familiar of all his
gestures, he lifted the hand tenderly to his mouth.
He kissed her knuckles. "I talk no more of wine. Not
today. We will drink a glass or two. In Tuscany, I will
make *no* judgments, positively." He kept his promise
for another thirty seconds. Then, he was off again.
"Such a scoundrel, your friend Mick Tyler. You

know, Clarissima, that Montebanque was not half bad."

"Why did he do it?"

"I truly do not know. He never would say. I think . . . that Mick had a suspicion too, about the Pinjattas and *his* accident in the Bay. We would know more if the monster Otis Cheroot had lived." No loss, Otis Cheroot had died in a jailhouse fight within days after the Montebanque debacle. "So curious," Henri mused. "Cheroot, the villain, so soon dead, as if the Devil retrieved his own. Yes, it *is* curious. The wine was *not* so bad. Not a Montebanque, I think. Perhaps another Gitane Flambé in masquerade."

"We'll never know about that either," Clara said. "Nobody else got a chance to taste it."

In the several seconds of bedlam that followed Victoria's demise and Steve's going off like a fire alarm, the three Bertram Hill heavies had lumbered across the dance floor. Supposedly taking charge of the semicomatose Franco, they'd made sure to smash the imperial on the floor. Nurse Astrid had made herself scarce at the same time.

"Such an *histoire*. But at least," Henri said, "I think that I am at last free of the Pinjattas."

"They've got to be finished in California."

"Perhaps in New York as well. They have scandal enough for a lifetime."

Indeed. The Pinjattas were very busy with the law. Carmen, Maxey's high-strung daughter, stood accused of murder in Bordeaux, France. Nurse Astrid, close enough to Franco to be considered family, was on the run from charges of attempted murder. Even though the buckshot evidence was pretty circumstantial, nobody bought Franco's lame story that Astrid had been giving him a Jungian brain-wave treatment at the time of the attack. And taking flight was not exactly an indication of innocence. Oh yes, said Officer Flange, Astrid Wunderlick's wounded posterior would be in plenty of hot water should she show up again in Sonoma County.

The humiliation they'd suffered in the matter of the Montebanque imperial had by itself been enough to send Maxey and Franco scurrying. Then, it turned out that another item in the auction, the case of Pétrus from the cellars of the late Maurice Cumberbum, was also questionable. Seems the Pinjattas had assembled that particular donation for a Flemming client who would remain nameless, and charged him accordingly. But, upon inspection after the auction, half the bottles in the case hadn't passed muster. This matter had been referred back to France.

Worse yet for the Bertram Hill organization was that Werner Flemming's death had ignited a federal investigation into BHill's involvement in Flemming's California Cellar, in particular the precise financial relationship of the deceased with the Brothers Pinjatta.

But absolutely worst of all was the doubt now being cast upon the manner of Werner's death. The knife wound to the stomach, nonfatal by itself, might reasonably be blamed on Victoria—but the bullet in the back of the head? That was a different but to the police all too familiar kind of killing. Had Werner known too much? Had he threatened to talk?

And Victoria? Was she really a suicide?

At the moment, Franco was reportedly in the American Hospital in Paris and unable to do much talking himself. Maxey was said to be vacationing in Acapulco, Mexico. Perhaps, by now, Nurse Astrid had taken over his care and feeding. Steve Pinjatta had been reassigned to Bilbao, Spain.

"Clarissima," Henri said after a bit, "you know, we are very lucky we survived all this. . . . If I am ever so careless again, I give you my full permission to—"

"Henri, no, I will not. I refuse to kill you. In a few hours, we'll be in Rome."

He leaned way over and kissed her resoundingly. "Thank you for having me alive in the Holy City."

"*Ahem . . .* excuse me . . ." The flight attendant was leaning over them. What? Was she going to say kissing was not allowed on transatlantic flights? "Your friends up front . . ."

Yes. Mina and Hugo, in first class. Henri had gotten himself and Clara business, for saving some money, he explained, and also to keep them out of range of Mina, who would want to talk to Clara all the way across the ocean, leaving Henri to sparkling conversation with Hugo.

"Are they okay?" Clara asked.

"Oh, fine. They're sending you a bottle of wine. . . ."

Clara groaned.

"Hey! I get the feeling you two are on your honeymoon. Am I right?"

"No, no, not us . . ." Clara pointed toward the front of the aircraft. "They're the ones on the honeymoon. . . ."

"Well, yes! Now that you mention it . . . I'll be right back. I'll get the wine."

"Clarissima, you are a *devil!*"

In a moment, the attendant reappeared with a bottle of red wrapped in a napkin, and two glasses.

"Shall I pour?"

"No, no." Clara took the bottle. "We're experts."

"Enjoy . . ."

"All right, Henri, don't look." Keeping the bottle well wrapped, Clara poured him half a glass, the same for herself. She sipped and sniffed and swished and swirled, through the complete Lamarque routine. "Good. I love it. It has a big nose . . . a *huge* nose. The bouquet is spectacular, like all the flowers at a wedding, there's a bushel basket of fruit. The aftertaste is like being dragged by a truck. . . . If you say any different, I *am* going to kill you. . . ."

Henri drank. Straight off. "You are right. It is fine."

Clara took away the napkin. "Château Montebanque . . . I don't believe it!"

"Wait, Clarissima. Look! There is another label underneath. . . . *Regards!* Château Lafite! But wait, Clarissima, yet another!" He ripped away the Lafite. "*Mon Dieu!* It is a *Clara Morelli Reserve* . . . a wine for you."

"Henri . . . you arranged this with Mina, didn't you?"

"I do not deny it," he said. "Fun, no? Are you bored?"

This required deep thought. "Henri, if I am *ever* bored, I give you permission . . . yes, I require, I demand—"

Henri crossed her lips with his finger.

"Have no fear. Lamarque will unbore. Like the blink of an eye, you will see, Lamarque, *le Supernose*"—he was laughing hard—"to the rescue of so beautiful a Tuscan maiden. . . ."

Clara kissed his glass with her own.